MARY-MARGARET
and the CASE of the
Thieving
BARMAid

MARY-MARGARET
and the CASE of the
Thieving
Barmaid

A Pint of Trouble Mystery

DESMOND P. RYAN

LEVEL
BEST BOOKS

To The Deadly Dames: Joan O'Callaghan, Sydney Leigh, Melodie Campbell, and Cheryl Freedman. Thanks for walking through this manuscript with me, chapter by chapter.

Chapter One

"Michael, 'tis yer mother."

"Yes, I know. I recognize your accent," Michael said, rubbing his forehead.

Mary-Margaret O'Shea pulled the cell phone away from her ear, looked at it as if she had been talking into a zucchini, and then returned it to her ear to continue.

"'Tis not an accent. And 'tis yer mother's voice ye recognize. Honestly, me son, I worry about ye."

"And you called me on my cell while I'm in court to tell me this?"

"Ach, Michael. Don't be daft. I'm callin' ye because Arthur is missin'."

Michael rolled his eyes. Arthur had been sent over by the cleaning agency Michael had contacted years ago to help his mother for a few weeks after her surgery. He was a terrible cleaner, but he and Mary-Margaret had become thick as thieves.

"Missing?"

"Yes!" Mary-Margaret hollered into the phone. "Can. Ye. Not. Hear. Me. Words. Me. Son? Is. It. The. Technology. Or. Is. It. Ye."

"I can hear you, Mom. You don't have to yell," Michael said calmly, as was his way when he received such calls from her. Despite almost thirty years as a police officer, he considered life with his mother, especially since she had moved in with him a few months ago, to be the greatest schooling for dealing with challenging individuals. "They're motioning to me that court is about to start up again, so I've got about a minute. What is it that you expect me to do about Arthur?"

1

Mary-Margaret pulled the phone away from her ear a second time and stared at it for a long moment before returning to the call. *And to think I have to connect the dots for he who ought to have been Police Officer of the Year many times over if he'd just stop gettin' his noggin bashed in at every turn.*

"I'm expectin' ye to find him, luv," Mary-Margaret said slowly before quickly adding. "Ye are the police, are ye not?"

"I'm a police detective, yes. But I am not *the* police."

"Ye know, of all me four children, I don't recall ye bein' the obstinate one." She walked from the kitchen at the back of Michael's house into the living room to look out the front bay windows for any sign of Arthur. "Maybe I should go easier on yer sister if I–"

"What I'm trying to say, Mom, is that…well…what makes you think Arthur is missing?"

"Well, he's not here, is he?" *And to think this lad actually thinks he can shoulder the responsibility of rearin' a teenaged son on the cusp of manhood without a wife. It's beyond the scope of consideration.*

"Apparently not. But is he supposed to be there?"

Mary-Margaret rolled her eyes as she considered the situation she was in, living as she was, albeit temporarily, in a Victorian house that was far too big for one man and his son but likely not big enough for the three of them. *Had Carmen not run off with that boy toy of hers, none of this would likely be happenin'. Never did like that one.*

"Sure as this is Thursday mornin' and yer house needs cleanin'."

"Then why are you calling Arthur?"

"Don't be cheeky, Michael. He's a good lad. He might not be the best cleaner, but he's a good lad," she said, running her fingers across the mantle, swiping off a layer of dust that had likely taken more than a few weeks to gather.

"I was joking."

"And at a time like this, then? Where is yer compassion?" She shook her head. *'Tis true: a man without a wife–even a poorly chosen one–is useless, plain and simple. And a man with a teenaged son without a wife is a recipe for disaster.*

"Sorry. Let's start again. Arthur is supposed to be at your house—"

"*Yer* house, lad. Why would he be goin' to *my* house when no one is there? Honestly, me son, I think ye might want to consider takin' a desk job or maybe even early retirement. The pressure of it all seems to be affectin'—"

"Right. *My* house. I forget sometimes because you're always there."

"As I should be," Mary-Margaret said. *And here I'll stay until suitable arrangements can be made.*

Sensing that she might have spoken in a tone of voice unlikely to cause her Michael to want to help her, Mary-Margaret erupted into a violent fit of coughing.

"Are you okay?"

"Oh," Mary-Margaret sputtered after another few deep coughs, "as well as can be expected at me age and all, given that I've got this wee bout of the pneumonia."

"Have you been in to see the doctor yet?"

"And why would I be doin' that, lad? I've got the pneumonia and there's nothin', but bedrest can rid me of it." *And the doctor would surely tell us all that I'm as fit as a fiddle on a Saturday night at the pub. Enough so that ye'd be sendin' me and Wee Phil packin' if ye only knew.*

"I just thought—"

"Save yer thoughts for the business at hand. Where is Arthur, and how shall we bring him to safety?"

There was no response.

"I can only imagine him," Mary-Margaret continued, walking back to the kitchen, "bein' held hostage by one of those gangs of ruffians that hang about at the docks—"

"What are you talking about?"

"Ye know exactly what I'm talkin' about."

"No, Mom, I don't. Let's start at the beginning," Michael said, his words becoming clipped as he switched from son to investigator. "When was Arthur supposed to be there?"

"This morning. Now."

"And how late is he?"

"He's not."

3

"I thought you said—"

"He's not late, Michael. He's missin'," Mary-Margaret corrected with a huff that was matched in frustration levels with her son's audible sigh.

"Ach, Michael. Can ye hang on a minute? Wee Phil is dancin' like yer uncle Seamus after last call. I'm thinkin' ye didn't take him out to the jacks before ye left for work this mornin'?"

"He's not my dog," Michael said pointedly. In fact, the little Jack Russel belonged to Sally, the flight attendant who lived next door to Mary-Margaret's own home. Given Sally-next-door's long hours and single-woman lifestyle, Mary-Margaret had offered to take in Wee Phil as required. When Mary-Margaret installed herself at Michael's house after seeing the mess his life was becoming, Wee Phil was simply part of the package.

"And I'm sure your neighbor would be happy to have him—and you—back," Mike continued.

"And there was me this mornin' before ye left, lyin' in what very well could have been me death bed, what with the pneumonia and all, and ye couldn't find it in yer heart to take a wee pup out for a piddle. Ach...."

"Mom, I have to get back into court. I'm testifying—"

"Well, ye can say a word or two at me wake as well, after ye wipe up the puddle of piddle Wee Phil will no doubt be leavin' beside me coffin because ye couldn't be bothered—"

"Mom, I have about thirty seconds before I have to go. What do you want to tell me about Arthur being missing?"

Just as Mary-Margaret was about to repeat what she had already told Michael, she heard the sound of a key fumbling in the lock of the solid back door in the kitchen. She looked through the stained glass window beside it and saw a large figure wearing what looked like a pale blue house dress, the likes of which she and every other housewife had sworn off sometime in the mid-'60s. Mary-Margaret flung open the door to see Arthur, his outfit completed by white runners, white gloves, and a white purse, making him look like a cross between Alice B. Davis and Jackie Kennedy if either of them had been six foot four inches tall and more than a bit overweight.

"Oh, me stars," she said, looking up to the heavens as she crossed herself.

"Mom, I have to g—"

"Of with ye, then. There's nothin' needs doin' now that Arthur has just been found. Except that, ye might want to have a word with Max."

"Why? What's going on with Max?"

"I'm not sayin' that yer out of touch with yer only child, Michael, but ye might want to talk to him about what can be called nothin' short of an organized crime ring that's runnin' rampant in his school."

"What?"

"Oh, sure and all. He told me just this mornin', but it's obviously been weighin' heavily on his mind for some time, poor lamb. Anyway, I'm off. Bye-bye bye bye-bye-bye."

Mary-Margaret ended the phone call with a tap of her finger.

"MM, you'll never believe what just happened to me," Arthur said breathlessly as he began to remove his gloves.

Chapter Two

"Sticheedoon," Mary-Margaret instructed Arthur. "Judgin' by the looks of ye, I'd say a good cuppa and a biscuit is in order."

"I *so* cannot deal with wiping up dog urine right now. Here," Arthur said, putting his gloves back on before clipping the leash on the frantic dog's collar, "let me take Phil out first."

"When ye come back and explain yerself, remind me to tell ye about what somethin' else that we need to deal with."

"I don't think I can manage another thing right now, MM," Arthur said, his lower lip trembling.

"After a good cuppa, ye'll be right as rain. Off with Wee Phil before he bursts a gasket."

Once he stepped away from the back of the house, Arthur dropped the leash to let the Jack Russell run along the back laneway to the end and then along the pathway that led to another laneway. The dog hurried from one bush to another, sniffing every raised surface in between until he found just the right spot to empty his full bladder.

Mary-Margaret watched Arthur and Phil for a moment, wondering what the sight must look like to the neighbors: a paunchy thirty-six-year-old man wearing a dress and carrying a purse accompanied by a tiny dog peeing like a racehorse. *Ach, 'tis no business of anyone's anyway. As if anyone around here would take notice.* With that, she turned from the open door and put the kettle on. She rummaged around in the cupboards looking for the biscuits but came up short. *'Tis a wonder Max manages as well as he does, livin' in these conditions. Clearly, I cannot leave the poor lamb. I've got to stay on at least until*

6

the lad goes off to college or his da smartens up and marries that lovely Bridget Calloway, whichever comes first. Ach!

"I've a wee bit of bad news," Mary-Margaret said with a slight cough as Phil bounced back into the kitchen with Arthur not too far behind.

"Ugh," Arthur said, his shoulders dropping. "Can this day get any worse?"

"Indeed. I cannot find the biscuits."

"Fear not, MM," Arthur said, puffing out his chest as he unclasped his purse with a gloved hand. "You can't find them because you were out of them. But, voilà. I've got a new package right here for us."

"Ye are a lifesaver, no matter what me Michael might say," Mary-Margaret gushed as Arthur handed them to her.

She set them on the counter just as the kettle began to whistle. She then dropped two Barry's tea bags into the teapot before filling it with boiling water and setting the timer on the stove for five minutes. Always five minutes. Anything less would be a waste of a tea bag, and anything more would murder it.

"Before we begin, luv," Mary-Margaret said, looking Arthur up and down. "I realize that yer...what did ye call it...pansexual? Yes. I realize this. Havin' been a young widow left to raise four smallies on me own in poverty, but for me secretarial callin' at St. Francis, I've seen a lot in me day. I've no issue with ye or who ye see yerself as. It's just that—"

"Oh, this?" Arthur said with a pirouette.

"Indeed. Ye look...lovely. I'm just flounderin' about in my mind, wonderin' if this is one of those times when I'm not to call ye Arthur, and, if not, what...?"

"Lucille will do

"Lucille?"

"Yes. I feel like a Lucille today. She. Her."

"Brill. Lucille, it is. So...Lucille. Do ye want to tell me yer news, or shall I start in on—"

"Let me go first," Lucille said, and then, seeing the look in Mary-Margaret's eyes, quickly added, "Not that I don't care about what's going on in your life. I do. But I don't want to forget anything and, with trying to get myself here on time this morning and everything, I may have used too much hairspray, and it may have—"

"Go on then," Mary-Margaret said.

"Okay. Thanks. So there I was, en route to your place, MM—"

"*Michael's* place," she corrected, the sound of Michael's words still nipping at her heart.

"Well, yes. Michael's place. Anyway, there I was, en route, when I noticed this super weird-looking guy over by the wooden fence back there where Phil ended up urinating, between where your laneway dead ends and that little spot before the laneway where the old guys drink their wine starts."

"And ye would know about this how?"

"I have eyes, MM."

"And ye have seen me Michael's neighbors drinkin' out back, then? Ach. What have we become?"

"Oh, that. No. You told me about that. I thought you meant about that little path or whatever. Anyway, about this weird-looking guy—"

"And that's another thing," Mary-Margaret said, looking Lucille up and down again. "What, in your opinion, would constitute 'weird'?"

"Oh, it's all about aura, MM. Totally the aura."

"I'm not much on that myself—"

"I disagree," Lucille interrupted.

"Do ye now?" Mary-Margaret said with a smirk as she turned to get two mugs from the dishwasher.

"You are one of the most fae people I know."

"Ach, go on with ye," Mary-Margaret said proudly, straightening up as she gave the mugs a closer look. "I'm not sure me Michael's dishwasher is doin' its job. Wash them by hand, I always did, but not our Michael. No. He shoves everythin' in the machine and, as me eyes are showin' me now, clearly hopes for the best. No way to run yer life, in my opinion. Wishin' on a star—"

"All of you have it. The Irish, I mean."

"Have what? Dirty dishes?"

"No. The gift. You know…the magic."

"Not all of us," Mary-Margaret said, wiping out the mugs with a dishcloth.

"Point in case. Now, get on with yer story."

"Right. So," Lucille continued, stepping into the middle of the kitchen to begin her oration, "I'm walking along the laneway where the old guys—"

"Yes, yes," Mary-Margaret interrupted. "We all know the ne'er-do-wells drink their tinnies and their wines there. Tell me about—"

"I'm trying, MM," Lucille said.

"Sorry. 'Tis either me patience or me aversion to ill-chosen comportment gettin' the best of me, I'm thinkin'. Carry on."

"You're not upset with me coming here looking like this, are you?" Lucille said, looking down at her apparel.

"And why would I be?" Mary-Margaret demanded. "Ye have as much of a right to wear a dress as anyone else does, although, if ye are askin', I would have picked somethin' a little more…flatterin'."

"I know. But I did come over to clean, after all. Otherwise, I would have worn this killer little black dress I have that makes me look like Audrey Hepburn in *Breakfast at Tiffany's*."

Mary-Margaret stared at her friend.

"You're sure it's not more like Katherine Hepburn in *Pat and Mike*?"

"Hardly," Lucille said with a nod of her head. "But anyway, I was walking from that laneway into the other at the back, just there, when I practically run into this guy. We both jump back, and I see that he has a plastic grocery bag in his hand. He takes another look at me, drops the bag, and pushes past me to run through the laneway on the other side and out onto the road."

"Did ye call after him, then?"

"Well, no. I was too surprised. And he was too fast, not that I couldn't have outrun him under normal circumstances, but by the time what had happened registered with me, he was already out onto the street, and this dress is *not* ideal for a foot chase. I mean, I suppose I could have pulled it up, but I don't think I'm wearing the appropriate undergarment…"

The timer on the stove began to make an awful grinding noise.

"Hold that thought while I get our tea, Arth—Lucille. Would ye mind puttin' a few of those McVitie's on a plate? We might as well take this saga out to the livin' room and make ourselves comfortable."

9

Lucille reached around Mary-Margaret to get a plate from the cupboard and then unloaded the entire bag of biscuits onto it. Mary-Margaret looked at Lucille with raised eyebrows.

"This story might take a while," Lucille advised.

Mary-Margaret poured the tea, and they each took a mug. Lucille carefully balanced the near-capacity plate of biscuits and followed Mary-Margaret into the living room, placing the plate down on the coffee table before settling into one of the two wingback chairs by the front bay window.

"Now," Mary-Margaret said, settling herself in across from Lucille, "this bag. Did ye pick it up, then?"

"Of course, I did."

"And where is it?"

"Just outside on the stoop at the back there," Lucille said, gesturing to the back door.

"And why would ye be leavin' it outside?" Mary-Margaret said in disbelief.

"Because I wasn't sure where I'd put a bag full of bones."

"Bones? This whole thing is about bones? The lad likely picked them up from the butcher 'round the corner for his dog. Ach, luv. I think ye might be havin' yer gloves on a bit too tight this mornin'."

"They don't look like animal bones, MM," Lucille said quietly.

"And just what kind of bones *do* they look like?" Mary-Margaret whispered back, half-mockingly. "Because ye would know the difference how?"

Lucille sat upright. "Well, as you may or may not know, I have been a rather exceptional student of forensic anthropology from a very young age. In fact, my grade seven science teacher said that I had a knack for it, which I've obviously enhanced through online learning courses since then."

"Ye were studyin' forensic anthropology in grade seven then, were ye?"

"I went to a special school."

"Now that, I'm sure of."

"Anyway," Lucille continued, ignoring the comment as she popped a biscuit in her mouth, "it's always been an interest...no, a passion...of mine, and I have to tell you, these aren't any animal bones."

"And just whose bones do ye think they are, then?"

"Well, I can't say for sure without doing a complete analysis—"

"And ye plan to do this how?" Mary-Margaret asked.

"With my analysis kit."

"Indeed."

"Even without the kit, I'd bet next week's rent that these are *human* remains."

"Ye pay yer rent by the week?"

"That's as far in advance as I can afford. You're kind of my only client. I'm going through a bit of a ...rough patch at the moment."

"I see," Mary-Margaret sighed, reaching for a biscuit. "And how long do ye think it would take for ye to sort out whether or not we'd be carryin' someone's beloved in that bag out there on the stoop?"

"Hmmm," Lucille sighed, his eyes widening as he looked just over Mary-Margaret's head. "Depends on how quickly the chemicals react to the DNA in the structure of the—"

"Ye have chemicals stored in yer place that ye are renting by the week?"

"Oh, you have no idea what I have there, MM."

"No, luv. I do not," she said, leaving the biscuit on the plate. "And I'm beginnin' to thank me lucky stars for that. But about these bones?"

"So, assuming this is a garden-variety bag of human bones—"

"Are there any other type?"

"You have no idea."

"Clearly."

"But assuming these are garden-variety bones," Lucille continued, "I'd say I could know by later today."

"That soon?"

"Absolutely. Assuming I went home right now."

Mary-Margaret glanced around the room, all thoughts of the criminal activity going on at Max's school having left her mind. "Well, no point wastin' time flappin' our gums. Ye best get to it."

"Right," Lucille said, shoving a few more biscuits into her mouth as she got up to take her mug to the kitchen sink.

She pulled on his gloves and picked up her purse before turning back to

Mary-Margaret.

"I hate to ask, MM, but…"

"I'll e-transfer the money over to ye within the hour. Ye did show up to work. 'Tis not yer fault I sent ye on another task."

"Thanks, MM."

"If it's clients yer lackin', ye might want to consider talkin' to Father Miguel at the church. I hear they're lookin' for a cleaner. I'd certainly put a word in for ye. Better yet, I'll give him a ring in the next moment and get ye the job," she said, nodding her head confidently. "That is, if ye want it."

"Oh, don't you know it, MM. And being a custodian at the church would be my dream job. Imagine the outfits I could wear. Ohhhh!" Lucille grasped where her pearls would be had she been wearing any.

"And ye promise to keep comin' here to clean even after yer a Big City Church Custodian?"

"Absolutely. I will never forget the little people," Lucille said, holding up an imaginary award.

"Ach, be off with ye then," Mary-Margaret said with a chuckle, opening the back door for her friend. "And mind yer step. Don't be crushin' that bag ye left there."

"Right. The bones."

"Oh, and luv?" Mary-Margaret said, giving Lucille's arm a little squeeze. "Don't think it's a bank error when ye see a little extra in that e-transfer. I'll be payin' ye in advance for the next several weeks."

Lucille lowered her eyes and smiled before practically skipping down the alleyway, swinging the bag of bones in one hand and the white purse in the other.

Mary-Margaret closed the door and went upstairs. As promised, she transferred the money before pulling the vacuum out of the closet, plugging it in, and beginning to clean.

No different from usual. I'd be hooverin' afterwards, regardless, she thought, pushing the vacuum around as she wondered if she'd have time to finish the police procedural she was reading before tonight's book club meeting.

Chapter Three

It was a lovely evening, and Mary-Margaret half wished she didn't have to spend it inside, but, after Arthur's discovery this morning, she was particularly keen on speaking to the coroner her book club had arranged to have at tonight's meeting. Hopefully, there would be no discussion around the last few chapters of *Man at the Door*, the book they had chosen, because she'd been too busy to finish reading the book.

"Can we all get seated, please," Abby Regan's shrill voice called out to the small but dedicated group as she moved to the podium set up at the front of the small parlor. "We've got a very special guest this evening, and we don't want to keep him waiting."

The dozen or so women and the handful of men who made up the book club at St. Francis of Assisi stopped their chattering and shuffled to their usual seats, and quickly settled in on the hard folding chairs arranged in three rows of five. All eyes looked expectantly up at the young woman standing before them.

If me Michael knew I was out and about like this, Mary-Margaret thought, beginning to fret as she looked over her shoulder at the others. *Well, it's not like the pneumonia is contagious, and I could always say I needed to get out for some air if anyone said anythin'.*

"Tonight," Abby began, looking down at the notes she had prepared, "we have a more…unusual, shall we say?…speaker. As some of you may know, Norm Goodier, our alter guild chair, grew up in a small town just east of the city with his brother, Raymond. While we are blessed that Norm decided to build his life here at St. Francis with us, his brother chose a different path.

After completing medical school, Dr. Raymond Goodier returned to his hometown and became the county coroner."

Everyone began to look around the room for an unfamiliar face and then back to Abby when they didn't see one.

"And tonight," Abby continued after allowing for these few moments of anticipation, "we are lucky to have Dr. Goodier with us to discuss anything and everything you ever wanted to know about dead bodies but were too afraid to ask."

On cue, an older man, who Mary-Margaret thought should have looked distinguished but did not, walked into the room from the hallway and stood beside Abby, but not before making a very loud noise as he shuffled his gum-soled shoes along the dull tile floor.

Ach, that reminds me. I've got to call Father Miguel and get Arthur in as the custodian here before we are all consumed by filth.

"H-h-hello," the man stuttered, looking down as he pulled some papers out of his tweed sports coat pocket, his lip twitching into a smile that disappeared as quickly as it had appeared.

"I'm sure you've got lots to say, Doctor, so I'll leave you to it," Abby said with a flourish, reaching out to touch the man's elbow but changing her mind as he pulled away.

"Y-y-yes," Dr. Goodier said, clearing his throat. He looked up at the expectant room before quickly dropping his gaze down to the papers he was fumbling with. "M-m-my name is Dr. Raymond Goodier, and I am— was—the regional, n-n-not county– coroner for Northumberland County."

There was a polite round of applause as he set the papers on the podium.

"'Tis good this lad works with the dead," Mary-Margaret said a bit louder than she had intended to the woman beside her. "I don't suppose he has much of a bedside manner."

Dr. Goodier looked at Mary-Margaret, who was sitting directly in front of him, and flashed a quick, almost warm, smile.

"Y-y-you're absolutely right, M-M-Mrs...?"

"O'Shea. Mary-Margaret O'Shea."

"Mrs. O'Shea. I-I-I decided very quickly on in my medical career that

14

working with the deceased w-w-was a better match for me than with the living."

"Ye are a wise man," Mary-Margaret said with a nod, a wave of empathy washing over her.

"Yes, w-w-well," he said, pulling a pair of black-rimmed reading glasses from his coat pocket and then clearing his throat again. "I-I-I have been a coroner for over forty years. In fact, th-th-the only reason I retired was because I can't drive anymore, and my w-w-wife isn't too keen on the idea of driving around the countryside looking at corpses, human remains, and homicide scenes."

He waited a few seconds for a laugh and, when there was none, tousled his obviously dyed black hair that looked like an overgrown crew cut before clearing his throat again and continuing.

"Um, I-I-I've never spoken in front of a group like this b-b-before. I usually only talk to the b-b-body on the table."

Again, when he was met with nothing but blank stares, he heaved a big sigh and continued.

"As Miss...?"

"Regan. Abbey Regan. Mrs. Regan," the moderator called out with a smile as awkward as the coroner's demeanor.

"Yes...Mrs. Regan. As Mrs. Regan said, I graduated from medical school and then, realized that I lacked in the most b-b-basic of social skills—"

A roll of laughter came from the group.

"Tha-tha-that wasn't the funny part," he said, looking over his glasses. "I w-was being serious."

A few people cleared their throats, but Mary-Margaret caught the sparkle in his eye.

"Right. Wh-wh-why don't I get d-d-down to business, then. So," he said, taking a deep breath, "when someone d-d-dies, the coroner is called. As the coroner, I attend to the b-b-body, whether in their home or at the hospital—although most of the larger hospitals have their own coroner's, thank goodness—or at the location wh-wh-where the b-b-body was found. My p-p-primary responsibility is to confirm that the p-p-person is d-d-d-dead. Sometimes, it's p-pretty obvious. Well, usually it is, which is w-w-why I was called in the first place."

Dr. Goodier looked up at the audience who, despite his speech impediment, were now hanging off of his every word.

"Tha-tha-that was supposed to be funny."

A polite tittering was heard.

"In any event, I then issue a d-d-death warrant and a d-d-death certificate. The certificate is to certify that the b-b-body is of a d-d-deceased individual, and the warrant is like," he fumbled, "a ticket to ride. Feel free to hum that song in your heads for the next several d-d-days."

Assuming by the silence in the room that his stab at humor had failed, Dr. Goodier continued.

"I am not a p-p-pathologist, which is to say, while I can d-d-declare the cause of d-d-death, I d-d-d-on't—"

"I'm sure ye would know what it was before the pathologist gets to the body though, wouldn't ye?" Mary-Margaret asked.

"W-w-well, yes and no, which is to say, my opinion is not considered… uh…what is legally construed as 'expert' in the c-c-case of a homicide. I just have a quick look at the scene. I d-d-don't do autopsies. I'm afraid it's not very exciting or sexy, b-b-but that's what I d-d-do. D-d-does anyone have any questions at this p-p-point?"

"I do," Willow Anderson said from the back row. "If you go to a scene and you think it's a murder, do you call the police?"

"Unlike television, I d-d-don't often stumble across b-b-bodies. It's usually the p-p-police who call me. B-b-but," Dr. Goodier continued, "there have b-b-been times when I've been called out to scenes where there have b-b-been human remains found, and I have suggested to the officers that it could b-b-be a homicide."

The small group of crime readers sat up.

"Y-y-yes," he continued, his eyes nervously scanning the faces in front of him, "I often get called out when what appears to be human remains are found, only to d-d-determine, of course, that they are the bones of a large d-d-dog or a d-d-deer or something like that."

The small group slumped down again.

"Tell me," Mary-Margaret asked as she raised her hand. "How long would it take for the skin to rot off of human bones?"

"Well, that's-that's-that's an excellent question," the coroner responded, his eyes beginning to brighten up. "It d-d-depends on where the remains were left. For example, is it p-p-possible that an animal may have eaten the f-flesh off of the bones, unless the body was f-found inside a dwelling or other enclosed space, in which case, insects—"

"What about acids and the like?" Mary-Margaret continued, her eyes narrowing.

"W-w-well, it d-depends on what type of acid and—"

"Planning on killing someone and getting rid of the body, Mary-Margaret?" Abby asked with a laugh.

"Are you working on another murder?" Willow called out.

"Are you a p-p-police officer?" Dr. Goodier asked with a cordial nod.

"No, luv. Me son Michael is. Would be Police Officer of the Year if he just applied himself. Hard workin' lad, but not always the brightest light in the laneway, if ye know what I mean."

"Yes. Yes. I see."

"What I would like to know, however, and ye can answer this, I'm sure, is how often are human bones found?"

"D-d-depends on where you are," Dr. Goodier began, stepping away from the podium. "If you're in the country, wh-wh-where people w-wander off, and there are a lot of p-p-predatorial animals and not very many p-p-people, it's not unheard of. Here in the city, however, I would think very f-f-few human bones would be found."

"And why is that, then?"

"P-p-population. People tend to stumble across b-b-bodies before they've been dead very long, which doesn't give the animals—"

"Do raccoons eat people?" someone called out.

"Th-th-that's not really my area of expertise, but I d-d-don't believe they d-d-do," Dr. Goodier said and then looked down at the papers in his hands. "Now, let's get b-b-back to what I had p-p-prepared for this evening..."

Despite sitting not more than six feet from the man, Mary-Margaret did not hear a word of his presentation. She was increasingly convinced that the bones Arthur had found were not human but rather, as she had suspected, had come from the butcher's shop around the corner. Hopefully, Arthur would be able to tell her soon, assuming his analysis kit was accurate, and she could put the matter out of her head.

He did say he'd call when he had the results, didn't he? Or did he?

Out of deference for the coroner standing in front of her, Mary-Margaret exercised more self-control than usual by refraining from reaching into her purse and pulling out her cell phone to check for messages.

Ach, this is worse than having to go to the jacks before the final few minutes in a football match. But of course! I can excuse meself to go to the jacks and then...

"Now, y-y-you seemed to be quite interested in b-b-bones, Mrs. O'Shea," she heard Dr. Goodier say.

As her mind returned to the events around her, Mary-Margaret noticed that all eyes were on her.

"Me? No. Well, yes, now that ye mention it. Ye see, I've found, well, I've not, but these bones have been found in a bag in me son's yard—"

"Likely animal b-b-bones," Dr. Goodier cut in, nodding knowingly.

"And that's exactly what I told Arthur, who was Lucille today."

Dr. Goodier stared down at her.

"They're pansexual," Mary-Margaret said, looking behind her at her book club. "Me house cleaner. The logic behind it is too complicated for me mind to unravel to ye in this moment, and it matters not to the present conversation, so let's get back to the bones. Animal, then? Just as I thought. Thank ye, Doctor."

"W-w-well, I'm not d-d-definitively saying that they're animal b-b-bones, but, in a city the size of this one, the likelihood that they are human remains is slim."

"So they might be human?" Mary-Margaret asked, raising one eyebrow.

"P-p-possibly, although unlikely."

"Ye are not exactly the lad I'd want leadin' my charge," Mary-Margaret chortled.

"W-without the b-b-bones," Dr. Goodier began as the otherwise polite gathering began to murmur. "If I could look at them, then I could give you a d-d-definitive answer."

"So ye are sayin' that if I had the bones with me just now, ye could have a wee peek, and ye'd know?"

"Yes. I feel comfortable saying that."

Mary-Margaret looked around the room and, like a magician pulling a rabbit out of a hat and with the same level of audience anticipation, pulled her cell phone out of her purse.

"This is getting really good," a voice behind her said.

The phone rang twice before an automated voice told her to leave a message. *Ach, where could the lad be? And, on second thought, do I want to know?*

"Arthur, luv," Mary-Margaret said loudly, looking at the people around her, "'tis me, Mary-Margaret. Pick up yer phone, lad. I've got the coroner here and…"

"MM?" a voice at the other end broke in.

"And who else would it be? Bring the bones—"

"Yes, bring the bones!" a man in the group said.

"Why would I bring them anywhere? Oh, and by the way, they're human."

"Are ye sure, lad?" Mary-Margaret whispered, leaning down in her seat.

"No doubt in my mind. As you know, I was always—"

"I'm sure. Ta, luv. I'll call ye later. Bye-bye bye bye-bye."

Everyone in the room was looking at Mary-Margaret as she sat up again in her chair.

"Let's suppose," she began, looking casually around the room before directing her attention back to the coroner, "that someone had, in their possession, some…human bones…that they found."

"She's got another murder on the go," another voice behind her said. A wave of murmurs followed.

"Th-th-then the police need to be called right away. Might not be a homicide. Might be a theft from a g-g-grave site, might be a number of things. R-r-regardless, something illegal has h-h-happened."

19

"I don't know why we don't just have Mary-Margaret as a speaker," another man in the group said.

"That's all we need," someone else groaned.

"Well, I was only just supposin'. And, as ye all know, I've not been feelin' meself lately. A touch of the pneumonia, as ye may know, so I'll be off now. Excuse me."

With that, Mary-Margaret gathered herself up and hurriedly left the parlor. She raced down the hallway as fast as her heavy legs could carry her and crashed out the side doors of the church to the parking lot where her eggshell blue Renault Dauphine was parked.

"Jesus, Mary, and Joseph, Daphne," she said to the car after fumbling with her keys to start the ignition. "We've got ourselves another homicide."

Chapter Four

One of the luxuries Mary-Margaret refused to give up, even if it did mean driving across the city, was her Friday morning massages. While there were massage therapists who were much closer—some even in Michael's neighborhood, as he was fond of reminding her—she only went to Louise. Everyone else in Mary-Margaret's neighborhood also went to Louise, which made the appointment an excellent opportunity to gossip without saying so.

"I would have thought that all of your knots would be gone now that you're retired, but," Louise said, massaging Mary-Margaret's left leg, "such is not the case, although...."

For someone who had just passed her sixty-fifth birthday, Mary-Margaret was in good shape, despite her feigned ailments that would lead anyone who was unfamiliar with Mary-Margaret's well-intentioned mind to believe that she was a hypochondriac. And then there was the matter of her weight. If the BMI charts splashed all over the internet were to be trusted, she could stand to lose a few inches here and there, although her own doctor had never said anything, and Louise regarded Mary-Margaret as one of the healthiest people she knew.

"Ach, 'tis another murder I've got on the go," Mary-Margaret replied as she felt a wave of relief wash over her.

"Another one? You're a regular Miss Marple," Louise said, moving to the other leg.

"If only it was that easy, Louise."

"Easy? Those were hard cases to crack."

"Ye just had to keep readin' the book to crack 'em, luv. Nothin' like real life."

"I see you've given up the crutches," Louise commented.

"Indeed. Ye can only have a broken foot for so long."

"You mean Mike figured it out?" Louise said, recalling that Mary-Margaret had feigned a broken foot to stay longer with her son.

"And what do ye mean by that?"

"Nothing at all," Louise said. "I'm just glad you're not using the crutches any more. I imagine they threw your alignment off, which is why your legs are so tight."

"Well, if that's all that's tight, I'd say I'm doin' okay," Mary-Margaret replied with a chuckle. While she was not prone to over-indulge, Mary-Margaret maintained that the secret to her vitality and well-being included the occasional shot of whiskey, a weekly half pint of a crown float at O'Leary's Pub, and a steady diet of family involvement.

"And what does your Michael have to say about this latest murder?"

"Me Michael? I've not the slightest. Except that he thinks I'm daft. And have the pneumonia. Ye won't tell him otherwise, will ye?"

"Not to worry. Our paths don't cross. And a good masseuse never tells. Now, roll over onto your back, please."

Louise stepped back as Mary-Margaret, holding the sheet up to her chin, managed to turn her ample body over on the small massage table.

"Don't worry, Mary-Margaret. I'm sure there's nothing I haven't seen before, and I'm not looking anyway," Louise offered, attempting to make her friend feel less self-conscious.

"Nobody needs to see what's under here. Trust me. Keep tellin' yerself that ye'll be young and beautiful forever, but I've got proof to the contrary right here under this sheet," Mary-Margaret said with a half-laugh.

"Every body is beautiful. Now, let's try to get these shoulders loosened up a bit."

The massage therapist settled into a rhythm of kneading and rolling as she worked in silence for a few minutes.

"Ye know, it's not like I go lookin' for this sort of thing. Murder just seems to fall into me lap. And then there's me Michael. It's not like I *want* to implant meself into his life at this stage of the game, but, honest to God, Louise, if I hadn't just let me job at the Church and found meself with a clear dance card—"

"There are no coincidences in life."

"So ye've said."

"Let's start with the murders. You've lived here for years, and nothing. You leave the church, and that lapsed parishioner ends up dead. And now...?"

"It's not like I'm doin'—"

"You don't have to. It's fate."

Mary-Margaret looked over at Louise.

"Consider why you're directed to all of these murders. Is it because your Michael is a detective? And how did he become a detective? Is it because it's in his DNA? And where did he get that DNA from?"

"Well," she said, settling her face back into the face cradle, "most of it is mine, I must admit."

"Exactly. So, in a nutshell, you are the actual detective. He's just a genetic offshoot."

"Don't tell him that, poor lad. He gets beaten down enough as 'tis."

"You were the one who solved that last murder. The police—"

"Ach, don't get me started—"

"But you needed to be close to Michael to get close to their investigation."

"I don't think so," Mary-Margaret objected half-heartedly, knowing that Louise was right.

"It's all about energy. The universe needed the two of you to be close to channel that energy, which is why the universe had sent you to stay with him." Louise gave Mary-Margaret's shoulder a particularly intense squeeze before returning to the previous rhythm. "And now, the universe has trusted you with another murder."

"Do ye read tea leaves as well, then?" Mary-Margaret said with a full laugh.

"You've got your church. I've got my coven."

Again, the room was silent while Louise dragged her fingers up Mary-Margaret's neck onto the back of her head.

23

"So what happened?" Louise asked.

"Arthur, who was Lucille at the time, and was wearing a horrible frock, even just for cleaning, I might add,found a bag of bones out in the laneway. Didn't say much about it until after he took Wee Phil…." Mary-Margaret stopped mid-sentence. "Wee Phil. Oh, me stars. I forgot to let him out before comin' here. Louise, I know it's against policy, but can ye reach inside me handbag and get out me cell phone. I've got to make a call. It's an emergency."

Knowing her friend too well, Louise complied.

"Michael, 'tis yer mother. I know ye are asleep, or maybe ye are in the courts. Regardless, when ye get this message, can ye either just let Wee Phil out the back or get yerself home to let him out because I'm…at the doctor's. Yes. The doctor has called me in to have a listen to me lungs. Routine for someone with the pneumonia. Who's my age. Yes. That's what the doctor has said. I'm alright, but ye can never be too careful. Again, quotin' the doctor. But nothin' a wee bit of extended bed rest at yer place won't cure. Ta, luv. Bye bye-bye bye-bye-bye."

Mary-Margaret handed the phone back to Louise, who dropped it back into the handbag.

"Yes, I know," Mary-Margaret said, sensing a wave of disapproval from Louise, "I've told a wee bit of fib. But me Michael, ach, honestly, luv, the lad is losin' the plot. If I weren't there, he and all that's around him would fall into a heap at our feet."

"I'm sure his work keeps him very busy."

"Indeed. So much so that me grandson might as well be an orphan, poor wee soul. I don't know what he'd be eatin if I wasn't there to shove somethin' into his gob, and, with all that's goin' on at his school—a regular organized crime ring over there, what with lads breakin' into lockers durin' the day, stealin' cell phones and laptops, all right under the administration's nose—and no one seems willlin' to do a thing about it. Not even his da, me Michael, a Big City Police Detective. I don't understand it at all. Unless—"

"Does he know about it?"

"Who? Me Michael? Of course, he does! He's the police!"

Louise grunted as she tried to relax the re-engaged muscles that she had

24

just finished massaging.

"Ouch!" Mary-Margaret hollered in protest.

"Sorry," Louise said, but continued to press hard into the older woman's flesh. "I'm sure you'll sort it out, Mary-Margaret."

"I've a feelin' that I'm goin' to have to. There's nothin' left but to see for meself, I'm thinkin'. But honestly, though, I'm at me wits' end, what with all the mayhem around me."

"Well, I'm sure a visit to the school will—"

"'Tis a regular organized crime ring in full operation, I'm thinkin'. Likely gang-related. And me own wee grandson is caught in the crossfire, I'm sure of it."

"Why don't you wait until you speak to the principal before you get—"

"Are ye suggestin' that I'm over-reactin', Louise?"

"No," Louise said, trying to work a new knot out of Mary-Margaret's neck. "I'm suggesting that you're literally tying yourself up in knots."

Mary-Margaret remained silent while Louise concentrated on the knot.

"And then there's the bones—"

"Quiet," Louise said. "I've almost got this thing under control."

"Sorry. It's just the less I talk, the more worked up I get in me head."

"How about the church? How are things going there?" Louise asked, hoping to find a neutral, if not more positive, topic.

"Oh, thanks for remindin' me. I was to make a phone call and forgot. I'll pop by after this."

"Another bazaar coming up?" Louise asked.

"No. I told Arthur that I'd get him the job as the custodian. I know Father Miguel's been lookin' for a while."

"I thought you've told me before that he wasn't a very good cleaner."

"He's not, but he's a good lad, and I think he'd keep Father Miguel in line."

"Is that a good thing?"

"Indeed. He's gettin' a bit too big for his cassock. I've never seen a man of the cloth as driven as he to become pope."

"Do you really think so?"

"Ach, there's not a doubt in me mind. Why else would someone with so little ability such as he land himself in such a parish as ours? I realize that Father Brian was no saint, but we'd have been better takin' Father Ted or any of the other bumble heads from Craggy Island than this power-hungry poser. But I've got great faith that me God won't allow such a martinet to overturn His work."

After a few more minutes trying to work the knots out of her neck, Louise turned from Mary-Margaret and walked towards the door.

"Take your time getting up. Shall I book you in for another appointment next week?"

* * *

After such a vivid vision of Father Miguel's plan to take over the Catholic Church, Mary-Margaret found herself even more annoyed with the traffic that made an eleven-mile journey from the clinic to Michael's house a forty-five-minute drive than usual. The only upside of it all was that she had plenty of time to shift her annoyance from Father Miguel in general to Michael's lack of interest in all things important to Max's inevitable victimization by persons unknown within that organized crime ring to the matter that she knew should have been front and center her mind: the origins of the bones in the laneway.

It was too early for the neighbors to be out in the back having a drink, which gave Mary-Margaret the opportunity to check in the bushes for clues.

"Lose your marbles, Mary-Margaret?" Doug called from the back gate of his yard, his golden retriever looking lovingly up at him.

"Ye should be the one talkin'," she called back. She could feel the muscles in her neck that Louise had worked so hard to loosen tightening up again.

"I'm only kidding. Is there anything I can help you with?"

"A bit early for a tinnie, wouldn't ye say?" she shot back, preparing for a full-on back spasm.

"Oh, that," Doug said with a boyish grin. "Do you know, we started that about twenty years ago when we all moved in. Dave was the one who started it, actually. He's gone now. Marge is still in the house, but she doesn't come out much."

"And it's something yer proud of then? A bunch of grown men, drinkin' in the laneway?"

"It was a nice way of having a drink after work with the neighbors. Of course, since then, we've all retired, but it's become a nice tradition."

"Did ye not think of takin' it inside?"

"Nope. And if it's raining, or in the winter, we just don't do it."

"Well, at least ye have some standards."

"Perhaps you'd like to join us later today. I'll even bring a beer out for you, if that's what you drink."

"And what if it isn't?"

"I'll bring whatever you'd like out for you," Doug said, the grin returning to his face.

"I only drink crown floats. Or a wee dram of whiskey if I'm feelin' poorly. Or it's cold outside."

"I don't know what it is, but I'll have a crown float for you this afternoon at five."

"Half a pint, mind. I don't go mad with it."

"Half a pint of a crown float at five p.m. Come on, Red," Doug said to the dog behind him. "Time for your walk."

I'll be out at five, but there'll be no crown float, Mary-Margaret thought as she began poking the bushes growing on both sides of the fence dividing the two laneways where Arthur found the bag of bones back. *Miscreants, the whole lot of 'em. I don't know why Michael loves this neighborhood so. Not a workin' church in sight. And the pub around the corner is likely no O'Leary's. Not that I need to go to a pub or drink tinnies like—*

Her train of thought screeched to a stop when she saw a torn yellow shopping bag amidst the bushes that had been tied at the top and still contained something that the animals were unable to tear out.

Slowly, she reached in and plucked the bag out, careful not to let whatever was still in it roll out of the tear the animals had made. The bag began to drip a reddish liquid, causing Mary-Margaret to set it back down much quicker than she had picked it up.

She hastily pulled the cell phone out of her pocket and fumbled to press the numbers.

"Arthur," she whispered.

"MM, what is it?"

"I've found something."

"I'm sure you have. Where are you, and what is it?"

"'Tis no time for bein' clever, lad. I'm in the laneway. Where ye were. I think I've found the head."

"Don't move. I'll be right there."

"Shall I call the police in the meantime?"

"No. Wait until I get there. It may be nothing—"

"Should I call me Michael, then?"

"I'm just around the corner, MM. I just need to get dressed. I'm at a play partner's—"

"I don't want to know. Just get here," Mary-Margaret said, as close to tears of fear as she recalled ever having been in recent history.

Chapter Five

"I don't even want to ask what ye are pretendin' to be at this moment," Mary-Margaret said as she saw Arthur rushing up the laneway, his ample girth jiggling under what appeared to be a purple body suit.

"I...never...pretend...and," he replied, bending over, hands on knees as he gasped for air, "I'll have you know, this emo suit cost—"

"Is that what ye call it, then? Well, ye look more like a Telletubbie than whatever it is ye are bein'. And this is all a part of yer play, then?"

"Yes. It's—"

"I don't want to know," Mary-Margaret said, trying desperately not to be overly judgmental. *Matthew 7, Mary-Margaret. Just remember Mathew 7.* "Have a look at this, lad."

"Where is it?" he asked, sucking in his belly while he wiped his brow, scanning the bushes.

"Mind yer step!" Mary-Margaret shouted just as Arthur was about to step into a pool of what she assumed was blood.

"Yikes," he said, leaping to the side.

"'Tis in there," she pointed, stepping back from the bushes.

Arthur stood where Mary-Margaret had been and plucked out the yellow bag. He held it up, and the outline of a face could be seen against the plastic.

"It's a head, MM. Someone's head is in this bag," Arthur whispered.

"Jesus, Mary, and Joseph," Mary-Margaret gasped, her hands over her mouth. "What do we do now?"

"Are you okay, Mary-Margaret?" Doug called out, having heard the commotion. "Is that...person...bothering you?"

"Call the police," she called back, her voice cracking.

"I am right now," Doug replied, rushing towards her with his cell phone in one hand and a large stick he had picked up in the other.

Unaware of Doug's approach, Arthur carefully set the bag down where he'd found it. The bag rolled slightly until it settled about half an inch away from Arthur's right foot. In that split second, when the bag was in motion, and much to everyone's surprise, Mary-Margaret let out a shriek.

Hearing her shriek, Arthur shrieked.

"You leave her alone," Doug yelled, rushing towards them while dropping the phone into his pocket before having placed the call.

"It's only me. Arthur," the younger man said, holding his hand to his chest. "And we're alright. A little taken aback, but—"

"I don't care what your name is or how you feel. You leave that woman alone!"

Within striking range now, Doug grasped the stick like a baseball bat. Before anyone could say anything, he whacked Arthur across the back, knocking him to the ground.

"I'm calling the police, so don't even think of getting up," Doug said, fumbling in his pocket for the phone, his body shaking as much as he was shaking the stick over Arthur's head.

"Ughhhh," Arthur groaned.

"Are you alright, Mary-Margaret?" Doug said, turning his attention to her. "Has he hurt you? I saw everything from—"

"Are ye daft, lad?" Mary-Margaret bellowed, looking up at Doug as she fell to her knees beside Arthur, oblivious to the yellow bag only inches away. "I think ye've killed him!"

"Not. Dead. Yet," Arthur moaned, rolling onto his back, eyes closed, arms outstretched.

Mary-Margaret put the back of her hand to Arthur's forehead, then took his wrist to check his pulse. She nodded the count for about fifteen seconds, multiplied the number of pulse beats by four, and, satisfied that he was, indeed, not yet dead, set his hand down on his chest.

She then got up and stood toe-to-toe with Michael's stick-brandishing neighbor. She did not say a word, nor did she have to. Her fiery blue eyes said it all.

"Look," Doug said, stepping back to point the stick at her, still holding the phone up to his ear, waiting on hold for the emergency call-taker to pick up. "You're bleeding."

Arthur opened his eyes and looked up.

"Blood? There's blood?" he wailed.

"I am *not* hurt," Mary-Margaret corrected in a tone that every man who's had a mother would recognize. Both Arthur and Doug recoiled slightly before she continued. "Nor am I bleeding. 'Tis Arthur who is hurt, and no one's bleedin'. And put the stick down before ye truly do hurt someone."

"*Else.* Hurt someone else," Arthur corrected, still lying face up on the ground. "I'm already hurt, remember?"

"You know this...guy?" Doug asked, dropping the stick.

"Of course, I know him. 'Tis Arthur. The lad who cleans me—Michael's—house."

"Bi-weekly. Openings available if you're looking—"

"But your knees," Doug said, pointing to the blood on her legs.

"Ach, 'tis the blood from what's in the bag. Look at me now, makin' a mess of it all."

"What bag?" Doug asked.

"The one that almost rolled out onto the laneway but for me shriekin' it back into hidin'. 'Tis there. In the bushes. Now, have ye got the police on the line or not?"

"Right," Doug said, holding his phone to his ear. "Yes. Oh, hello...I need the police, please. I've got a...I—I'm not sure what I've got."

Arthur groaned loudly.

"Ye have a head in a bag and a lad that likely needs lookin' at," Mary-Margaret told Doug. "Here, give me the—"

"Needs immediate medical assistance," Arthur corrected, slowly sitting up.

"Stay where ye are, luv. Might be some spinal—"

"There goes my custodian career."

"Lie back," Mary-Margaret said, pushing Arthur down before directing her attention to Doug. "And ye: just tell them what I said."

"I've got a head in a bag and a fellow in a purple leotard that needs looking at," Doug said into the phone.

"Ach, I should have just called me Michael straight away. He would know what to do."

* * *

The first to arrive was the ambulance, driven by an old paramedic with an even older partner in the passenger's seat. They both waited inside their vehicle for the moment or two it took for the police car to pull up. Both paramedics then got out, methodically pulling on their latex gloves and putting on their masks before approaching the scene.

By this time, the uniform officer, who looked too young to even have a driver's license, was already standing beside the threesome.

"I'm horribly sorry, officer," Doug began. "I thought this…person…was attacking my elderly neighbor—"

Mary-Margaret shot Doug a glance that would have killed him had he been looking at her.

"And I hit him with this stick. It was done to protect her, or so I thought. And now I'm thinking that I've committed a crime. I suppose that's assault with a weapon, isn't it? Hitting an innocent person with a stick? Do I need to get a lawyer?"

"Let's just figure out what happened first," the officer began with a sigh before saying something into the mic clipped to the epaulet on his shoulder.

The paramedics looked at each other, and then the one with more gray hair knelt beside Arthur.

"What happened, bud?"

"Well, like this man said—" Arthur started.

"How 'bout you, ma'am?" the other paramedic said. "You hurt? What happened to your legs?"

"Me legs are fine. 'Tis just the blood from the bag with the head in it is all."

"I think this one's for you, Matt," the more senior paramedic said as he stood up and looked over at his partner. They both rolled their eyes.

"You don't need any medical attention, do you, bud?" Matt asked without making any attempt to get closer to Arthur.

"I don't think he does," the other paramedic said.

"No. I'm fine. I am an experienced martial arts master and have an exceptionally high threshold for pain as a result—"

"Good," Matt interrupted, nodding to his partner, who had already turned to go back to the ambulance. "I think our work here is done, George. Let's go."

The young police officer held up his hand. "Would you guys mind standing by for a couple of minutes, just in case I need you to transport one of them as a mental health apprehens—"

"The man said he was actin' in good faith, lad," Mary-Margaret said. "And Arthur is fine. There are no mental health issues here."

"We'll stand by," both paramedics said in unison.

"Perhaps ye know me son, Detective Michael O'Shea?" Mary-Margaret said, stepping forward, looking the young officer up and down.

"Ah, no," he stammered, pulling out his memo book from the side pocket of his uniform cargo pants.

"Well, ye must be as new as ye look, then. Me son is quite a legend, even though he's never been Police Officer of the Year. They save that for the likes of ye, who'd probably dive into the lake just before it ices over to rescue drowning rodents and such, not heroes like me son, whose risked life and limb."

Arthur stood up and dusted himself off as the officer looked blankly at Mary-Margaret.

"Regardless," she continued, "I am Detective Michael O'Shea's mother, and that, over there, is his house. I'm just stayin' with him on account of the pneumonia that I'm presently afflicted with."

The young officer stepped back and looked at the rear of the houses in the laneway before taking another look at Mary-Margaret, Arthur, and Doug.

"Pneumonia?" Matt asked.

"The very thing," Mary-Margaret said with a nod, puffing her chest out.

"And I should know. There've been more than a few of me people die from it over the course of time."

"Maybe we should have a listen to your lungs then, ma'am," he said, pulling his stethoscope from around his neck. "Just a precaution. Given your age and the circumstances."

"Me age?" Mary-Margaret gasped. "And just what age do ye think I am that I need me lungs checked as a matter of routine? And by a stranger in a back alley, no less?"

Without waiting for confirmation, the paramedic poked the stethoscope under her blouse and, just as Doug was about to protest on her behalf, held his hand up for silence.

"Stay still, please, ma'am. And don't speak. Any of you."

The officer, the other paramedic, Arthur, and Doug all froze while he looked at his watch, gently holding the bell of his stethoscope to listen to Mary-Margaret's lungs.

"Sounds pretty clear to me," he said, quickly disengaging. "Who told you that you had pneumonia?"

"Well, it's the wanderin' pneumonia."

"You mean walking pneumonia?"

"Indeed. It only flares up when I'm walkin'."

"I don't think that's exactly what that means, lady," George said with a chuckle.

"We can stand here all day splittin' hairs over the difference between wanderin' and walkin' or we can look at what's just at me feet here. Which will it be, lads?" Mary-Margaret asked, glad that they weren't taking her blood pressure because she could feel that it was surely rising.

"Just point to it, please. We don't want to disturb it," the young officer directed, reaching into his cargo pant pockets for rubber gloves.

"A bit late for that," Mary-Margaret said, pointing nonetheless to the yellow bag.

"What else do you have in there?" Arthur asked, taking a closer look at the officer's uniform.

"What makes you think there's a head in this bag?" the officer asked, ignoring Arthur.

"Because I picked it up, took a look, and that's what I saw. And so did Arthur, didn't ye, luv?"

"Absolutely. And I have the bones of the body it belongs to at home."

The officer looked sorrowfully up at the sky and took a deep breath.

"If it's a head, we can put it on our gurney and take it over to the morgue for you. Otherwise, we'll do the transport for the mental health—"

"'Tis definitely a head," Mary-Margaret said. "And no one here is mental."

The three first responders exchanged glances with each other.

"Here," Mary-Margaret said. "Look for yerselves."

With that, she reached into the bushes and pulled out the bag so aggressively that it caused the already compromised plastic to split open and its contents to fall onto the ground.

"Oh my god! I know her! It's Cassandra Lewis!" Arthur cried.

"I think I'll have that wee whiskey now, if it's all the same to ye, luv," Mary-Margaret said to Doug, who looked almost as gray as she was sure she did.

Chapter Six

"I'll be gettin' ye the usual, then, shall I? Although, by the looks of ye, ye could likely use a full pint this evenin'," Maeve O'Leary said when she saw Mary-Margaret come into her pub.

"I think ye may be right, Maeve, although I've got me car," Mary-Margaret replied from her side of the bar.

"Ah, yer still at yer Michael's, are ye?"

"Indeed, luv."

"A bit of a jaunt, then. Are ye plannin' on sellin' up or—"

"Never. It's just that me Michael needs me. Ye know how lads are on their own."

"Don't get me started. Big John, is more work than wee Nolan now that Mammy O'Leary has passed. Probably always was and I just didn't notice. Now that I see it in his da, I'm fearin' that me Johnny's no better," Maeve said with a laugh, carefully pouring the Guinness on top of the Strongbow. "It's like a full-time job just managin' the two of them, never mind rearin' a smallie and runnin' the pub. Oh, and a life of me own? Never."

"And since when are ye behind the bar?"

"A minute, luv. I've got to concentrate. Don't want to muck up yer crown float. I'll never hear the end of it from Johnny if I do."

Mary-Margaret looked over to see that her regular Friday night table was unoccupied and then back at Maeve. While she couldn't have been more than thirty-five and was a bit tightly wound, Maeve O'Leary seemed to have a good mind for business, and Mary-Margaret was very glad when she and Johnny, Big John's son, had taken over the pub.

"Tell me it gets better than that," Maeve said with a smile, handing the pint glass to Mary-Margaret.

"Sláinte!" Mary-Margaret raised the glass, took a sip, and sat down on the stool in front of her.

"So, me behind the bar," Maeve said, pulling the cloth from her shoulder to wipe her hands. "Since Johnny had it out with Cassandra and the stupid girl quit is when. And here am I, with wee Nolan upstairs in front of the telly until Johnny can call someone else in."

"Quit? But she's not been here long enough to want to quit."

"I'll take that in me stride, Mary-Margaret," Maeve said, giving her the side-eye. "Seems our girl had light fingers."

"Ach. Hand in the till, was it?"

"Aye. And in the cash I keep upstairs in me drawer as well. Ye trust these ones and this is how they repay ye." Just as Big John and Maureen had lived in the flat above with their brood, so, too, did Johnny and Maeve with their only child, Nolan.

"How did she get upstairs, then? I know ye've got a lot of empty rooms up there, but—"

There had been great speculation amongst the regulars around the reasons why the younger Mr. and Mrs. O'Leary weren't filling the bedrooms as rapidly as the senior O'Leary's had, but that ended abruptly when Maeve got wind of it and threatened to ban the lot of them for life.

"Johnny had her run up and get me the other night when it got busy down here. I'd just put Nolan down so off I ran. Never thought Cassandra was too far behind me until the next mornin' when I went to get me cash from the drawer to pay the fella that washes the windows and found it gone."

"Ye can't know it was her."

"And why not? Turns out our girl had sold us quite the bill of goods, sayin' she was new to the neighborhood, needed a job to support herself and her disabled mother. Turns out, the only one she was supportin' was her drug dealer."

"Ach, ye don't want that in yer place," Mary-Margaret said with a nod.

The patrons at O'Leary's enjoyed the timeless familiarity of the pub. There was never any trouble except for the occasional flair up that was quickly dealt with by John until his knees went. Johnny takes care of things now. Back in the day, if it turned really ugly, Mammy O'Leary would take over. Now that she's gone, Maeve sorts matters out in jig time.

"No. Not at all. But ye know Johnny. As trustin' as the day is long. He even hired her brother's band to play here tonight on account of her sad story. Said we should consider havin' a band in every Friday night goin' forward. To stay current, apparently."

"A band? On a Friday night? But we all come here to talk, not shout ourselves hoarse over some fandoozle players who think they'll be the next U2."

"I know. And I've a feelin' they don't play what we're used to at our Sunday céllis, but it's too late to cancel them, so here's hopin'."

"It's not like we can just unplug them, I suppose," Mary-Margaret said, referring to the old jukebox in the corner. After Maeve had put an abrupt stop to their baby speculating, patrons of O'Leary's turned to betting on how long it would take between the time someone picked a song on the jukebox and the time someone else unplugged the music box.

"I'm dead set against it, for the record. Like ye said, Mary-Margaret, people come in here to talk, not listen to some wannabe Shane MacGowan screamin' their lungs out."

"I'd have to agree with ye there, Maeve."

"And with Nolan upstairs. Not like it isn't hard enough to get the whelp to sleep as 'tis. But we don't have to worry about that now that she's gone, thanks be to God."

"And a good evenin' to ye," Frank Maloney interrupted, walking over from the other side of the bar with a half-empty pint glass in his hand. "Mind if I take a seat? And what's the worry?"

"Are ye just noticin' yer luv now?" Maeve said with a cheeky grin.

"Away with ye, Maeve! 'Tis not like that 't all," Frank said, deciding not to sit.

"Aye. Love among the ruins, 'tis, and I'll leave ye to it," she replied with a wink before sauntering over to pick up an order from the kitchen window.

"Francis," Mary-Margaret said with a curt nod. "What brings ye in on a Friday night?"

"Aside from this Guinness an' th' chance o' layin' me eyes on ye? Nuthin'."

"Ach, off with ye," Mary-Margaret said, her voice softening now that Maeve was out of earshot. While it was no secret that the morgue assistant had been pursuing her since Michael had introduced them one evening at the pub many years ago, Mary-Margaret didn't want her personal life to become gossip fodder. "And besides, I've me night with Eleanor and Angus this evenin'. Our night is tomorrow."

"Indeed 'tis," Frank admitted, taking a sip of beer before turning away. "Perhaps I'll jus' make me way back o'er yonder—"

"Although," Mary-Margaret said, reaching out to grab his arm, "ye might be interested in the story I have to tell me friends."

"Does it have t' do wit' a head wit' no body?" he said, turning back with a grin.

"And ye would know this how?"

"Are ye forgettin' where 'tis that I work, luv?"

"So ye mean to tell me that ye remember every detail of every moment of yer work day?"

"Ye don't suppose a head delivered on its own t' th' morgue wouldn't stand out in me mind, then?"

"All the same, there could be more than one."

"In all me years, Mary-Margaret," Frank said, moving closer to her, "I think I can count on all the fingers on me foot th' number o' times I've seen tha'."

"Are ye ready for another, Frank?" Maeve said, standing at the tap handle directly across from him, pulling a pint for another customer. "Honest to God, sometimes I think the reason Johnny brought me from Ireland was because I could pour a proper pint."

"'Twas for love," Frank said.

"Love me arse," Maeve said, leaning back to listen for a moment. "More like cheap labor. So. Another pint, then?"

"Not yet, luv. But I see that our girl over 'ere has a full one on th' go. What's the occasion?"

"Suit yerself," Maeve said just as the glass began to overflow. "Jesus! Don't breathe a word, or I'll ban ye both!"

"Yer secret's safe with us, Maeve. And ye mind yer own business, Francis. But while I'm thinkin' on it, is it all right if I leave Daphne in the lot for the night, luv? The last thing I need is to be callin' me Michael from the cells on account of bein' found pie-eyed behind the wheel in the ditch somewhere."

"I'll make sure me Johnny knows," Maeve said. "If he ever gets down here. Ah, no! Look at the time, will ye? Nolan's either conned him into stayin' up 'til all hours, or he's fallen asleep beside him. Never mind. I'll manage. I never thought I'd hear the words come out of me mouth, but I do miss Big John behind the bar."

"I can jump in if ye need a man behind the bar," Frank offered.

"I don't need a man behind the bar, Frank. What I need is me Johnny to do his job, but thanks anyway."

"So there's no problem with me car?" Mary-Margaret asked. "And be sure neither of ye go off and tell me Michael that I've been out to the pub tonight."

"Of course, ye can leave the car," Maeve replied, "but Michael already knows yer here, does he not? 'Tis Friday night, after all,"

"Well, truth to be told—"

"This should be good," Angus Corrigan said, looking at the pint in Mary-Margaret's hand as he and Eleanor walked the couple of steps past her towards their table. "Giving it your all tonight, are you?"

"If ye had the day I had, ye would be hard pressed to be standin' upright at this point," Mary-Margaret shot back at her old friends who, through so much shared history, were as good as family.

"I can hardly wait," Angus said with a smile, pulling out the chair for Eleanor.

"But about me Michael. Thank God he's workin' tonight, to be honest. Otherwise, I don't know what I'd do."

"Aside from havin' yer dinner here with Angus and Eleanor? Just like any other Friday night? Except that there's somethin' yer wearin' close to yer vest so let's hear it," Maeve said, noticing a group of four coming through the front door. "As ye can see, the pub's fillin' up and I've no time for foolishness."

"Well, it seems that me Michael thinks I've got the pneumonia—"

"What do you mean *he thinks*?" Maeve asked. "Ye either have it, or ye don't."

"Me Michael has been under a lot of stress lately. What with the murders he investigates and the bashin' abouts he seems to get himself involved in. Not quite on his pins lately."

Without providing anything further, Mary-Margaret joined Angus and Eleanor at the table near the bar, leaving Frank watching Maeve pouring pints.

"Are you joinin' us, or are ye just goin' to stand there like a lost dog all night?" Mary-Margaret called out to him.

"You'd better get yerself over there, before the offer's gone," Maeve said with a smile.

Not wasting a moment, Frank all but leapt toward Mary-Margaret and her friends, pulling in a chair for himself from the empty table beside them on the way.

"Of course, ye know Eleanor and Angus. Fresh off the boat at the same time as me and me Jimmy, God rest his soul—"

Eleanor, Angus, and Frank lowered their heads slightly, crossed themselves, and mumbled 'God rest his soul'.

"—and ye would know Francis Maloney, I'm sure. He works at the morgue."

"Can't say I've ever been there," Angus said, smiling as he ostentatiously checked his pulse.

"Are we ready to order, then?" Angus continued when no one laughed.

"We always have the Fish & Chip," Eleanor said. "I expect you'll be having the same, Francis?"

"What else would I be eatin' on a Friday night," Frank said. "An' most o' th' people 'round here just call me Frank."

"Grand. Fish and chip for us all then, Maeve," Angus called out to the bar over his shoulder.

"No need to call across the pub," Maeve said, rounding the bar towards them. "Are ye that hungry? And what about drinks? Unless ye are content to watch these two lovebirds imbibe."

"And just who are ye referrin' to?" Mary-Margaret demanded as Frank looked away.

"I'm just callin' it as I see it," Maeve said, winking at Frank. "Now, a wine and a pint, is it? I don't know why I bother to ask."

After Maeve returned with the drinks, Mary-Margaret told her friends what she had found.

"And," she concluded, "Francis here is lookin' after the case on the morgue side of things.

"Well, I wouldn't quite say tha'."

Maeve appeared again and quickly placed the four plates down before hurrying back to her customers at the bar.

"And why not? Ye are the pathologist's right-hand man, are ye not?"

"We don't like t' refer t' employees as body parts at the morgue," Frank said softly.

"The morgue," Eleanor said, resuming her trained voice. "That must be… unusual."

"Well, let's just say it's not the job for everyone."

"So what I'm hearing now," Angus said, taking a sip of beer to wash down a mouthful of battered fish, "is that you've got yourself involved in another murder, Mary-Margaret. Let's hope the police solve this one before you get all of us tangled up in it."

"She's not exactly involved," Frank began.

"Then what, exactly, is *she*?" Mary-Margaret said.

"Technically, ye are a witness to th' discovery o'—"

"Regardless of yer technicalities, Francis, I'm sure our Mandy will be glad that *I* was the one who found the remains."

"Mandy? Do ye mean Detective Sergeant Black?" Frank asked, referring to one of the most respected and, arguably, feared investigators who also happened to have the highest clearance rate and, without a doubt, stiletto heels in the homicide unit.

"The very same."

"Oh, I don't think she'll be handlin' this one," Frank said, taking a sip of beer.

"And you would know this how?" Mary-Margaret demanded.

"Had her in th' other day on an autopsy. She's at the bottom o' th' list now. I'm thinkin' it will likely be Detective Sergeant Gill."

"Jesus, Mary, and Joseph. Not Billy Gilly!" Mary-Margaret cried out. The two had met during a previous investigation. It had not gone well.

"Well, I can't be sayin' for sure, but, if memory serves," Frank continued, "I do believe he's up after Detective Sergeant Black."

"In that case," Mary-Margaret said, taking a large swallow from her pint glass, "perhaps I *will* be investigatin' another murder."

Chapter Seven

"Wasn't expecting to see you up this morning, Mom," Michael said, looking over his shoulder from the stove. Seeing the Jack Russell dancing at his feet, he added, "I see that dog's still here."

"And the same could be said of ye," Mary-Margaret said, stopping in her tracks.

"What, that I'm up, or that I'm here?"

"Both."

"I live here and—"

"And until further notice, so, too, does Sally-next-door's dog. And you well know that his name is Phil, not 'that dog.' And what's more, clearly ye did not take him out to the jacks this mornin'. Can ye at least open the door there so the wee thing can have a piddle before he explodes?"

Without putting down the spatula, Michael reached over to the back door and opened it. The dog took off into the laneway like a shot.

"What do we have goin' on here, then?" Mary-Margaret said, peeking over Mike's shoulder.

"I'm just making some breakfast. Do you want some?"

"I don't hear any bacon sizzlin'."

"I'm not making bacon."

"Nor do I see any eggs on the counter."

"I'm not making eggs."

"Oh, for the love of God, me son. Step aside while I make us a good fry-up."

With that, Mary-Margaret elbowed Michael away from the stove to commandeer the frying pan.

"And what is this mess ye have in the pan, then?"

"I was just making some—"

"Ach," she said, opening the back door and scraping the breakfast Mike had been preparing out onto the back step. "Somethin'll eat it, but it won't be us. Get me out the bacon. And the carton of eggs. And I think there's some sausage there as well. And grab a few potatoes that ye can cut up while yer there. Where is yer bread, Michael?"

"I'm trying to cut down on carbs. And aren't you supposed to be in bed?"

"Carbs? Why don't they just come out and say they hate bread and want us all to hate it as well? And why would I be sleepin' at this hour of the mornin'? 'Tis a wonder I've slept this long."

"You need sleep, don't you? Remember? Because of your pneumonia?"

Mary-Margaret paused for a moment and then stepped away from the stove to begin a lengthy coughing spell.

"Here," Michael said, reaching around his mother's shoulders with one arm while cupping her elbow with the other. "Why don't you sit down out here at the dining room table, and I'll get you a glass of water."

"'Tis alright, me son," Mary-Margaret choked the words out, allowing herself to be led from the kitchen. "'Tis only me lungs clearin' themselves of the vile phlegm that'll no doubt be the death of me. That's what it's come down to, this hellish ailment. Just fluid in me lungs, like the spittle of the Grim Reaper himself, fillin' me up as he counts the hours until it can drown me as I sputter t—"

"Let me get you a glass of water," Michael said after gently but firmly pushing his mother into the chair.

"I've just said I've got fluid on me lungs, Michael. Why in God's name would I want to ingest more fluid?" Mary-Margaret hollered after him and then added, "A cuppa would be more what I'd be needin'."

"Here," Michael said, placing a glass of water down in front of his mother. "Take a sip of this, and I'll get the tea on the go for you. And then back to bed."

"And a wee bit to eat as well before I make me way up to what may be me death bed? Somethin' that includes...carbs?"

"Sure. I'll put some bread in the toaster."

"Bread in the toaster. What about the fry-up?"

Just then, Phil bound in through the open backdoor and up onto Mary-Margaret's lap. He was licking his lips.

"Do you think that's a good idea right now?" Michael asked.

"And what do ye mean by that?" Mary-Margaret said as she moved Phil off her lap. "If I'm goin' to die, the least ye can do is give me a good fry-up first. Have ye ever heard of a dyin' man requestin' just a bite of toast for his last meal?"

"Speaking of which," Michael said, "have you been to the doctor lately?"

"For what? To have him tell me to do exactly what I'm doin'?"

"Wait. Weren't you there just the other day, Mom," Michael said, returning with a cup of tea.

"Ach, I'm seein' the game yer playin', tryin' to trip me up like that. I thought ye were taught never to interrogate yer mother."

Michael stopped and looked a little closer at Mary-Margaret. Before he could say anything, she broke into another violent fit of coughing.

"The fry-up, luv," Mary-Margaret sputtered between coughs. "That's all there is for it."

Michael dutifully returned to the kitchen. He put the sausages, the bacon, the eggs, and some potatoes onto the counter along with a loaf of bread he pulled out of the freezer. He set everything out beside the stove and began to prepare a proper breakfast for two. Mary-Margaret, meanwhile, alternated between sipping her tea, cooing at the little dog, and coughing.

"And since we're havin' a moment, did ye sorted things out with our Max yet?" she called to Michael after Phil decided to follow his nose into the kitchen and began circling around Mike's feet.

"What things?" Michael asked, poking his head around the doorway.

Wee Phil let out a yelp as Michael almost tripped over him.

"Jesu—"

"Ach, for the love of life itself, me son. The organized crime ring that's runnin' rampant through his school and likely the cause of generational anxiety for your descendants. And can ye not manage yerself around a dog after all these months?"

"Has it been that long?" he asked, looking down at Phil, who snarled back at him before becoming distracted by his own tail and giving it a good chase. "And what are you talking about, organized crime?"

"Yer helpin' Max catch the rovin' band of banshees who are breakin' into the lockers and stealin' computers and the like, are ye not?"

"No," Michael said, returning to the sizzling frying pan, careful to step over the dog, who had collapsed in the middle of the floor after his brief stint as a whirling dervish. "He hasn't said a word about it to me."

"And therein lies your problem, me son. Lack of communication. The two of ye—like ships in the night, are ye. Ne'er a word—"

"Not quite," he said, placing two plates loaded with food down on the table, Phil following at his heels.

Mary-Margaret stared at the plate in front of her.

"What?" Micheal asked, sitting down at the head of the table, Phil on the floor beside him, his tiny tail wagging madly.

"Are we not gettin' a fork or knife, or have we lost all sense of civility since yer last wife left? I never thought I'd be sayin' a good word about her, but Carmen did bring an element of refinement to ye that I've noticed lackin' in ye as of late, me son. Which leads me to me next question: how are things goin' between ye and that Bridget Calloway?"

"There is nothing *going between* me and Bridget Calloway, and Carmen didn't bring...oh, never mind," he said, getting up and returning with the cutlery before sitting down again, Phil shadowing him. "A guy forgets to bring a fork to the table, and suddenly he's—"

"A hopeless cause. There. Ye've taken the words right out of me mouth, and now we're all in agreement."

"Hardly," he said, stuffing a forkful of grease-soaked deliciousness into his mouth and then pausing. "You know, I've missed these breakfasts."

"Hmmm," Mary-Margaret said, taking a bite of sausage. "Not bad. Mind ye don't give any to Wee Phil. Gives him gas."

"Good to know," Michael said, looking down at the expectant dog. "Although I think he ate the eggs you scraped out onto the back porch before coming in."

"God help us," Mary-Margaret said, rolling her eyes. "Now, this business with Max."

"He hasn't said a word about it to me, Mom."

"Well then, I will. Seems there's been a number of lockers broken into at his school durin' the day while the lads should be in class. Sure, they've got video cameras in the hallways, but according to our Max, they haven't picked up anyone. And now Max is afraid to leave his things in his locker, so he's luggin' them around to all his classes, poor lamb."

"I'm sure the school's reported it to the police," Micheal said, enjoying the breakfast he'd made. Phil continued to look up, eyes pleading for a morsel.

"I doubt it."

"And why's that, Mom?"

"Well, ye don't know about it, do ye?"

"Mom," Michael said, taking a deep breath while tossing a bit of sausage down to Phil, "I'm not the police. I'm a police officer—"

"Detective, and we're all payin' for that lapse in judgment by those responsible for puttin' ye in charge of investigatin' anything, as is evidenced here today."

"I'm sure it won't kill him, Mom. Anyway, I don't hear about every crime that goes on—"

"Clearly."

Micheal stared at her.

"Yer no Mandy is all I'm sayin'."

"I'm sure the school has reported it to the police, and the officers in the division where Max's school is are working on the case."

"So ye can follow up with them, then?"

"No," Mike said, returning to his breakfast.

"Why not?"

"Because they don't follow up on my work."

"Maybe they should."

Micheal stared at his mother again.

"Listen, Michael. This involves yer own son."

"Exactly. Which is another reason why I'm not going to get involved."

"So we just let the criminals take over the school, then?"

"No, we let the investigators in that division do their jobs."

"Well, we've all seen how well some investigators do their jobs, haven't we?" Mary-Margaret said before taking a big bite of fried potatoes.

"What's that supposed to mean?"

"Well, I don't want to blow me own horn, but it was me who solved a few murders that yer lads couldn't—"

"I hardly think that's true, Mom," he said.

"Really? I guess yer right then. Yer lads would have figured out who killed Jane Ann Hill eventually, I suppose. And ye and Mandy would have figured out how to sort things out with the murder of our Sibby Mac...sooner or later."

The two ate in silence for a moment.

"Since we're talking about murders," Michael said, letting the words hang as he took another mouthful of food, "I understand there has been some other excitement around here."

"Oh?"

"Well," Michael said between chews, "first there was that bag of bones, and then I understand you found a skull yesterday."

"Did I then?"

"Mom...."

"Word travels fast in that police force of yers."

"Word doesn't travel fast, Mom. It just travels. What do you know about it? And why didn't you call me?"

"And why would I call ye? Ye've just finished tellin' me about when things are personal. It doesn't get any more personal than findin' bones in yer own back yard, I don't imagine. And ye are not a homicide detective. How many times have ye told me that? And truly, what's to tell? There was a bag, it had a head in it, and yer lovely neighbor, Doug, offered me a wee dram of whiskey. Beginning. Middle. End. Are ye happy now?"

Mike looked down at his empty plate.

"Anythin' else ye want to know about me comin's and goin's or am I free to go, Big City Detective?"

"Where were you last night?"

Mary-Margaret was about to glare at her son when she suddenly remembered her car still being in O'Leary's parking lot. She shot up from the table.

"Oh, me stars," she said. "I've got to go."

"Go where?"

"None of yer business, Michael O'Shea. And for future reference, when yer mam says she has someplace to go, that's more than what ye need to know."

"How are you going to get there?" Michael said, suppressing a smile.

"What are ye smilin' at over there?"

"Where is your car, Mom?"

"Remember what I said about interrogatin' yer mam. And since ye seem to be so interested, can ye give me a lift across the city to O'Leary's."

Unfazed, Michael cleared the plates from the table and returned to find his mother at the front door, ready to go.

"Michael," she said, "are ye comin' or am I to call an Uber?"

"Mom, I know you. Don't even think about getting involved in this investigation."

"Right now, I'm involvin' meself in getting me car from O'Leary's parking lot."

"And why would it be there, Mom?" Michael asked with a smirk.

"Because this is Saturday mornin', and last night was Friday night, and I go to O'Leary's every Friday night."

"Even when you have pneumonia and should be in bed."

Mary-Margaret stopped for a moment.

"As ye well know, Michael, people die of the pneumonia. More than a few of yer ancestors certainly have. And so, if it is the pneumonia that is goin' to kill me, I wanted to make sure that I was prepared to see me maker. There was not a bite of fish to be had in yer house and so I had no choice but to go to the pub to have me fish on Friday. Now, are ye comin' with me to pick up me car—?"

"Did you have a few drinks, then, Mom?" Michael said, no longer able to suppress a grin.

"Michael. I am yer mother. I do not *have a few drinks*. After having me fish, I felt too weak to drive on account of the pneumonia, and I had Angus and Eleanor drive me home."

"So you went to the pub and met your friends for dinner—"

"Ach, Michael, the logic behind it is too complicated for me mind to unravel to ye in this moment. Are ye comin' with me or not?"

"Mom, I don't care whether you have pneumonia or not. I'm just—"

"And there's the truth of it. Lad doesn't care if his own mother lives or dies. Well, that's grand, isn't it, Wee Phil? Put us both out on the street, would me Michael. Stand by while I get yer lead. Just like a couple of Travelers now," she said, reaching for the leash that was by the front door. She clipped it onto Phil's collar.

"Mom—"

Mary-Margaret paused for a moment and then unclipped the leash. Phil darted up the stairs, a foul odor having been left behind.

"Get yer keys, Michael. I'll meet you beside yer truck. And bring yer wallet. Since ye've been goin' on for so long, it'll be almost time for lunch by the time we get there. Luckily for ye, O'Leary's does a lovely Saturday lunch."

With that, Mary-Margaret grabbed her coat from the rack, opened the front door, and then stopped as the Jack Russell terrier came bounding back down the stairs.

"Before ye do, it wouldn't hurt to let Wee Phil out the back for another piddle and perhaps to expel some of that gas, unless it's ye...?"

Mary-Margaret closed the front door behind her, marched down the street, and stood beside Michael's locked truck.

Chapter Eight

"We've got to stop meetin' like this," laughed Maeve. "Pretty soon, people are goin' to say we're besties."

"Hardly," Mary-Margaret sniffed as she walked towards the near-empty bar.

"Hello, luv," Frank said with a nod. "Maeve here was just tellin' me tha' ye and yer Michael just left—"

"Oh, and are you gettin' too big for me pub, then?" Maeve said, the smile still on her face. "I was only just tellin' Frank about how—"

"I'd appreciate ye not broadcastin' me comin's and goin's," Mary-Margaret said, stepping up to the bar to look Maeve directly in the eye. "And ye call yerself a barmaid."

"I," Maeve said, the warmth disappearing from her voice along with the smile on her face, "am *not* a barmaid."

"Maeve didn't mean anythin' by it," Frank said. "She was just waggin' her chin while I was waitin' for—"

"Indeed, but yer not the only one she's waggin' her chin at," Mary-Margaret said, pursing her lips. "If this keeps up, Maeve O'Leary, then I think it's time we consider findin' ourselves another local, Francis."

"Another local? Come on, luv."

"No. Away with ye, then," Maeve said, raising her voice. "Before I ban ye."

"Girls!" Johnny called as he came down the stairs into the bar.

"Don't 'girls' me," Maeve said. "I want this woman out!"

"Out? Have you lost your mind, my luv? I know it's been stressful in here with the murder and all, but—"

"What murder?" Mary-Margaret said.

"You mean Mike didn't tell you?" Johnny asked. "He was here around closing time until almost morning questioning me and Maeve."

"Well, that explains why yer missus was givin' us the stink eye when me Michael and I were here at lunch," Mary-Margaret said, looking Maeve up and down. "And thanks again for letting me park the car for the night."

"I wasn't giving ye the stink eye, ye unsavory—"

"Well, then ye've just got a horrible tick," Mary-Margaret spat, giving Maeve a piercing look before turning her attention to Johnny. "And what was me Michael on about last night, then?"

"About our former barmaid, Cassandra. Apparently, she was murdered."

"Another murder?" Mary-Margaret said, looking over at Frank.

"The same," Frank corrected.

"And ye know this how?"

"'Twas the head ye found in the laneway."

"Wait. Cassandra," Mary-Margaret said, the penny starting to drop. "That wouldn't be Cassandra Lewis, would it?"

"It would. Was," Johnny said, pulling Maeve close.

"And yer just tellin' me now, Francis?" Mary-Margaret said.

"I hardly had a moment, did I?" Frank replied. "What, with ye attackin' our Maeve and all."

"'Tis bad enough yer Michael was interrogatin' me and Johnny until all hours without the likes of ye havin' a run at me," Maeve added.

"Havin' a run at ye?" Mary-Margaret repeated.

"What Maeve is trying to say," Johnny began, "is that Mike seems to think that me and Maeve might have something to do with it."

"Do with what?" Mary-Margaret shot back. "Don't tell me me Michael thinks ye've murdered yer girl? Honestly, I'm truly believin' the lad has slipped a gear."

"Yeah. Imagine that. Me a suspect for murder," Maeve cut in, her short, straight hair snapping at her face as she spoke. "What with a pub and a smallie upstairs, not to mention an old man—"

"Steady," Johnny cut in.

"Ye know what I'm sayin'. Like I don't have better things to do with me time than kill off me barmaids. Speakin' of which, have we got someone comin' for later tonight? I can't keep runnin' up and down the stairs ye know, and yer da's knees aren't ready for him to be runnin' around after a smallie yet."

"Why don't ye just bring wee Nolan down?" Frank asked.

"Oh, wouldn't that just be grand! The booze police would have a field day with that one. It's not like back home, Frank," Maeve said. "Not to mention that we've a murderer amongst us. So who's comin' in, Johnny, because I'm not stayin'—"

"I've got Finn coming in," Johnny said.

"Finn? He's like a bull in a china shop," Maeve said, her eyes darkening. "Why wouldn't ye call in Lesley? Or Kate? Or—"

"Because I figured we might need a strong guy behind the bar, given this band we've got coming in. I checked them out online, and I don't think they draw the kind of crowd we're used to having here."

"Jesus," Maeve moaned as she began to wipe down the bar.

"And there was me Michael in askin' the questions, was he?" Mary-Margaret asked.

"Yep. This big guy in a suit came in first, sat down right there, looked us over, and then Mike appeared out of nowhere," Johnny replied. "At first, I didn't really connect Mike with the suit and thought maybe he was just dropping in for last call, and I even pulled him a pint, but he pushed it aside. That's when I knew things were serious."

"And he didn't pay for it either, did he," Maeve said, glaring at Mary-Margaret.

"Well, if me Michael owes ye any money," Mary-Margaret said, pulling her purse onto the bar. Johnny pushed it back to her.

"Mike doesn't owe us a dime. Maeve served his pint to someone else anyway, if I recall correctly," Johnny said, not looking over at his wife. "And I know you told Maeve not to say anything about you being here last night, but I was sworn in or whatever they call it, and I had to tell them everything. I'm sorry if that caused you any trouble, Mary-Margaret."

"Give me a moment, lads," Mary-Margaret said, her eyes narrowing. "Did the big fella happen to give ye his name by any chance?"

"Yes, and he gave me his card. I've got it here in my wallet," Johnny replied, reaching into his back pocket.

"Name wasn't Gill, was it?" she continued.

"Yes. Do you know him?"

Mary-Margaret rolled her eyes.

"So, is this a crime scene now, is it?" Mary-Margaret asked.

"Thank God, no," Maeve chimed in. "Can ye imagine seein' that all over the papers? 'Murder At O'Leary's: Landlords Prime Suspects.' That would be the end of us, wouldn't it be?"

"Just because this isn't a crime scene doesn't mean yer not..." Frank began and then, thinking better of it, let the words die off in his mind.

"So what kind of questions did they ask ye?" Mary-Margaret asked.

"Things like how long did we know her, and did she have a boyfriend. Was she a good employee–"

"Standard fare," Frank said, taking a casual sip of his beer.

"I said she wasn't, but that I didn't think it was worth killin' her over," Maeve said with a laugh.

"And they asked what kind of chemicals we used to clean the place," Johnny said.

"We don't use any, I told 'em," Maeve stated. "Just vinegar and water and some good old elbow grease. Don't want that commercial shite on my skin, and, since I'm the one down on me hands and knees scrubbin'...."

"Chemicals?" Mary-Margaret said. "Why would they ask about that?"

"*They*? 'Twas yer Michael," Maeve said, crossing her arms over her chest. "Treatin' me husband over here and me like common criminals. The big lad sat all quiet and proper like. And I have no idea. Maybe you'd best be askin' him."

"Because chemicals were used t' clean th' bones," Frank said quietly.

"Right," Mary-Margaret said with a nod. "And here's me Michael, not sayin' a word about any of this to me. But then again, ye never said a word when I was in earlier with me Micheal, either," Mary-Margaret said, looking at Maeve.

"Contrary to what ye may wish to believe, I've got more to do than keep ye updated on the comin's and goin's of yer son. Or anyone else," Maeve snapped and then, glancing at Johnny, added, "And yer Michael told me not to say anything about it when he left. Said it was police business. Imagine me surprise when I saw the two of ye sittin' right over there orderin' me lunch special. Never mind a tick. Was a wonder I didn't go into seizures tryin' to keep it all to meself."

"Here's his card," Johnny said, passing it over to Mary-Margaret.

"Well," she said, shaking her head, "ye'd be best to tell me everythin', then. With Billy Gilly as yer main man, it looks like I'm in for a pound even if they think I'm just in for a penny."

"Will it be another full pint tonight, then?" Maeve said, all having been forgiven. Before Mary-Margaret could answer, Maeve stepped back from the taps to answer the phone on the wall behind her. "O'Leary's....No, luv. I don't know where yer iPad charger is. Why are ye callin' me? Ask Granddad...no, no, don't wake him. Now, did ye look under the couch?.... Look again. And get yerself off to bed. I'll be up in a sec to get ye a snack.... What?.... The whole bag?.... No, Cheetos is not proper food.... I don't know what 'tis, me son, all I know is.... No, ye can't come down and sit with me behind the bar.... Because yer too old for doin' nuthin' and too young to be workin'."

Maeve hung up the phone and looked at her husband.

"Finn. Yer lad Finn. When is he gettin' here?"

"Half a pint is fine for this evenin'," Mary-Margaret said. "I can see that I've got to keep me wits about me goin' forward."

* * *

"Sláinte," Mary-Margaret said as she and Frank sat at the same table they had occupied the night before.

"Sláinte," Frank said and then took a gulp of his beer. "If 'tis any consolation, 'twas a quiet day at the morgue."

"Did ye know it was Cassandra when ye saw it? The head, I mean."

"I had an idea, yes."

"And the bones. How did they tie the bones in?"

"'Tis not for sure yet, but, t' the trained eye—"

"Yer eye?"

"Indeed. Looked like the bones were too…new…t' be that clean, and th' pathologist laid them all out like they would be if they were a complete skeleton."

"Were they all there?"

"Except fer the skull, more or less, yeah. We looked at th' neck bones there, and then looked at th' head we had, and it all kind o' fit together."

"But yer not sure."

"We'll have t' wait for th' lab work to come back to say that th' bones and th' head are from th' same body. DNA and all, but me money would be it bein' the barmaid, yeah."

"Enough to be investigatin' Johnny and Maeve for murder?"

"Well, Maeve's temper is no secret, and th' girl did work here. I don't know what was said, so maybe yer Michael were just askin' some questions. Routine-like. Regardless, leave this to th' police. I don't think yer quite up to this one. It cuts a little too close to home, don't ye think?"

"I've had four children, and me husband, God rest his soul," Mary-Margaret crossed herself, as did Frank, "died when they were babes in me arms. There isn't much I can't handle."

Frank looked down at the table and nodded.

"Is that you, Mary-Margaret?" a young woman almost shrieked.

"I take it back," Mary-Margaret said to Frank, forcing a smile.

"Ashleigh. From St. Francis. My brother is the bass player in the band that's playing here tonight. I totally forgot that this was your…what do you guys call it…local? That is *so* adorable. Oh, this is my husband, Justin. Justin, this is the old woman from the church who was there while we were on our honeymoon."

"Pleased to meet you," he mumbled, extending his hand, beads of sweat forming on his shaved head.

"And ye." Mary-Margaret did not extend her hand.

"And who is this silver fox?" Ashleigh said with a smile as she looked Frank up and down.

"Francis Maloney," Frank said, standing up and offering his hand to her, which she took with a squeal.

"O. M. G. You two are just too quaint. Why don't you order us a drink at the bar, lovey. Remember, no alcohol for me for the next few months."

The recent bridegroom smiled weakly and went to the bar.

"I don't know how I'm going to manage a new marriage, organize the new house, *and* work full-time."

"I'm sure ye'll manage. Most of us have," Mary-Margaret said, not getting up from her seat.

"All that while being pregnant."

"Well, now. That's…lovely," Mary-Margaret sputtered. "And ye just back from yer honeymoon and all. Ye must be very…blessed."

"I know. My ObGyn seems to think I'm a little further along than I should be, if you know what I mean, but we're cool with that. I mean, Justin's parents would love a grandchild. They won't care. And it's not like we'd never had sex before."

"Clearly," Mary-Margaret said, her right eyebrow arching well up on her forehead. "Did ye say yer brother was in the band?"

"Yeah. And so is the brother of one of the servers here. Isn't that random?"

"So ye knew the girl?"

"*Knew her?* You mean do I know her. And yeah, Cassandra's dating my brother. I kinda figured she'd be working tonight," Ashleigh said, looking over at the bar.

Clearly, no one's told her, Mary-Margaret thought, standing up in preparation to be the bearer of bad news.

"I guess not," Ashleigh continued. "You know, I wish our culture was more like yours, Mary-Margaret."

"How's that?" she asked absently, wondering if this was the time or the place.

"Well, don't they practically encourage you to drink while you're pregnant *over 'ome?"*

Mary-Margaret stared at this silly girl for a moment.

"Only if ye knew the only way ye could have married as well as ye did was because ye misrepresented yerself, and ye felt pangs of guilt," Mary-Margaret said, consciously trying not to wag a finger in Ashleigh's face. "Or the father of the baby yer carryin' isn't yer husband. Otherwise, no, not really. We just do what we do...over 'ome."

"OMG. You are *so* funny," Ashleigh squealed. "I don't know why Miguel has such a hard time with you."

"Miguel?" Mary-Margaret echoed, stepping back.

"Yeah. Father Miguel, although I can't seriously call him Father. He's like, what? Six years older than me? And what a hottie."

Mary-Margaret caught her breath as she fell back against Frank, blinking her eyes several times.

"I got you an orange juice," Justin said as he returned. "I hope it's okay."

"Ugh. I hate orange juice. It gives me heartburn. Especially now. Take it back and get me a ginger ale."

Without making eye contact with either Mary-Margaret or Frank, Justin slunk back to the bar. Mary-Margaret and Frank glanced quickly at one another.

"Honestly. You'd think he'd know me better by now," Ashleigh said with an exaggerated sigh. "Anyway, I was kind of thinking of telling Miguel that I can't work full-time anymore. I haven't said anything about that to Justin yet because we just bought a new house, and he kinda can't afford it on just his salary, but I'm sure he'll be supportive of my decision."

"He seems like a very...supportive...lad," Mary-Margaret commented.

"Ginger ale for you, a good old Irish Guinness for me," Justin announced as he returned for the second time, his back a little straighter. "Do you want to hang out with your friends or get our own table and have a little date night?"

"Nice meetin' ye, lad, and good luck to ye," Mary-Margaret said, moving away from the young couple. "Poor sod."

Chapter Nine

To say the band was loud would be an understatement. To say they were terrible would be kind. Fortunately, Johnny gave them their money for the evening and ushered them off after their first set with a promise to the regular, who hadn't been driven away by the noise that a band would never appear at O'Leary's again.

Mary-Margaret and Frank did not hear this promise, however, because they were a part of the exodus of regulars who had left before the first set ended. Not that the promise would have made any difference. They'd be back the following Saturday regardless.

"I'd offer ye a wee sip, but I don't know what me Michael has on hand," Mary-Margaret said after they got in the door. "Ach, Wee Phil! Ye are waggin' like yer goin' to explode."

"'Tis not a worry, luv. I'm drivin', and a liquor drink would be out of th' question. Unless I was to stay th' night…?" he said with the slightest twinge of hope in his voice.

"I'll put the kettle on, then. Come on, Wee Phil. I'll let ye out the back."

"Right ye are," Frank said with a sigh, sitting on one of the wingback chairs by the front window.

It wasn't long before the water was boiled, and Mary-Margaret returned from the kitchen with a tray carrying two mugs of tea and a plate of McVitie's. Wee Phil, all the while, was darting around her feet, causing her to stumble slightly.

"That dog will be th' death of ye," Frank commented. "When does Sally-next-door want him back?"

"Ach, I don't know. As a stewardess—"

"Flight attendant," Frank corrected.

"Flight attendant," Mary-Margaret said with a nod. "She's away more than not, and it's not fair to the dog. And to be honest, I think it's good for Max to have a pet."

"Speaking of th' lad, where is he?"

"Out with his mates, as he should be at his age."

"Ah, yes," Frank began, taking a sip of his tea. "I remember bein' seventeen. Although, truth t' be told, it wasn't me mates I was spendin' time with."

"Times have changed, Francis. These days, they're not interested in girls until they're in their twenties."

"Not interested or not gettin' caught?"

"Is that what happened to ye, Francis?"

"In me father's house, luv, ye didn't dare get caught because if ye did, ye were gettin' married, and that was th' end of it."

"Don't I know that story too well," Mary-Margaret said, nodding in agreement.

"Do ye think yer girl Ashleigh got caught?"

"Hardly," Mary-Margaret said. "I'm thinkin' it's the other way 'round, poor lad. And her, wantin' to go part-time at the church. Might as well just pack it in and call it a day. Imagine callin' the priest by his first name. Who does she think she—"

Suddenly, there was a loud rap at the back door. Phil barked madly, and Mary-Margaret jumped.

"Expectin' anyone?" Frank asked, suddenly on his guard as well.

"At this time of night? Max would have called if he'd forgotten his keys, and me phone is on," Mary-Margaret said as she got up, pulling her phone out of the purse she'd hung up by the front door to check.

There was another knock, this time louder and sounding more urgent.

"Do ye want me t' see who 'tis, then, luv?" Frank asked as he got up from his chair.

"I've told me Michael a million times to put a peephole or somethin' in that back door so ye can see who's there. Granted, the stained glass window he's put in beside the door is lovely, but ye can't see a thing through it and have no way of knowin' who 'tis pounded down yer door."

"I'll go check."

"What if it's the murderer returnin'?"

"Returnin' to what? Ye don't actually believe whoever killed Cassandra did it here in th' laneway, do ye?"

"No, but—"

"MM! Open up. It's me, Arthur," a loud voice called out.

"Oh, for the love of God," Mary-Margaret said, stomping into the kitchen, unlocking the door, and flinging it open. "What are ye doin' here at this time of the night, and what in God's name are ye wearin'?"

Standing in front of her was a paunchy six-foot-four man in a bathrobe.

"I," Arthur announced, "am a Ninja Warrior."

"Ye," Mary-Margaret countered, "are a lad in a bathrobe. Come inside before the neighbors see ye."

"What th'—" Frank said, stepping into the kitchen.

"What is *he* doing here?" Arthur asked.

"I think the question on everyone's mind is what are *ye* doin' here," Mary-Margaret shot back.

"I am here to protect you, MM."

"From what?"

"From the murderer."

"If it's keepin' her safe you're talkin' about, lad, I believe I've got that sorted," declared Frank, puffing up with pride.

"How did ye know we'd be here at this hour of the night?" Mary-Margaret asked.

"I stopped by O'Leary's first, and the guy at the bar said you'd already left."

"Dressed like that, were ye?"

"MM, I am a Ninja Warrior."

"So ye've said. Well, come inside and sitcheedoon in the livin' room. I'll pour another cuppa. Might as well catch ye up to speed on the news."

"Have we got another investigation on the go, MM?"

"No, ye do not," Frank stated.

"And who are ye to be tellin' me what I am or am not doin'?" Mary-Margaret said sternly. "The lot of ye can go into the livin' room now and we'll chat."

The two men slunk away while Mary-Margaret made a cup of tea for Arthur.

"Are ye not havin' a seat, then?" Mary-Margaret said, seeing that Arthur was standing by the front door.

"I'm on alert, MM. From here, I can see up the stairs, down towards the back door, and I've got the front door covered."

"Suit yerself. Sure you don't want a cuppa?" she said, handing him a mug of tea.

"Thanks," he said, taking it from her. "And can I have a biscuit, too?"

"Francis, pass the lad the plate."

Frank passed the plate of biscuits to Arthur, who, rather than taking one or two from it, took the entire plate and set it on the third stair to the left of him.

"Now," Mary-Margaret began. "In answer to yer question, Arthur: given that Billy Gilly is likely to be the lad from Homicide—"

"Why don't we ever get that Mandy girl you're always talking about?"

"Because God is testing me. I don't know. Regardless, if Billy Gilly is our man, then yes, we have another investigation on our hands."

"Mary-Margaret," Frank said, "I'll not be standin' by again if ye are intent on gettin' yer nose in where it doesn't belong."

"And the alternative is what?"

Having her question met with silence, Mary-Margaret continued.

"It seems that the Cassandra Lewis, who we saw a bit of in the laneway, and Cassandra the thieving barmaid from O'Leary's are one and the same."

"We don't know for sure that she's a thief," Frank said.

"Say what ye will about her, but if Maeve O'Leary tells me that the girl's a thief, then she's a thief. Money problems, no doubt. Apparently, she had a drug problem."

"Oh, she had no drug problems, MM," Arthur said.

"And you would know this how?"

"As much as I hate t' admit it, I'd have t' agree with the lad," Frank said, looking Arthur up and down. "She served me a few times. Looked right enough. If she was related to that clatterin' lot we saw on the stage tonight, though, I'm wonderin' if it wasn't one of them's habits she was supportin'."

"They certainly were below subpar, weren't they?" Mary-Margaret said.

"Oh, she wasn't supporting them, either," Arthur said.

"But we don't know 'twas for drugs," Frank continued, ignoring Arthur's comment. "She could've just been an honest girl who's livin' too big for her britches."

"Makes sense, and she wouldn't be the first, what with all this click-and-buy business on the computers now," Mary-Margaret considered.

"She was a drug dealer, MM," Arthur stated.

Both Mary-Margaret and Frank stared at Arthur.

"A dealer? At O'Leary's?" Frank finally said with a laugh. "And just who do ye think she'd be dealin' to at O'Leary's?"

"She doesn't deal there, *obviously*," Arthur said, looking disdainfully at Frank. " Maybe that's just where her supplier does the exchange."

"Are ye sure yer not tyin' yer bathrobe a bit too tight, lad?" Frank asked, shaking his head.

"Ninja. I am a ninja," Arthur said, shooting a menacing look at Frank.

"Whatever the reason, lads," Mary-Margaret cut in, "we've agreed that our girl's a thief and that it's her head sittin' on its own in the morgue. And we know that me Michael has already deceived me and cannot be trusted. Now tell me how ye know she was a drug dealer."

"We never agreed that she was a thief, and I don't think Michael's deceived ye—" Frank offered, glaring back at Arthur.

"Lied, then. I was tryin' to be kind, but clearly, me own son has lied to me. And if Maeve says the girl was a thief, then the girl was a thief."

"And a drug dealer," Arthur said, moving his attention to the plate of biscuits before stuffing a handful into his mouth. "My woommate bought fwom her all the time."

"You're roommate?" Mary-Margaret said. "Don't tell me ye are involved—"

"Not my scene," Arthur said, swallowing the mostly unchewed biscuits.

"So me Michael will be wantin' to talk to ye, then," Mary-Margaret said. "Unless he already has?"

"No, but I'm supposed to go to the police station to give a statement about finding the bones. And the head. And I suppose they'll want to know about the drug dealing thing," he sighed, as if providing such information was a daily occurrence for him.

"With the way things are goin', luv, be sure to have a lawyer when ye go," Mary-Margaret said.

"Oh, I don't need a lawyer, MM. I've bailed more than a few friends out of jail and, if you ask me, this getting a lawyer thing is just a money grab."

"Out of jail?" Mary-Margaret exclaimed. "What kind of friends do ye have, lad?"

"Well, not exactly a few times," Arthur conceded. "Maybe more like once. And he had a lawyer. And just needed a ride home. But I still think I'll be fine."

"A man who is his own lawyer has a fool fer a client," Frank said.

Both Mary-Margaret and Arthur stared at Frank.

"Don't be lookin' at me like that. 'Twas Abraham Lincoln who said it, not me," Frank said. "I'm just quotin' the man."

"Brill," Mary-Margaret said with a huff. "Now, can I get on with me story?"

"As you wish," Frank said with a sigh.

Mary-Margaret proceeded to outline her understanding of the events, adding a liberal dose of editorial insights.

"What if the killer is some regular at the pub who had a thing for her, and she blew him off?" Arthur suggested.

"Have ye been to O'Leary's, luv? The median age is well past that foolishness."

"Are ye sayin' I'm beyond havin' a love interest?" Frank said.

"No. I'm sayin' yer beyond bein' a fool about it," Mary-Margaret shot back.

"What if Ashleigh's the murderer?" Arthur asked.

"Not that I'd put it past her, but I doubt it."

"What about Maeve?" he continued.

"Again, I wouldn't put it past her, but she has a lot to lose, and she knows it. I also don't think she'd flourish in prison. Can ye just imagine herself, havin' a row with one of the other inmates, then tryin' to banish her from the cell block?" Mary-Margaret said with a laugh.

"What about the boyfriend, MM? It's always the boyfriend."

"Ach, too easy."

"The brother?" Arthur suggested.

"And why would a lad kill his own sister?"

"Money? Jealousy? Ultimate sibling rivalry? Or maybe over drugs," Arthur said. "Maybe he's a dealer, too."

"Now yer talkin'," Mary-Margaret said, her eyes narrowing.

"Talkin' rubbish," Frank said.

"Rubbish? And what, then, do ye have to offer to the mix?" Mary-Margaret asked.

"Nothin' because there's nothin' t' add. Let the police do their jobs. Now let's talk sense. I can see th' hour is gettin' late, and with Michael not home, I'd feel much better if someone was here overnight with ye."

Both Mary-Margaret and Arthur looked at Frank.

"And I'm offerin' me services," the older man continued.

"Well, I thank ye for yer chivalry, Francis, but I hardly think it proper that ye be spendin' the night."

"I didn't exactly mean *spendin' the night*, although–"

"What are ye sayin' then?" Mary-Margaret asked.

"I could sleep down here. In this chair."

"Unless ye announce it when ye leave, what difference would that make? The neighborhood would be all a-buzz with gossip when they see you waltzin' out of the house in the morning. And what sort of lesson am I teachin' me own grandson? That it's acceptable in his gran's eyes to have gentleman-callers spend the night? No. I can't have that!"

"He's gone for the night, isn't he? And I don't recall ever bein' called yer gentleman caller before, but if that's what ye're sayin'…"

"Well, yer not, but let's not muck up the soup."

"I think *I* should stay," Arthur said.

When no one responded, he continued. "At least until Mike gets home. I'll stand right here. Like this."

Arthur assumed a ready stance.

"Well, if 'tis protectin' I'm needin', I think Arthur is the better bet. Not that I don't trust yer intentions, Francis, but the night gets long and—"

"Don't I know it," Frank said with a smile.

"—ye are likely to fall asleep," Mary-Margaret concluded. "I don't know what time me Michael will be home or if he'll be home before mornin'. As such, Arthur, ye are goin' to have to stay alert."

"I will."

"Grand. And as ye've rightly noted, 'tis quite late. I'm off to bed. Take the dishes to the sink before ye leave, Francis. Goodnight, lads."

With that, Mary-Margaret ascended the stairs. Before she was halfway up, she stopped and called over her shoulder. "And can ye let Wee Phil out to the jacks before ye go, Francis?"

* * *

"What the—?"

Michael pushed the front door a little harder so that he could get inside. He then turned on the front hall light before stumbling over Arthur, who was fast asleep on the floor by the front door.

"Hiiii…YAAAAA!" Arthur yelled, leaping to his feet as Michael fell to the floor. As if to compensate for allowing the intruder he had yet to recognize to breach the threshold, Arthur quickly turned around and, with great vigor, jumped on top of Michael.

Phil came bounding down the stairs, barking excitedly.

"Get off of me!" Michael yelled.

"Oh. Sorry. I didn't know it was you, Mike."

"Who else would it be? And what are you doing here, anyway?"

Now, at the bottom of the stairs, Phil began licking Michael's face.

"And get this dog away from me."

"Michael? Is that ye, lad?" Mary-Margaret called from the top of the stairs, a hurley in her hand.

"Of course, it's me. What's going on here, and where did you get that bat?"

"It's not a bat. It's a hurley. And if ye'd gone to the Irish Club instead of whatever else it was ye did as a lad, ye'd know. Now, what are ye doin' on the floor?"

"Can you call your dog, please?" Michael said.

"'Tis not me dog. 'Tis Sally-next-door's. Honestly, son, I think—"

"Well, it might as well be your dog. Can you call it, please?"

"He. The dog is a he. Come on, Wee Phil. Up the stairs, my pup. There's a luv."

The dog darted up the stairs, tail wagging madly.

"And now, can you call Arthur off, please? And can you at least do up your bathrobe, Arthur? Nobody needs to see that."

"Uh, sorry, Mike. It must have come undone during your attack."

"Attack of what? Never mind. Just everyone. Please. Go away."

"Ach, 'tis the stress of the job, isn't it, luv. Let me put on a kettle for ye," Mary-Margaret said, leaning the hurley against the wall before coming down the stairs. "Do yerself up, lad. It…diminishes…the fierceness of yer Ninja Warrior look otherwise."

Arthur turned away from Mary-Margaret and directly towards Michael as he pulled the bathrobe around himself and then tied the belt.

"No, Mom," Michael said, averting his eyes. "It's the stress of…never mind. I just want to go to bed."

"I'll warm up some stew for ye, too, luv. Always were a bit gnarly when ye were hungry. What do the young people call it? Hangry?"

"Mom, it's the middle of the night. I'm not hungry. Or hangry. Or anything else but tired. I don't want a cup of tea. I just want to go to bed."

"Don't worry, Mike. I'll get myself home," Arthur said.

"At this hour of the night? And lookin' like that? Hardly. Michael, drive Arthur home. Yer food will be ready for ye when ye get back," Mary-Margaret directed, then walked past the two men into the kitchen.

"Honestly, I can get myself home," Arthur offered.

"I've got my coat on now. Let's go."

"Would you mind, then, dropping me somewhere else?"

Michael stopped in the doorway and looked at Arthur.

"No, I'll drive you home. I'll be back in about half an hour," Michael called to his mother.

"Grand. Be quiet when ye come in. I'll likely be in me bed sleepin'. 'Tis the middle of the night, dontcha know. And take Wee Phil out the back before ye go. He'll need to piddle now, havin' been woken up by the lot of ye."

Chapter Ten

For a Sunday morning, there were very few parishioners of St. Francis of Assisi Catholic Church and most ranged in age from sixty to death. During its heyday, when Mary-Margaret had been church secretary, the place was so full that if you didn't arrive early, you would likely have to either stand in the back in the narthex or sit in the front pew. It was no coincidence, according to Mary-Margaret, that attendance declined dramatically after the loss of Father Brian and her own retirement. While the latter was inevitable, transferring Father Brian to another parish and acquiring Father Miguel—brought in theoretically to attract the 'younger crowd'—was a colossal mistake. Aside from being considered a *hottie* by Ashleigh, her successor, Father Miguel, had added no value to the church at all. Or so thought Mary-Margaret.

Despite her keen, albeit subjective, observations, neither of the aforementioned staffing changes were the reason for the decline of parishioners. In fact, what had happened was that many of the single-family homes filled predominantly with large Catholic families that the parish St. Francis of Assisi served had been knocked down and replaced with exorbitantly priced multi-use condos full of either career-oriented couples with small designer dogs or tourists opting for Airbnbs rather than the much pricier hotels.

Unlike most of her neighbors and their homes, Mary-Margaret and her house had remained. And, despite living at her son's for the foreseeable future, Mary-Margaret would rather leave her house empty than have a stranger sleep in her bed, regardless of how much they were willing to pay to do so.

After receiving communion on this particular Sunday morning, she got up from the altar rail and noticed the dust on it.

Thank ye for the reminder, God.

A few minutes later, Mass was over, and Father Miguel was standing at the back of the narthex, arm outreached, limply shaking hands with each of the exiting congregants. Mary-Margaret hung back, seeing this as her opportunity to introduce the idea of hiring Arthur as the church custodian. The smell of freshly brewed coffee wafted through the sanctuary, indicating that all was in order for the weekly social gathering in the gymnasium.

As Mary-Margaret reached for Father Miguel's hand, however, she hesitated.

Has he met Arthur before? If so, what was the lad wearin'? Has he seen him as Sister Augustine? No, 'twas only the daycare ladies when he brought down the lunches for the smallies. Or was Father Miguel there as well that day? Ach, I can't remember. Never mind. If he's not met Arthur in any way, shape, or form before, I've got a better chance. But if he has—

"Mary-Margaret," Father Miguel said with tightened lips, snapping her back to this world.

"Father," she said, deciding that she'd have to rely on her innate charm to overcome this potential complication. "'Twas a lovely Mass ye gave today."

"And to what do I owe this unexpected compliment?" Father Miguel said as he reluctantly took her hand, forcing a smile, the left side of his mouth beginning to twitch.

"Ach, ye can read me like a book," Mary-Margaret said, reciprocating the handshake with an equal lack of enthusiasm before quickly withdrawing her hand.

"I'm thinking more like a psalm. 120:2 comes to mind," he said, looking beyond her to the cross above the altar.

Deliver my soul, O LORD, from lying lips, and from a deceitful tongue, they recited in muted unison.

"Well, since we are not mincin' words," Mary-Margaret said as she locked eyes with him, "I understand that ye are lookin' for a cleaner—a custodian—for the church."

"And...?"

"Well, I've a friend, his...her...name is...Sister Augustine and she is a fine cleaner."

"I am looking for a cleaner, not a nun, Mary-Margaret. And if I'm not mistaken—and I'm not—parishioners do not recommend nuns."

"Well, Father," Mary-Margaret began and then grabbed her chest and began to gasp for air.

Rather than assist her or call for help, Father Miguel blinked slowly twice and sighed. To his credit, he did not roll his eyes.

"'Tis nothin' to worry yerself about, Father," Mary-Margaret wheezed, holding up her hand in protest of any assistance Father Miguel might decide to offer. This gesture was in vain, however, because he didn't move.

"Just the pneumonia," she continued. "Me body is practically consumed with it at the moment. Which is why I'm stayin' at me Michael's, as ye know."

Still no offer of assistance.

"Grabs me chest every now and again, does the illness. Doctor says I should be in me bed, but ye know me: never miss a Sunday."

"Yes, sadly."

"But I'll be fine, Father. Don't ye worry."

"I won't," Father Miguel said, unmoved.

Sensing that Father Miguel was not the least bit worried or even interested in her illness, feigned or otherwise, Mary-Margaret completed her Oscar-worthy performance by rubbing her chest, giving it a pat, and straightening herself up again.

"A glass of water, Father. Have ye got a glass of water?"

"I believe there is water in the gymnasium," he said, lifting his head up to pull underneath his collar, as if it had suddenly become too tight for him.

"Indeed. Well now. I'll be makin' me way, then. And sendin' Sister Augustine in to see ye tomorrow mornin', say around nine, should be fine."

"Why?" Father Miguel asked, but it was too late. Moving much faster than one would expect from someone with lungs full of fluid, Mary-Margaret was already out of the church proper and almost to the gymnasium doors, missing Father Miguel's parting words.

"Why do I even bother," he said, shaking his head slowly. "Ashleigh can deal with this Sister Augustine."

* * *

"Well, if it isn't Murder Mary." Eric Switzer's gravelly voice could be heard above the chatter of the social gathering when she entered the gymnasium.

"Another murder?" Irene Ashford asked, mincing her way towards her friend in a tight pencil skirt and inappropriately fashioned cashmere sweater, a plate of pinwheel sandwiches in hand. "Do tell."

Mary-Margaret stopped and smiled in the doorway of the gymnasium, basking in the moment, and then made her way to the refreshment table just inside.

"I bet you could *murder* a cup of coffee," Laura-Jean McQueen squealed and then followed up with a high-pitched laugh from behind the table, holding out a Styrofoam cup. "And maybe *kill* some time with we regular people who are *dying* to hear all about it?"

"Ta, luv, but a cuppa would be much better," Mary-Margaret replied, reminding herself that the gymnasium she stood in was still a part of God's house and that responding to that daft Laura-Jean McQueen in a manner more in keeping with her foolishness would be inappropriate, especially on a Sunday.

"So, come on, Mary. Spill," Eric said, scratching his slicked-back, unnaturally black hair as he moved closer to her than necessary. While she tried to never get close enough to him to know for sure, Mary-Margaret always had the feeling that he smelled of B.O., or had lice, or carried something equally undesirable on his skin.

"Does yer obtuse nature not even get Sunday's off?" she asked, stepping away from him while rubbing her arm, as if to soothe an abrasion. Logic told her that her unfounded and irrational concerns about Eric's personal hygiene were likely false, but one could never be too careful.

"Give the girl a moment," Monique Prudhomme said with a smile, taking the cup of coffee out of Laura-Jean's hand while picking up a cup of prepoured tea for Mary-Margaret.

"I second Eric's request," Irene said, giving him a quick wink before pushing the plate of sandwiches at Mary-Margaret. "I want to know the deets."

"Well, there's not much to tell—" she began, taking a sip of the tepid tea Monique had handed to her as her friends crowded around her. *You'd think she'd know enough to keep the tea in the pot, the daft girl.*

"So says she who lives with a homicide detective," Eric said, winking back at Irene.

"Just a detective. Me Michael is just a detective," Mary-Margaret retorted, taking what she hoped was a cucumber sandwich off the plate.

"A detective who just happens to be involved in every murder in this end of the city," Irene said with a smile, setting down the tray to adjust her sweater. "Has his divorce come through yet?"

"And ye'd be asking why?"

"Do you have to ask?" Eric said with a smirk.

"Me son is a devoted father with no time for the likes of that," Mary-Margaret snapped back, giving Irene the once-over. *In God's house, there are many rooms. And if there was a brothel next door....*

"Every man needs some—" Irene began.

"Says who? Besides, he's too young for you, Irene," Eric said.

Irene flinched, as if a glass of cold water had been thrown in her face.

"I'm sure he's far too busy anyway, dear," Monique said. "You'd be better with a man who can be there for you."

"Me son was a fine husband," Mary-Margaret announced. "'Twas the trollop he was—"

"No, I-I didn't mean—" Monique stammered.

"Yeah. Whatever," Eric cut in, scratching underneath the red suspenders that held his pants up over his bulging belly. "We want to know about this bag you found in the laneway."

Mary-Margaret jerked back.

"It's been all over the news," Eric said. "So go on, tell us what that dame on the TV won't."

"Ach, there's not much to tell because," Mary-Margaret said, regaining her composure, "as I'm sure ye are all well aware, this is an ongoing police investigation, and I'm not at liberty to discuss the details."

They all nodded to one another, considering what she had said, while Mary-Margaret stepped closer to the refreshment table to get rid of the not-cucumber sandwich before taking a sip of her now-cold tea.

"Makes sense," Monique said.

"But you're not a cop. You're not bound by any gag order. Tell us what you know," Eric persisted.

"Indeed, I am not," Mary-Margaret said, looking squarely at Eric. "But I am bound by a moral duty to do me part by tryin' to assist in findin' the killer, which means—"

"That you'll be doing your sleuthing thing again?" Laura-Jean McQueen said with an inappropriate tone and volume that suggested to Mary-Margaret that Laura-Jean was forgoing her prescription in favor of self-medicating again.

"That I will be keepin' me nose out of places it doesn't belong," Mary-Margaret corrected.

"Somehow, I find that hard to believe," Norm Goodier said, joining the group. "I just hope they find out who did it. Got any more of those pinwheel sandwiches, Irene?"

With that, Norm reached over and snatched three of the tiny sandwiches off the plate Irene was holding and stuffed them all into his mouth at once.

"My brother said this will be a good one," Norm said once he'd swallowed the sandwiches. "Lot of variables."

"How would your brother know?" Eric demanded. "Is he a cop?"

"Better than that. He's a county coroner. He and the missus are in town for a few days. Staying at my place. He said he'd spoken to you the other night at Abby's book thing here at the church, Mary-Margaret. Maybe you'd like to pop by later today, and you and him can compare notes."

"That's a lovely offer, Norman, but I've got the family comin' 'round for dinner this evenin'." While chatting about the whys and wherefores of dead bodies might be of interest to a county coroner, she was more interested in discussing the criminal end of things. And she didn't know how much of

Dr. Goodier's stammering and stuttering she could put up with. *Forgive me, Father, but I've got me limits, too, as Ye know.*

"Well, can't say I didn't offer," Norm said, reaching for another handful of sandwiches as Irene gave him a disapproving look and pulled the plate away from him.

"Duly noted," Mary-Margaret said with a nod. "Now, if ye'll excuse me, I've got some corned beef to put on the boil."

Chapter Eleven

"Is the corned beef to yer likin', Allan?" Mary-Margaret asked, completely unconcerned about his reply.

"Mom, why...?" Teaszy began, wishing that the ever-widening rift between her mother and her husband could be set aside, even if just for one meal.

Mary-Margaret inhaled the unmistakable aroma of boiled corned beef and cabbage as she admired the plate of it in front of her.

"I'm sure it's going to be fabulous, Gran," Paulie deadpanned. "Just like it was last Sunday. And the Sunday before that. And the Sunday—"

"Poisoning the lad against me dinners now, are ye?" Mary-Margaret said, scowling down the table at Allan, who was seated as far away from his mother-in-law as possible.

"I hardly think he needs my hel—"

Mary-Margaret broke out in a fit of coughing.

"You okay, Mom?" Katie, Mary-Margaret's youngest, also known as the postscript, asked.

"I will be, me luv," Mary-Margaret finally gasped. "'Tis just the pneumonia rearin' it's ugly..."

Mary-Margaret's words were cut short by another fit of coughs. Teaszy rose from the table and headed into the kitchen to get some water.

"No, luv, sitcheedoon," Mary-Margaret whispered hoarsely, waving for her older daughter to return to her chair. "'Tis just the nature of the beast."

"Should you even be up out of bed?" Ahmed, Katie's partner, asked.

"Ach, such a lovely lad, is your Ahmed, Katie. Always thinkin' of his mother-in-law."

"Mother-in-*like*," Ahmed corrected with a smile.

"At least one of ye cares," Mary-Margaret said, rubbing her chest with one hand while passing a serving dish full of mashed potatoes up the table to no one in particular.

"Wait," Max said, reaching towards his grandmother to intercept the serving dish before it was out of reach. "I want some more."

"And I see the corned beef is almost all gone, so it must be to someone's likin'," Mary-Margaret said, surveying the table after giving Max an approving nod.

"That's good to hear because I'm sure it's even worse cold," Allan muttered.

"Come on, All—" Teaszy began.

"In fact, it's lovely cold. On some rye bread. With a wee bit of that fancy French Dijon mustard. Would ye like me to pack ye a sandwich, then, Allan?"

"Hrumph," Allan said.

"Or shall I just set the plate across from ye?" Mary-Margaret continued.

"In the place for the Unknown Soldier?" Allan said, giving Mary-Margaret the side eye.

"'Tis a place set for an unexpected guest," Mary-Margaret shot back with not nearly as much venom as she felt Allan deserved.

"*What* unexpected guest," Allan said with a sigh. "The one that's not sitting at the empty place at the head of the table?"

"*That* would be for Jimmy, God rest his soul."

"God rest his soul," everyone but Allan mumbled as they crossed themselves.

"Does anyone else find that...odd?" Paulie asked with a wince, looking around the table.

"Time to clear the table," Teaszy said, feigning cheerfulness as she looked over at Paulie and Max. "That means you two, boys. Let's go."

"But I'm still—" Max began.

Allan shook his head and returned to his dinner.

"So does this mean we're *not* clearing away now?" Max asked his aunt.

"And why would ye? We're right in the middle of Sunday dinner," Mary-

Margaret said, continuing with her meal.

For the first time that evening, everyone at the table was silent.

"Now that we've got that straightened out," Mary-Margaret continued, "what of this lunatic on the loose, Michael."

"There is no lunatic on the loose, Mom," Michael replied, reaching across Katie to the plate of corned beef.

"Ach, 'tis not a boarding house I'm runnin' here, Michael. Ye can ask yer sister for the plate to be passed."

"Sorry," Michael said, withdrawing his arm. "Katie, would you please pass me the corned beef?"

"Gladly, dear brother," Katie said with a smirk. "Would you like some mashed potatoes as well?"

"And how would ye know there's not a lunatic out and about? Here's me, pullin' heads out of the garden, and me son says not to worry. Clearly, there's a murderer in our midst, and ye, sittin' over there, are more interested in stuffin' yer gob than catchin' a murderer."

"Yes, I would love some more mashed potatoes, Katie. Thank you," Michael said, the sarcasm dripping off his words.

"Is that true, Dad? Is there a crazoid on the loose?" Max asked, eyes wide open.

"Unless you consider your gran a crazoid..." Michael began.

Allan chortled. Teaszy kicked him under the table.

"And what else could it be?" Mary-Margaret cut in. "But mind we don't say too much," she continued, patting Max's arm as she glanced up the table at the rest of her family, "in front of young ears."

"I'm almost eighteen, Gran," Max said.

"Barely seventeen," Mary-Margaret corrected.

"I'm sure he's heard worse," Allan said with a sigh. Teaszy gave him another swift kick.

"Maybe they're targeting you, Gran," Paulie said, a twinkle in his eye. "Like, let's kill off all the Irish immigrants. The one's who thought they could escape The Troubles."

"Paulie!" Teaszy called out to her youngest son, wishing she was close enough to give him a swift boot as well.

"Wasn't the victim from that pub all of you ex-pats go to? The papers are saying—"

"The papers don't know anything," Michael said, swallowing a particularly chewy piece of corned beef.

"And neither do ye, by the sounds of it."

"Mom, I'm not in Homicide."

"But ye were over at O'Leary's grilling poor Johnny and Maeve. Makin' them feel like they had anythin' to do with it."

"I was over at O'Leary's talking to the last people who likely saw her alive—"

"Exactly. Ye think one of them did it."

"If I may continue, Mom?"

"Not likely," Katie said just before Teaszy gave her a look that, as the youngest, she was all too familiar with.

"The last person who saw her alive…except for the murderer," Michael said. "Homicide has everything well in hand."

"Well in hand? With who mannin' the wheel?"

"Detective Sergeant Gill will be—"

"I rest me case. Pass the mashed back down, will ye, Ahmed."

"Oh, she's going for a double helping of mashed. This should be good," Paulie commented.

"Paulie!" Teaszy snapped.

Mary-Margaret looked over at Paulie, and with a nod, scooped a huge mound of mashed potatoes onto the serving spoon and plopped it down on her plate.

"Am I right or am I right, ladies and gentlemen?" Paulie said, crossing his arms as he leaned back in his chair.

"Ye were always the perceptive one, Paulie," Mary-Margaret said, shoving the bowl towards him. "Unlike yer uncle over there, Mister Big City Police Detective. And it wouldn't hurt ye, me wee luv, to have another serving—or would this be yer first?— of mashed."

"No thanks, Gran. I'm on a diet," Paulie said, rubbing his stomach.

"You?" Katie asked. "A guy at your age?"

"Totally. Now that I'm single—"

"Again?" Ahmed asked. "What happened to—"

"*He-whose-name-shall-not-be-spoken?*" Paulie cut in. "Gone, girl. So now I have to be in top form."

"I think you should spend your time working on getting a decent job," Allan said.

"Speakin' of the same, Allan, any more word about ye gettin' let go?" Mary-Margaret asked.

"I was never getting let go," Allan replied slowly.

"Well, that's not what I'm hearin'. All of these IT jobs are bein' moved out of the country. Open yer eyes. The writin's on the wall, lad."

"Allan's job is quite secure, Mom," Teaszy said.

"Is there any more of those mashed potatoes?" Ahmed asked.

"Of course, there are, luv," Mary-Margaret said, her voice softening. She motioned for Paulie to pass the plate up the table. "May it never be said that a potato couldn't be had in the O'Shea house. But ye see, I knew I should have made more corned beef."

"You know no one actually eats this back in Ireland, right?" Allan said.

"And ye would know this how?"

"I don't," Allan conceded.

"No, ye don't. Now. About this lunatic who's likely intent on killin' us all. Why isn't our Mandy leadin' the investigation? Ye know, if she was, the murderer would be behind bars by now, and she'd be sittin' in that empty place across from Allan. *Enjoyin' me corned beef.*"

"Because she's already working a case, I suppose. I don't know, Mom. I'm not in Homicide," Michael said, feeling that this was becoming more of a mantra for him rather than just a statement of fact.

"But ye are thick as thieves with Homicide when it comes to interviewin' yer own."

"Johnny and Maeve O'Leary are not 'my own.' The pub happens to be in the division I work in, and I was told to interview them. That's it."

"Ye were undercover, weren't ye? Puttin' an Irish lad in an Irish pub like that. Ye've been dropped in because there's a serial killer out there in the Irish community, just like Paulie said, and yer the only one who can crack the case, isn't that so?"

"No, Mom. I was asked to take some statements because the pub is in the division where I work, and it just happens to be an Irish pub."

"Ach, ye can keep that malarky for the likes of Janelle Austin and her telly friends, but amongst us family, it won't wash. Someone is targettin' we Irish. Again. Likely an Englishman."

Ahmed couldn't suppress his giggles any longer, and once he began, the rest of the table, except for Michael and Mary-Margaret, began to laugh.

"Laugh now, but don't ye come cryin' to me when ye start gettin' death threats. Although ye likely won't, Ahmed. Or ye, Allan."

"Why not me?" Allan asked. "I could be Irish."

"But yer not," Mary-Margaret snapped.

"Mom," Michael began with a sigh, "I sincerely doubt that this was a targeted murder. At least, not based on perceived ethnicity."

"Well, that settles that then, doesn't it?" Mary-Margaret said. "The Big City Detective has spoken."

There was an uneasy silence around the table, cut only by the sound of cutlery on porcelain.

"And what about the organized crime spree goin' on in our Max's school? Or are ye goin' to tell me that's just boys bein' boys?"

"She's on a roll tonight, ladies and gentlemen," Paulie said under his breath.

"Must have been a particularly rousing Mass this morning," Allan said, speaking a bit louder than Paulie.

"In fact, 'twas not," Mary-Margaret said. "Father Miguel lacks the fundamental ability to—"

"I don't think there's an organized crime thing going on at my school," Max said. "Just likely a few guys breaking into lockers—"

"And this is how it starts, doesn't it? A couple of lads doin' a couple of break-and-enters, and then before ye know it, they've become a gang of organized killers," Mary-Margaret said.

"How long does the doctor think you'll have pneumonia?" Katie cut in.

"And shouldn't you be in bed, resting?"

"It will last as long as it lasts," Mary-Margaret replied and then broke into a round of coughs. "And yer right. A good lie-down would do me a world of good."

"Do you want a cuppa before you head upstairs, Gran?" Paulie asked.

"Ach, such a lovely lad," Mary-Margaret said, softening. "I would, luv. I'll take it in the livin' room, while I'm still…livin'."

"That's one way to get out of the dishes," Allan quipped.

"That's one way to take care of someone ye love," Mary-Margaret shot back, plopping herself down in one of the living room chairs. "Speakin' of which, do ye want a ride to school in the mornin', Max?"

"Mom, I wish you'd let him—"

"'Tis not yer concern, Michael, and if ye must know, I'm goin' there meself to get this organized crime ring sorted."

"Ugh," Max groaned.

"Well, it's obvious that this matter is far too complex for yer da to sort out."

"I think you're being a bit unfair to Mike, Mom," Ahmed said.

"Or is it just beyond your scope of comprehen—"

"Oh, she's pulling out all the stops!" Paulie laughed.

"Weren't you going to make your grandmother a cup of tea?' Teaszy asked, her foot aching to give her son a kick.

"I think it's time for us to go," Katie said. "We'll let the big kids sort this one out."

"No, no," Mary-Margaret said. "Don't be leavin' on my account. I'm sure we'd all like a cuppa, wouldn't we, lads?"

"I'm not making tea for everyone," Paulie said.

"I think it's time for us to go as well," Allan said. "I'll get the car."

"And there's yer problem, Teaszy. Yer saddled with a man who would rather walk out than look after his family. I'll be sure to have yer room made up at me house for when ye need it."

Teaszy began to defend her husband while Michael began to advise Mary-Margaret to stay away from Max's school; Katie told Ahmed to get his coat, Allan told Paulie to leave the tea for Max to make, and Max began to object to no one in particular.

Perhaps it was the sound of the front door being opened, or perhaps he mistook the tension in the air for excitement. Regardless, Phil came bounding down the stairs, his tiny stub of a tail wagging five beats to the four.

"And, before I have me last cuppa and take me last breath," Mary-Margaret hollered, silencing the mayhem, "would someone take Wee Phil out to the jacks?"

Chapter Twelve

After dropping Max off the next morning, Mary-Margaret parked Daphne a few streets over and walked back to his school. One of the downsides of having such a distinctive car was that everyone knew when Mary-Margaret was around, which, when she reflected upon it, wasn't always a downside. But it was today because she wanted to get to the bottom of this organized crime ring situation discreetly. Not like it would happen, but Mary-Margaret was not about to risk having her Michael drop by the school and see her car parked out front. One could never be too careful.

From the doorway of the office, it was hard to tell whether the hair running halfway down the secretary's back had undergone too many home perms over the years or had cost the woman a small fortune, judging by the way it looked this morning. The denim jacket that she wore over an off-white chiffon dress also might have been a relic from a few decades ago or an overpriced reproduction. Either way, Mary-Margaret recognized that this thin waif was the gatekeeper of the organization and the first hurdle to get past on her quest to conquer the criminal element terrorizing her grandson's school.

"Can I help you?" the secretary asked as she looked up from her computer monitor. Her voice was gravelly in a way that Mary-Margaret knew came from too many hard nights over too many years. Her face didn't undermine that conclusion.

"Indeed. My name is Mary-Margaret O'Shea, Max O'Shea's grandmother, and I'm lookin' to speak with Mrs. Zalinski, yer principal."

"Is she expecting you?" the secretary asked, scrutinizing the visitor as much as the visitor was scrutinizing her.

"I don't know how she wouldn't be with all that's been goin' on at this school," Mary-Margaret retorted, straightening her back to maximize her full five-foot-two stature.

"I mean, do you have an appointment? If not, you may need to come back later because—"

A woman who looked a lifetime younger than the secretary swept into the office.

"Sue, can you be sure that I don't forget to send off...oh, hello. May I help you?" the woman said, stopping in her tracks.

"Only if yer Mrs. Zalinski," Mary-Margaret replied, looking her up and down. *Surely this can't be...*

"I am," she said, cocking her head sharply as she looked over at the secretary.

"No, she doesn't have an appointment. I was just telling her that she may have to—"

"Oh good," the principal said with a sigh, putting her hand to her chest. "I *absolutely* hate it when I make people wait to see me. No worries, Mrs...?"

"O'Shea. Mary-Margaret O'Shea. Max's gran—"

"Mrs. O'Shea. Come in. I've got a few minutes now, don't I, Sue?"

"You've got—" Sue began, looking at the datebook on her desk.

"I'm sure you can sort it out for me. Come in, Mrs. O'Shea."

Mrs. Zalinski motioned for Mary-Margaret to follow her through the doorway across from her secretary's desk. Assuming that Sue felt as she had every time Father Miguel would decide that he could organize his time better than she could, Mary-Margaret felt a kinship for the woman left at her desk, her mouth hanging open.

"I was a secretary for years, luv," Mary-Margaret whispered to Sue as she followed the principal into her office. "I know what these people can be like."

"Close the door, will you?" the principal said as she looked from her cluttered desk to a cozy seating area by the window, clearly unaware that she had disregarded the schedule her secretary had drawn up for her for the day. "And forgive me. I haven't formally introduced myself. I'm Leona Zalinski."

"Nice to make your acquaintance," Mary-Margaret said with a nod, extending her hand.

"Please," the principal said after shaking Mary-Margaret's hand. "Sit down. Let's go over to the comfy chairs. No need to talk over a desk, unless you've done something horribly wrong, and I need to make you feel bad about yourself?"

The principal lowered her head and looked over her glasses.

"No, not this time," Mary-Margaret said, choosing what she hoped would be a firm armchair over the overstuffed couch that sat kitty-corner to it.

"Excellent. Would you like a coffee? I'm dying for one, and it's no trouble to have Sue bring in one for you as well."

"No, thank ye. I'm fine."

"Wonderful. Sue?" the principal called as she opened the door slightly. "Can you get me a coffee, please? Are you sure you don't want anything?"

"No, I'm fine, luv. I mean…Mrs. Zalinski."

"Please, call me Leona," she said, taking the coffee that Sue handed to her and then closing the door again.

Has the whole world gone mad with these instant coffee machines? Mary-Margaret thought. *Whatever happened to having a wee moment to collect yer thoughts while it brewed? Or change yer mind?*

"Ahh, that's much better," Leona said, sinking into the couch as she took a sip. "Now, what brings you to the principal's office? You've mentioned that you're Max O'Shea's grandmother. I'm not familiar with the name, so I'm thinking it's not him we're going to be discussing."

"Well, in a way, it is. Ye see, Mrs. Zalin—"

"Leona. Call me Leona."

"Leona," Mary-Margaret corrected, her face flushing as she recalled the numerous and not-so-congenial visits she had paid to the principal's office in her youth, "it's about this organized crime ring ye've got goin' on."

"Hold the phones!' Leona held up her free hand as her body jolted forward so quickly that she almost spilled coffee all over herself. "What—what—what did you just say?"

"Organized crime. There's no other word for it," Mary-Margaret stated.

Leona Zalinski sat bolt upright, her eyes as big as pie plates.

"Me Max has been tellin' me about how these hooligans are terrorizin' the students right under yer nose by breakin' into lockers and stealin' cell phones and laptops, and it's got to stop," Mary-Margaret continued as quickly as possible, fearing that the poor woman might faint before she got all of the words out.

Mary-Margaret stared at Leona, waiting for her to either faint or respond. She did neither.

"That's why I'm here," Mary-Margaret concluded.

It took a few seconds for the principal to catch her breath, during which time Mary-Margaret couldn't be sure that she wasn't going to be asked to leave.

"Sue," Leona hollered through the door as soon as she was able to regain her composure. "Is Mr. Wiggins around?"

Quickly enough for Mary-Margaret to assume that she had been standing outside the door listening the whole time, Sue had the door open and was inside the principal's office.

"No. He called in sick today, remember? Maybe not. No. You wouldn't know. I don't think I've had a chance to tell you. Sorry, Mr. Wiggins called in sick. If you ask me, he'll likely be gone for the week."

"Oh, poo!" Leona said, squirming her way up and out of the clutches of the couch.

"It's a thing I have," Sue said, looking over at Mary-Margaret. "Kind of like a gift. Might be linked to my musical ear. I don't know, but I can kinda tell how sick someone—"

Suddenly recalling her feigned pneumonia, Mary-Margaret's face flushed.

"I wouldn't bet my last dollar on it," Sue said, noticing Mary-Margaret's apparent discomfort, "but I can just sort of hear it, you know?"

"But it's not for certain," Mary-Margaret confirmed.

"No, just a thing."

"Grand," Mary-Margaret nodded, giving a few throaty coughs.

"Now that—" Sue began, wagging a finger at Mary-Margaret.

"I need Mr. Wiggins," Leona cut in, beginning to pace the small room. "We need to make a united management decision. Maybe call him at home, Sue."

"If I may suggest," Mary-Margaret said, looking up at the two women while giving one final cough, "ye might want yer lady to sit in if it's information on these thefts that yer wantin'. A secretary knows more about what's goin' on than…well…never mind."

"No, of course. What would Wally know? He's just a vice principal anyway. You're right, Mrs. O'Shea. Sue, can you help us out here?"

As Mary-Margert had suggested, it turned out that the secretary was quite aware of the locker thefts and had already reported them to the police the previous week. Of course, Sue assured her boss, this was done on behalf of the principal.

"The bike cops—the ones in the cute shorts—even came by. They wanted to take a look at our video—"

"You didn't let them, did you?" Leona said with a gasp, and then, noticing the look on Mary-Margaret's face, added, "Privacy laws. We'd have to clear it with the Board first. Make sure we don't have to pixelate any faces. You know…."

"We couldn't even if we wanted to," Sue said. "Most of the cameras are broken."

"What good is that, then?" Mary-Margaret asked.

"None, but we can't get them fixed until the budget—"

"Oh no!" Leona interrupted. "I've got that silly budget meeting downtown this afternoon, don't I?"

"Yes, and I strongly suggest you attend," Sue said. "You've missed the last three, which may be why the cameras—"

"Yes, yes, yes. Did I know about this?" Leona asked, a wave of panic sweeping over her face.

"The funding has been—"

"No, the police being on site."

"No. You were at a Board meeting that day," Sue said.

"And you didn't think to tell me?"

"You weren't here," Sue said.

"You have my cell number," Leona countered.

Another one lookin' to climb the corporate ladder, Mary-Margaret thought. *Too busy lookin' after their own interests to look after those that actually need lookin' at.*

Sue looked down at the floor.

"Ach, 'tis the same all over, isn't it?" Mary-Margaret said, casually getting up from the armchair. "When I was at St. Francis of Assisi—that's the church where I was secretary for centuries—a lot went on that Father Miguel had no clue of. I mean, Father Brian, his predecessor, was quite good about bein' on top of things, but then again, he never left the church proper. Some of the congregants said it was on account of his dippin' into the blood of the—"

"Well, thank you for coming in, Mrs. O'Shea. I will follow up on this and get back to you," Leona said, suddenly sounding very official as she stretched out her hand. "Where can I reach you?"

"At me Michael's, Max's da's," Mary-Margaret said, taking Leona's hand in both of hers and holding on to it rather than shaking it. "I'm livin' with him for a wee while. His da, that is. Well, both of them, now that ye mention it, but it's his da that I'm carin' for."

"Mr. O'Shea is sick? Max never said—" Sue began.

"No, he's just a police officer," Mary-Margaret said, finally letting go of the principal's hand.

"I didn't realize you knew Max," Leona said.

"Of course I do. I'm the school secretary. I know everyone and everything. Max is a great kid."

"Thank ye," Mary-Margaret said. "I like to think I've had somethin' to do with that, but I think it's the strength of the entire O'Shea family that's kept that lad on the straight and narrow."

The phone on Sue's desk rang.

"Tell Max that the Old Bird is on it," she said as she stepped over to her desk.

"Tell Max," Leona corrected, "that he and all of the students here at St. Ignatius have the support of the administration and—"

"Yeah," Sue called over, resuming the conversation after having summarily dealt with whomever was on the phone, "that's what they call me. Because my last name is Bird. Used to call me Song Bird when I first got here. I used to be a singer before this gig, but it morphed into Old Bird. Because I got old. So tell Max that the Old Bird is always here for him."

"I will. Yes," Mary-Margaret said, nodding vigorously at this woman she felt was a kindred spirit as she turned to leave. "I most certainly will."

Chapter Thirteen

As she stepped in through the back door of Michael's house, Mary-Margaret could hear her cell phone jangling madly inside her purse. She reached in and pulled it out, instinctively looking at the caller ID before answering it. The number was blocked. The only calls she ever got from a blocked number were from Michael's work, and the only time Michael's work ever called her was when Michael was injured.

Her heart missed a beat as her fingers struggled to hit the answer key.

"Yes, 'tis Michael's mother here. What has happened to me son?" she demanded, leaving the traditional greetings for another day.

"MM, it's me. Arthur," an unsteady voice whispered into the phone.

"Arthur? What are ye doin' givin' me a scare like that? Have you no sense, lad?"

"I'm in jail."

"Is that a code name for one of your playgroups?" Mary-Margaret asked.

"No. I'm in jail. Real jail."

"That can't be. Are ye just tryin' to take the Mick out of me, as if I don't have enough on me plate at the moment. Because if ye were in jail, ye wouldn't be callin' me now, would ye? I'm not seein' the craic in this, lad."

"No. I'm serious, MM. I'm in jail," Arthur continued, his voice trembling as he blurted out the words, his eyes starting to tear. "They gave me one phone call, and this is it."

Mary-Margaret pulled the phone away from her ear and stared at it for a moment before continuing.

"Did they do a raid at one of those club things ye go to?"

"No. They think I killed Cassandra!" he cried, his voice at full volume.

"Have they met ye, luv?"

"I'm serious. They think I kidnapped her from the pub, killed her, boiled her body—although everyone knows that would take way too long to get the niggly bits off the bones—and—"

"Ye didn't tell them that, did ye?"

"Tell them what?"

"About how long it would take to get the niggly bits off?"

"Of course I did," he said frantically. "And I told them that I won First Place in my grade seven science..."

"They did tell ye that ye weren't obliged to say anythin' in response to the charge, didn't they?"

"No. They didn't have to," Arthur answered. "I recited it for them."

"And I'm thinkin' that impressed them to no end."

"I couldn't help myself, MM."

"I believe ye," Mary-Margaret said with a sigh.

"And now they think I killed Cassandra and couldn't get rid of the head, so I just planted it in the laneway on my way over to see you."

"Reasonable."

"MM! Whose side are you on?" Arthur yelped.

"Listen, luv, don't say another word. I'm going to call me Michael and get this sorted out. Is there a number I can call ye back on?"

"I don't think it works that way, MM."

"What, then? I can't call ye back?"

Mary-Margaret heard a couple of thuds and a voice call out, "You almost done in there?"

"I have to go, MM," Arthur whispered. "Wish me luck."

"Have ye got a lawyer?" she called loudly through the phone, as if Arthur was truly being walked away from her.

"No," he replied. "I thought I could—"

"Leave it with me."

* * *

93

"Detective O'Shea speaking. How may I help you?"

"Michael. 'Tis yer mother."

"Oh," he said with a sigh.

"I need yer help."

"Is it Arthur?"

"How did ye know?"

"Is he missing? Again?" Michael said, feeling a tension knot forming on the right side of his neck.

"What kind of a question is that, lad? He's sittin' right in yer cells, likely right in front of ye."

"What do you mean?" Michael said, sitting up a little straighter, the knot tightening.

"What do you mean *what do I mean*? I mean Arthur's in jail for the murder of that thievin' barmaid from O'Leary's."

"Hang on a minute."

Mary-Margaret heard a click, followed by the sound of canned classical music.

"Ach, Wee Phil," Mary-Margaret said as the Jack Russell began jumping at the back door. "'Tis a wonder ye don't have a urinary tract infection with the way they forget about ye around here. Off with ye, then," she said as she opened the door, the tiny dog bounding out and down the few stairs of the landing into the laneway, "and don't be bringin' back any bones or niggly bits."

"Okay, Mom," Michael said as he took her off hold, his voice sounding much more official. "Arthur is in custody, charged with murder."

"And?"

"This is a homicide investigation—"

"Clearly," she said.

"And so Homicide is investigating."

"Do they pay ye extra for bein' so bright in the sea of darkness the rest of us apparently float about in?"

"What I'm saying, Mom, is that this is a murder investigation that is being led by Detective Sergeant Gill…"

"Speakin' of a sea of darkness," she muttered.

"As I was saying," Michael said, rotating his neck slowly, "D/S Gill is in charge of this investigation. And that's all I'm going to say."

"So ye have nothin' to do with it then?"

"No."

"Can ye just pop yer head 'round the corner there and see how the poor lad is doin'? Maybe get him a sandwich or a cuppa?"

"No."

"Can ye at least see what he was wearin'?"

"Why?" Michael said, now rolling two fingers over the lump on his neck.

"I'm just thinkin' of Arthur. His pride. If he has any. He wasn't wearin' that Teletubby outfit, was he?"

"I have no idea what he was wearing when they arrested him, but he's likely wearing a white paper jumpsuit now."

"Well, at least he'll enjoy that."

"But if you must know," Michael said, giving up on relieving the pain in his neck while bringing the record of arrest up on his computer screen, "he was wearing a nun's habit when he was arrested."

"Oh, me stars," Mary-Margaret exclaimed. "Sister Augustine was supposed to see Father Miguel this mornin' about a job cleanin' the church. And now ye and yer lot have gone and arrested her. What a mess ye've made of this, Michael."

Before Michael could respond, Mary-Margaret hung up the phone.

* * *

I'll need a cuppa if I'm goin' to get through this mornin', Mary-Margaret thought as she filled up the kettle and fired up the back burned on the stove, dropping a Barry's tea bag in a mug. The whistle on the kettle began just as she heard a yapping at the back door.

Ach, Wee Phil. 'Tis a wonder ye've not run back to Sally-next-door's house, for all the attention yer gettin' here.

She let the Jack Russell in, giving him a second glance just to be sure he hadn't brought any bones or ligaments or other unwanted items in with him.

A quick call to The New Girl, and then I'm off to free Arthur, she thought, grabbing a McVitie's biscuits before taking the tea bag out of the mug. *How, I know not, but it'll come to me.*

She practically drowned her tea with milk and then tapped a familiar number on her cell without leaving the kitchen. This was not a social call and she wished it to be over as quickly as possible.

"Good morning. This is St. Fran's of A. May God shine down on you. Ashleigh speaking. How may I help you?"

"Ashleigh. 'Tis Mary-Margaret O'Shea. I need—"

"Oh, hey, Mary-M. O. How's it goin'?"

Mary-Margaret hoped Ashleigh could feel the coldness of her stare through the phone.

"You still there?" Ashleigh asked. Apparently, she could not feel the ice in the line.

"Yes. 'Tis Mary. Margaret. O'Shea. Put me through to Father Miguel immediately. Please."

"No can do, Mary-M. O. He's not in. Likely not around until later this afternoon."

"Not in? Not in? And who did the Mass this mornin' then?"

"Oh. Yeah. He did that, then was out like a shot. Said something about some nut or nun or something coming in and that I was supposed to deal with it. Never happened, so I have no idea what he was talking about," she said with a dismissive giggle.

"So he left ye in charge of hirin' Sister Augustine, then? Well, that makes life a lot easier, I suppose."

"I don't hire anyone. This job is just about answering the phone. You know that."

The New Girl that Father Miguel had determined to be a viable replacement for Mary-Margaret upon the latter's retirement had no idea how lucky she was that this conversation was being had over the phone. If it had been in person, and if looks could kill, she would have been dead several times over by now.

"In fact, I do not," Mary-Margaret declared, preparing to set this thick girl straight, but then, recalling the purpose of her call, continued in a much warmer tone. "But I've just now received a note from Father Miguel, as I do despite havin' given up me post, advisin' me to advise ye to regard Sister Augustine as the new custodian. She gets paid cash on Fridays."

"Say whaaaaat?" Ashleigh almost laughed.

"This is how we do things at St. Francis, luv," Mary-Margaret almost choked on the word of affection. "Father Miguel had mentioned to me yesterday after the service to make sure ye knew. We're in communication daily, he and I."

"Really?" Ashleigh asked.

"Truly." *Father, forgive me, but 'tis for the right reasons, as Ye already know.*

"Ah, okay. Makes my life easier, I suppose."

"Well," Mary-Margaret said with relief, "between waitin' for the phone to ring while sittin' down—practically multi-taskin' for someone like yerself, really—we girls have to stick together to try to make things as easy as possible for each other, don't we?"

"You know it."

"So just write down on a piece of paper that five hundred dollars a week is to be given to Sister Augustine."

"Five hundred dollars a week? We're lucky if we pull down a couple of C notes, even when Miguel goes on a tithing rant."

"'Tis not the Sister's fault that the Father isn't a good provider. I'm sure the Pope regards cleanliness in God's house as a priority. Besides, St. Francis receives a hefty subsidy to keep its doors open to those in need. Like Sister Augustine. Five hundred a week 'tis, and Sister Augustine will be there on Tuesdays and Fridays. Done deal."

"Uh, okay. I'll let Miguel know."

"*Father* Miguel clearly has enough on his offerin' plate as 'tis. Just ye make a note of it, pass it along to the Finance Committee, and we need never speak to each other again. I mean," Mary-Margaret corrected, "we need never speak *of this* again."

"Cool."

"Indeed."

Mary-Margaret hung up the phone, crossing herself profusely as she muttered, *"'tis easier to ask forgiveness than to ask permission, and ye are a very forgivin' Father."*

Grabbing the biscuit she had got for herself, she went upstairs, leaving her untouched mug of tea on the counter. Phil scurried behind, ahead, and around her, watching her sort through the numerous skirts and dresses she had hanging in her closet until she found the perfect outfit.

And now, ye have legal counsel, Arthur Lukowitz.

Chapter Fourteen

"I'd like to speak to my...client," Mary-Margaret said, raising the tone of her voice while puckering everything that could be puckered in her body in an attempt to sound like a pretentious criminal lawyer.

"Sure thing. Name?" the gruff voice on the other end of the phone said.

"Uh..."

"*Client's* name," he clarified impatiently.

"Mister Arthur Lukowitz."

"Oh. The guy in for murder. Sure. Hang on."

Not very professional, Mary-Margaret thought. *I'm going to have to have a word with me Michael about that.*

"Detective Sergeant Gill speaking."

"Oh," Mary-Margaret said, her voice dropping along with everything that was puckered.

"I'm the officer in charge of your client's case," he said.

"I know exact—" Mary-Margaret began and then caught herself. She cleared her throat, raised her voice again, and got back into character. "I mean, yes. You are. And I am...Tara Rafferty, Mr. Lukowitz' lawyer."

"Okay. Let me write that down, and I'll put you through."

Father, forgive me and give me strength. And a wee bit of legal knowledge wouldn't hurt at the moment, either.

Mary-Margaret heard the same tinny classical music that she had heard whenever Michael had put her on hold.

"Hello?" Arthur said, a quaver in his voice.

"Hello, Mr. Lukowitz," Mary-Margaret said, still using her newly developed lawyer voice. "This is Tara Rafferty, your lawyer."

"MM? Is that you?" he exclaimed, the broad smile that was spreading across his face evident in his voice.

"No. This is—"

"I'm in a super small room alone with the door closed. I know it's you, MM."

"And just how did ye—?" Mary-Margaret said, her voice back to normal.

"Tara Rafferty? Come. On. Who doesn't watch *Striking Out?*"

"Billy Gilly, apparently," she said with a chuckle. "And I should be thankful. In any event, before I forget, ye are to be at the church on Tuesdays and Fridays. They're payin' ye five hundred dollars a week, cash."

"Five hundred dollars?"

"I know, but it was a struggle to get that much out of them. It wasn't like this when Father Brian was—"

"No, I mean, that's great. Wow. Thanks!"

"The only problem is," Mary-Margaret began.

"Yes?"

"Ye actually have to *be* there and, given where ye are at the moment, that might be a wee bit of a challenge, so what are we goin' to do?"

"I didn't kill anyone."

"I know, I know. But Billy Gilly doesn't. Ach, I wish me Mandy was in charge. She'd know what to do. A wee word with her and ye'd be—Ach. That's it. I'll call me Mandy."

"Wait. What am I supposed to do in the meantime?" Arthur said, clutching the telephone receiver with both hands as a sense of desperation washed over him. "I can't stay here. I just can't, MM! Oh my god. This tiny room. A foreshadowing of the decades of prison time that lie ahead. A lifetime spent doing…what?"

"Have ye got a harmonica to play?" Mary-Margaret asked. "They always play harmonicas when they're on Death Row, don't they?"

"Not helpful, Mary-Margaret!" Arthur gasped. "Breath in, two, three, four, five. And hold, two, three, four—"

"Are ye hyperventilatin' on me, luv? Because, if so, this isn't the time."

"I know. Breathing. Two, three, four—"

"Should ye be callin' someone for help, lad?"

"Wait," Arthur said with a sudden calmness that negated any suggestion of actual hyperventilation. "I'm supposed to go to court soon. As my lawyer, aren't you supposed to be there, too?"

"Right," Mary-Margaret said with a nod. "Ye see? Now yer thinkin'. No need botherin' me Mandy. While ye're gettin' handcuffed to all the other criminals bein' taken to court, I'm goin' to see if I can find a few episodes of *Striking Out* on the telly and consider what Tara Rafferty would do."

"I'm not sure that's your most prudent course of action," Arthur said.

"This from the lad who thinks wearin' a nun's habit is a good idea?"

"I wasn't *wearing* a nun's habit, MM," Arthur said with all the sternness of any Mother Superior that ever was or will be. "I *was* a nun,"

"Well, in that case, I am not going to *watch* Tara Rafferty," Mary-Margaret shot back. "I'll *become* Tara Rafferty."

There was a moment of silence.

"I feel very confident, Ms. Rafferty. Thank you for taking on my case," Arthur said.

"Don't worry, luv," Mary-Margaret said softly before Arthur could hang up. "Ye'll be home in time for tea."

* * *

Despite having lived in the city for most of her adult life and despite her son spending most of his career practically living within these walls, this was the first time Mary-Margaret had even been to the courthouse. It was, however, just as she had imagined it, with its menacing gargoyles glaring down from their perches as a steady stream of police officers, lawyers, witnesses, and people whom she assumed were criminals filed in. Once inside, the marble floors were so polished that Mary-Margaret was surprised to find most people able to remain upright, although she did see the occasional well-dressed man in his fancy leather-soled shoes do a slider. And the glare from the brilliant light the chandeliers hanging from the thirty-foot ceilings offered didn't help those who would have benefitted from a good night's sleep.

"Empty your pockets, please," a man too young to be wearing such a uniform demanded.

"I beg your pardon?" Mary-Margaret said.

"Empty your pockets," he repeated.

"I don't have any pockets."

"Then put your purse on the tray and walk through, please."

"I'm not leavin' me purse behind," she said, starting to get a bit annoyed at this brash young man, uniform or not.

"You'll get it back on the other side."

"The other side of what?" she said, looking at the lineup of people that had quickly formed behind her.

"Jus' walk through, lady," a man called out from the crowd.

"This is worse than the airport," Mary-Margaret snapped, looking over her shoulder as she begrudgingly left it on the tray. "At least there, ye know yer on yer way to somewhere lovely."

"Sure ain't like that here," another man said. "I never ended up nowhere lovely after comin' here."

"Then why do ye keep comin' back?" Mary-Margaret said as she watched the uniformed man rummage through her purse with his latex-gloved hand. "And I'll thank ye to kindly—"

"Stand over here, please, ma'am," a much older uniformed man whose stomach hung over his belt said.

Mary-Margaret stepped to the side, allowing a steady stream of people to pass through the metal detector, but not before grabbing her purse from the younger man.

"Can you set it back, please," the older man said.

Mary-Margaret gingerly set the purse back on the tray. The older man nodded and then picked up what looked like a cattle prod from the desk.

"What in God's name is *that*?" she almost shrieked.

"Metal detector. Something on you is beeping," the man said calmly as he ran it up and down her body. "Can you remove your glasses frames, please?"

"Me what?"

"Glasses frames. On your face. You're wearing glasses frames."

"Oh. I am, aren't I? I mean, these are glasses, not just frames. Very expensive glasses. So expensive that ye can't see the...glass," Mary-Margaret said with a grin, removing them while the man wanded her again. Truth be told, she had completely forgotten that she had them on. As an added touch, she had found a pair of Max's designer sunglasses and removed the dark lens so that she was wearing only the frames. She felt it made her appear a bit more studious.

"Okay, you can go," he said.

"Stand over there, please," the first uniform said to a young tattoo-covered girl with various bits of metal sticking out of her face.

Mary-Margaret quickly picked up her purse from the tray, threw back her shoulders, and tried not to run into the open hallway in front of her.

While she had to admit that it could hardly be said that anyone would mistake her for the Tara Rafferty on the telly, Mary-Margaret felt that she did make a convincing criminal lawyer. And the decision to forgo the belt that came with her Sunday best gray dress provided a clean line, albeit somewhat rounded in places, that wasn't too far off the mark in keeping with the power suits of the men and women she saw in these hallways.

"Mary-Margaret?" a woman called out to her.

"Yes?" she instinctively responded, turning in the direction of the voice, then wishing she had not. As much as she liked Bridget Calloway, Mary-Margaret would have preferred to have as few witnesses to her current presence as possible.

Unaware of the impending and highly illegal deceit that the mother of a police detective she, as a seasoned crown attorney, collaborated closely with, was about to engage in, Bridget rushed towards her. Arms outreached, Bridget balanced a large coffee cup in one hand and a briefcase with hinges straining to remain shut in the other.

"What are you doing here?"

"Bridget! Imagine me seein' the likes of ye here!" Mary-Margaret stammered.

"It's been ages. How's Mike?" Bridget asked as she gave the older woman a hug, careful not to spill the coffee she was holding.

"Michael?" Mary-Margaret asked, quickly backing out of the embrace, "I barely see him. He's just so busy, as ye know…"

"I bet. Are you still staying with him?"

"Yes. Yes, I am. On account of the pneumonia, of course."

"Pneumonia? Oh no. Should you be out like this?" Bridget said, stooping down a bit to look closer at Mary-Margaret.

"I've got a…commitment that," Mary-Margaret said, starting to cough, "I've got to see through."

"Jury duty?" Bridget said, stepping back.

"More of–" Mary-Margaret began and then broke into a fit of coughing.

"I'm sure, if you tell the judge, you'll be excused. Here," Bridget said, motioning Mary-Margaret towards a wooden bench near the expansive stairway a few steps away from them. "Sit down. In fact, why don't you come into my office and I'll get you a glass of water. I'm just upstairs. There's an elevator over here."

"That's lovely, Bridget, but I've got to get to courtroom 101."

"Really?" the crown attorney said, cocking her head to one side. "That's not a trial room. Are you sure?'"

"Well, that's where I was told to be, yes," Mary-Margaret said, looking for a sign that would indicate which way to go.

"But that's where the in-custodies go to see if they can get bail."

"And how do they get bail then?" Mary-Margaret asked, realizing that this might be something she ought to know.

"Have a surety, or prove they're not a danger to the community, and usually agree to some conditions. Why do you ask?"

"Ye know me, luv. Always one to learn. Ach, look at me now, takin' up so much of yer time, and me cough has all but cleared up. Perhaps I'll stop by and see ye on me way out?" Mary-Margaret said with her best smile as she rose to her feet and started walking briskly in what she hoped would be the right direction.

"I've got a trial starting tomorrow, so I should be in my office all day. Yes.

Please do, but only if you feel up to it," Bridget called after her.

"Ta, luv. I just may," Mary-Margaret said, without turning.

Ach, thanks be to St. Expidutus. There's me courtroom there.

Chapter Fifteen

"All rise," the court clerk said as the occupants of the packed courtroom stood up. "The Honorable Judge Adelson presiding."

"Please be seated," the judge said, settling herself into her chair behind the bench.

Mary-Margaret heard the words that were being spoken, but was too busy looking at the judge to listen.

A woman of her age wearin' her hair like that? And she's had work done. Likely wearin' one of those big-name designer outfits under her robes, this one.

"Please be seated," the court clerk repeated, looking directly at Mary-Margaret.

"I'm here on behalf of Mr. Lukowitz," Mary-Margaret said, sounding to herself more like a common milkmaid than Tara Rafferty or any other learned Irishwoman, real or imagined.

"I believe all counsel are seated there," the judge said gently, pointing to a row of well-dressed men and one woman, all of whom looked suspiciously at Mary-Margaret.

"Ta, luv."

A titter of giggles rolled through the courtroom. The court clerk rolled her eyes.

"I mean, Ta, Your Honor," Mary-Margaret corrected herself as she sat down, squeezing between her bench mates before stretching her arm to shake hands with those closest to her. "Mary-Ma...Tara Rafferty. How do ye do?"

"Order in my courtroom, please," the judge said, nodding at Mary-

Margaret.

"Father, this is Yer chance to prove that the meek shall inherit the earth. I'm speakin' of Arthur now, of course, so let's get this business sorted. Oh, and don't forget about sendin' me that wee bit of legal knowledge," Mary-Margaret muttered loud enough for those on either side of her to give her the side-eye.

The gallery of the court was filled with a rotating group of family members intent on bailing their loved one out, police officers intent on keeping them in, and roving bands of teenagers clearly on a high school trip for some class or another. Mary-Margaret watched intently as one by one, each accused man was hauled up from the holding cells below the courtroom by a guard, hands cuffed in front, most wearing orange jumpsuits.

Upon seeing their client, one or another of her bench mates would leap up, introduce themselves to the court, and stand by as the crown prosecutor explained what the prisoner had done and why they should never see the light of day again. Each of Mary-Margaret's new colleagues would then give a variety of reasons—most of which included having committed their lives to rescuing puppies or some other saint-worthy cause—why their clients should be released from custody.

Mary-Margaret studied the words, gestures, and shallow courtesies exchanged between the defense, the prosecution, and the judge. She noticed what made the judge tap on her laptop keyboard and what made her look over the screen at the lawyers. She also paid attention to when the left corner of the judge's mouth twitched or the furrows between her eyebrows deepened slightly. As the morning progressed, Mary-Margaret's confidence grew, especially when she saw that the judge seemed to let almost everyone go.

And then she saw Detective Sergeant Gill come into the room.

Oh, me stars! Can it get any worse? she thought.

Janelle Austin, the reporter from Metro News, came in behind him.

Ye do enjoy testin' me, don't Ye, God?

Mary-Margaret was sure that Billy Gilly would recognize her, even with her glass frames. If he didn't, Janelle Austin certainly would.

"Next on the docket is Arthur Lukowitz. Could you bring him up, please?" the court clerk said.

Mary-Margaret didn't have time to think.

"State your name for the record, please?" the court clerk said.

"Arthur Lukowitz."

"Arthur Lukowitz, you are charged, on or about this date, with the murder of Cassandra Lewis. How do you wish to plead?"

"Not guilty?" Arthur asked.

"Very well. And do you have legal representation?"

"Um..." he began, looking madly around the courtroom.

"Yes. Yes, he does," Mary-Margaret said, suddenly shooting up from her seat. "My, uh, client—"

"Just a moment," the judge said. "Would you like to give us your name and stand up here at the podium?"

"Right. Yes. Of course."

Mary-Margaret nodded and smiled politely at the defence lawyers on either side of her.

"I'll just leave me purse there, right?" she said to one of the younger defence lawyers who pointed to the podium closest to her.

"Sure," he replied, shrugging his shoulders as his colleagues glared at him.

"Ta, luv. Tara Rafferty. And yer name is...?"

"Are we ready?" the judge said, looking first at the crown and then down at Mary-Margaret.

"Ach, right," Mary-Margaret said. *Strength, Father. And a wee bit of—*

"Please wait until you get to the podium and be sure to speak into the microphone so that the transcriber can pick up your words." the court clerk said.

"Right. Yes. Well."

Mary-Margaret stood silently at the podium. The courtroom was silent.

"Perhaps the Crown can get us started," the judge prompted.

"Absolutely, Your Honour. The accused, Arthur Lukowitz, has been charged with murder. He has no prior criminal record—"

"Well, that's good to know," Mary-Margaret said, not as quietly as she would have liked.

"—and is not considered a flight risk."

"Grand."

The Crown looked over at Mary-Margaret before continuing.

"However, given the severity of the charge, the Crown is proposing that Mr. Lukowitz be held in custody pending the outcome of his trial."

"Jesus, Mary, and Joseph."

"Is there something you'd like to say, Ms....?"

"Uh, Rafferty. Tara Rafferty, Yer...Honor."

"Yes. I've heard that. A few times. Is there anything you'd like to say on behalf of your client, Ms. Rafferty?"

"Excuse me," a voice called out from the gallery.

"Yes?" the judge said.

"I'm Detective Sergeant William Gill, the officer in charge of this case."

"Very good. Thank you for being here, Detective Sergeant."

"And this...woman...is not Tara Rafferty."

"I'm sorry?" the judge said.

"This woman is—"

"Ye know, I often get mistaken," Mary-Margaret began, putting on her brightest smile. "I am not *the* Tara Rafferty from the telly. 'Tis true. Although, in me younger days, I would have given her a right run for her money. No, luv. Ye are correct. I'm Tara Rafferty from the firm of...Malarkey, Dickery, and...Rafferty. I'd hand ye me card, but I've just this moment run out." Mary-Margaret turned to look directly at D/S Gill. "Ye lads must be doin' a poor job arrestin' the right people because me business is boomin' and I'm handin' them out right, left, and center now, aren't I? Regardless," she continued, turning back to the judge, "we're not here to talk about me business or the poor quality of yer man over there's work. We're here to get this lad out on bail, aren't we, yer Honor?"

"I believe we're here to provide a fair hearing," the judge stated.

"Exactly. So. Let's look at what we've got before we decide what we'll do, shall we?"

Mary-Margaret pushed her shoulders back, lifted her chin, and took a deep breath.

"I believe the Crown—" the judge began.

"No one in their right mind is disputin' that a murder occurred," Mary-Margaret cut in. "Ye'd be daft to go down that path."

"Madam Crown?" the judge said.

"No, I'm content to rest," the prosecutor said with a smile from behind her podium.

"And no one in their right mind is disputin' that this lad over here," Mary-Margaret continued, swinging her arm wildly towards Arthur, but miscalculating the distance between them and almost striking him. "Sorry, luv. Anyway, where was I?"

"I believe you had just said your client murdered—" the Crown offered.

"Indeed, I did not," Mary-Margaret said, giving the prosecutor a look that would stop a raging inferno. "In fact, yer holiness—"

"Your Honor will do," the judge said, trying to suppress a grin.

"Right. For a moment there, I thought...never mind. Anyway, ye'd have to be soft in the head if ye didn't see that this lad was plucked from the street—on his way to the church where God Himself trusts the lad to keep His house clean—and flung into a wee room after bein' stripped of God's own garments to wear this paper bag outfit we see him in now, where he sat, alone and hungry, until he was squeezed into a van and launched up the stairs and here he is. Am I right, or am I right?"

The judge paused before giving a slight nod.

"And no one is arguin' with anyone that the charge of murder is serious. Ach, it gets no worse than that, does it?"

Arthur glanced nervously at his friend.

"So why are we here?" Mary-Margaret said, turning to face the gallery, being sure not to make eye contact with Billy Gilly or Janelle Austin.

"We are here," she continued, her arms outstretched, "to see if it's fittin' to hold a man in the filthy bins these lads call jail cells until everyone's had their say on the matter because this lad may or may not be involved in some crime."

Mary-Margaret, still facing the gallery, held her arms up like Evita Peron facing her adoring countrymen. The clerk smirked. The row of defence lawyers all looked at each other. The Crown looked at the judge. The judge looked at Mary-Margaret.

"Could the defence address the Court, please?" the judge directed.

"Just a moment," Mary-Margaret said, not glancing over her shoulder at the judge long enough to notice that her patience was swiftly waning. "'Tis not rocket science, lads. The logic behind the defence I'll be providin' at a later date is too complicated for me mind to unravel to ye in this moment, and it matters not to the present conversation, so let's just all agree that me client will be released on the condition that he not get involved in any other murders. Thank ye for yer time, yer Honor."

Mary-Margaret nodded sharply before turning to face the judge and then return to her seat. She removed her purse from her seat, smiling at the young lawyer whom she had entrusted to keep safe in her absence while the people in the gallery erupted into applause.

"Order. Order in my court!" The judge commanded.

After several minutes and an unprecedented amount of gavel pounding, the room finally quieted down. With both the room and herself composed again, the judge made a concerted effort not to shoot Mary-Margaret a glare as she waited for her to take action.

"Um," the young lawyer whispered to her, "you need to stay up there."

"Do I now?"

"Yeah. You're not finished."

"Oh. Right. Much obliged. Purse?"

"Sure."

Mary-Margaret returned to her podium.

"Crown?" the judge said, looking at the perplexed attorney on her left.

"I—I have—nothing else to add."

"Very well. Mr. Lukowitz?"

"Um, yes?"

"There are a few points I would like to clarify."

"Sure."

"Thank you, Mr. Lukowitz," the judge said, her voice dripping with condescension while looking much more serious than Mary-Margaret thought was necessary.

Another roll of snickering washed through the courtroom.

"Your lawyer advises that you have full-time employment. Is that true?"

"Uh-huh."

"And what is it that you do for work, Mr. Lukowitz?"

"I make the world a better place."

An unabashed round of laughter erupted.

"Order!" the judge said, continuing once all was quiet. "And how do you do that, Mr. Lukowitz?"

"I clean, ma'am."

"Your Honor," the court clerk corrected Arthur.

"I clean, your Honor."

"You clean?" The judge asked.

"Yes. I take things that were dirty, and I make them—"

"I am familiar with what is involved in cleaning, Mr. Lukowitz."

"Oh, I don't think you are. Your Honor."

"Enlighten me," she said, leaning back in her chair.

"If I may?" Arthur said, moving slightly away from the guard on his left. "Your Honor, I, like you, strive to make the banality of everyday life more... enjoyable. Perhaps after a hard day sitting up there judging everyone, you escape to the theater or the ballet or the opera. But I need no such escape because I, unlike you, make everything I touch sparkle, shine, glow—"

"Is there anyone who will post bail for you, Mr. Lukowitz?" the judge said, cutting Arthur off as she looked down at her watch.

"Well," Arthur began, stepping back towards the guard. "How much are we talking?"

"We *are talking*," the judge began, "about two hundred thousand dollars."

"Oh."

"Does your client have anyone who can post that kind of bail, Ms....?"

"Rafferty. Like the lawyer on the telly."

"I don't think you should remind her of that," Arthur whispered loudly to Mary-Margaret.

"Ms. Rafferty," the judge said, ignoring Arthur's comment.

"Well, I could ask me Michael, if ye'll give me a moment?"

"I don't care who you ask, Ms. Rafferty. I am prepared to release this prisoner on bail if two hundred thousand dollars can be raised."

The judge stood up, rubbing her forehead.

"All rise!" the court clerk quickly called out.

The judge took a deep breath and nodded to the clerk as everyone in the room stood up.

"Court is adjourned for...?" the clerk looked up at the judge, who was walking towards the door that would lead to her office.

"Twenty minutes. Just give me twenty minutes. I'm sure I've got some Tylenol somewhere."

The judge disappeared behind the door as Arthur was whisked back down into the cells and everyone in the gallery made their way out the main door into the hallway. The Crown and the defense attorneys fumbled to gather up their paperwork before they cleared the courtroom as well.

"Is our girl goin' to be alright?" Mary-Margaret asked the court clerk on her way out.

"I think you broke her," the clerk said with a laugh as she headed towards the same door the judge had exited from. "Never seen a judge leave their own courtroom like that before."

"A good cuppa would likely—"

"Clear the court!" a court officer bellowed, looking at the lone occupant of the room.

Chapter Sixteen

"Ach, Michael!" Mary-Margaret exclaimed as she let herself in the front door, almost tripping over the threshold.

"Mom," Michael responded with a calmness that was in stark contrast to her mood.

"Well, I wasn't expectin' to see ye here. Ye scared me half to death, lad."

"I wasn't expecting to be here, either. But I was told to have a word with you."

"A word? Well, that's lovely now, isn't it," she said, taking her coat off and placing it on the hook behind the door, knowing that it would be anything but.

"How was your day?"

"'Twas...busy," Mary-Margaret replied, as she moved past her son towards the kitchen.

"I bet," he said, following her.

"What, with me bein' at the...hospital...all day."

"The hospital, was it?"

"Indeed. Where else would I be, me havin' the pneumonia and all?"

"Are you sure you weren't—"

Mary-Margaret erupted in a fit of coughs.

"Perhaps I'd be best just to go up to me bed. Max has eaten, I'm sure?"

"Perhaps you'd be best just to come clean."

"About what, me son?" she said, turning back to the stairs. "Now, mind yerself as I make me way past ye to me bed."

In a performance worthy of a Tony, Mary-Margaret ascended the staircase, clutching her chest with one hand, the banister with the other.

"Oh, hey, Gran," Max said, stopping short of bumping into her on his way down the stairs.

"Oh, me luv," she said softly, taking her hand from her chest and placing it on Max's arm. "Did ye get me text and order yerself one of those pizzas? Wasn't expectin' yer da to be home."

"Me neither, but I'd already ordered by the time he got here. I'm just going to pick it up now. I ordered two. Is that okay?"

"Of course, me lamb. And perhaps ye can bring a slice or two up to yer gran as I lay in me bed."

"Sure thing. Want anything to drink?"

"A wee whiskey might be in order," she muttered.

"I don't think they sell that," Max said, cocking his head to one side, the light had yet to go on.

"Perhaps I'll make me way back downstairs and get me own in a bit."

"You mean when Dad's not here?" he asked, his eyebrows raised with the realization that his gran was up to something. "And about that…I may have said something—"

"Indeed. Shh. Now do ye need me credit card, or would they take the order with just the number I texted ye?"

"Just the number worked."

With that, Max opened the front door and bounced out, leaving Michael to close the door behind him.

"You texted Max your credit card information?"

"Have ye been standin' there this whole time, evesdroppin' like a bookie in the shops?" Mary-Margaret asked, giving another noteworthy performance as *The Woman with the Pneumonia* before continuing. "Unless the lad has his own credit card, I didn't see any other way for him to get his dinner, what with the hours ye work. Never knowin' when ye'll be home and such."

"That's how fraud happens."

"Are ye callin' yer own son a fraud?" she asked as she took the final steps to the second floor.

"Wouldn't be the only one in this family, would he?"

Mary-Margaret stopped at the top of the stairs, grasped her chest as if to hold her heart inside of it, and looked down at her son, her eyes ignited with fury.

"I will *not* hear another word against the lad, Michael O'Shea. Now, if ye don't mind, I've got the pneumonia to deal with."

She stomped the few steps to her bedroom door, all the while sounding as if she was hacking up a lung. She considered slamming the door behind her, but held back, not wanting to be overdramatic.

"We're going to talk about this tonight, Mom," Michael called up the stairs.

"As ye know, I've got a plot beside yer da, God rest his soul," she called down from her room, the door only half-closed, "and be sure to have anyone but Father Miguel conduct the Mass. Perhaps Father Brian will come back to set me weary soul to rest."

"You're not dying, Mom," Michael hollered up.

"When ye become God, and God help us if ye do, ye can advise on such matters. In the meantime, if ye are intent on carryin' on, the least ye could do is pour me a wee dram of Jameson and leave it by the door. Max can bring it in with him when he brings in me pizza."

* * *

"Ah, ye are a rock star," Mary-Margaret said, taking the plate from Max as he opened the top pizza box. "Is yer da not havin' any? Honestly, luv, I don't know what the man lives on."

"No, he went out."

"Out? Where? Back to work, I hope."

"I dunno. I heard the back door open and shut when I came in the front."

"I'm hopin' he took Wee Phil out before he left."

Mary-Margaret pulled a piece of pizza out of the box and dragged it to her plate.

"Ye didn't happen to notice a glass by the door, did ye?"

"No. But the pizza came with six cans of pop. Do you want one?"

"I was hopin' for somethin' a little more…"

"Do you want me to pour you some whiskey?"

"I don't think yer da would approve."

"Not likely. Oh, hey, thanks for going to my school. I mean, I'm not sure it'll help, but—"

"Of course it will help, luv. And I'm glad ye've got an ally in that Mrs. Bird."

"I suppose," Max said, shoving almost the whole slice of pizza in his mouth.

"Mind ye don't choke on that. That's all we'd need. And, as blasé as ye seem to be about her, she seems quite fond of ye."

"Whatever," Max said, taking an equally large guzzle of pop. "I told her about how you solved that murder. She thought that was pretty cool."

"Did she now?" Mary-Margaret said with a smile.

"Yeah. She thinks you two are going to solve this big case!" Max said with a laugh before producing a substantial burp. "Excuse me."

"Certainly, me luv. And, if I can solve a murder, I can solve this matter. Ach, that wee dram would go well with this, wouldn't it?"

"I could always pour it for you. We don't have to tell him."

"Yer right," Mary-Margaret said with a wink. "The man doesn't have to know everythin' now, does he? How about ye take yer pizza boxes, and I'll take me plate, and we'll go downstairs and have a wee party."

"What if Dad comes home?"

"What of it? I'm his mam."

"Yeah, but he seemed pretty mad at you, and if he sees you day-drinking–"

"Hardly! It's dinner time. And what do you know about day-drinkin' and the like anyway?"

"I'm not a kid, you know. But he's really going to lose his mind when he finds out you've dropped in at my school."

"I don't think that's what'll push him over, lad," Mary-Margaret said with an equal blend of mischief and pride. "And, since it's all goin' to come out in the wash anyway, I might as well tell ye the whole of the day's events."

Before the two of them finished the first pizza, Mary-Margaret had given Max her version of what had happened in court. And then they heard the back door open.

"Michael?" Mary-Margaret called.

"Were you expecting someone else?" he called back.

"No, it's just that I thought ye were workin' this evenin'.'"

"I am," he said, pouring himself a glass of water before joining them.

"Not a word," Mary-Margaret whispered to Max with a wink. "Let's see what yer da knows. Maybe 'tis just about the school visit."

"Max, your grandmother and I have to talk. Do you want to take your pizza up to your room to finish?"

"Didn't realize they let ye work from home now, me son," she said, ignoring Michael's comment. "Sitcheedoon, then."

"*You* have become my work, Mom, and we're going to talk about it now," Michael said, not taking a seat. "You don't need to hear any of this, Max, so go on upstairs."

"If it's about me stoppin' in at the school, he knows. And if it's about the other business..." Mary-Margaret stopped.

Jesus, Mary, and Joseph. Ye've put yer foot in it this time, me girl. Might as well just keep runnin' with the ball.

"Too late. He knows," she said.

"Aw, Mom!" Michael sighed, collapsing into the chair his mother had offered. "Could you not have left him out of this?"

"I'm right here, Dad," Max said. "And, considering all the times you've almost been killed, and I had to find out from the newspaper, I think I'm okay with Gran being honest about pretending to be a lawyer."

Michael let out a huge sigh as he looked up to the ceiling, his shoulders dropping.

"'Tis not like I was the one on the stand, Michael. And besides, we all know that Arthur is innocent."

"No, we don't all know that Arthur is innocent. And you lied to the Court."

"'Tis easier to ask for forgiveness than to ask for permission."

"There is no forgiveness or permission involved in this, Mom. You misrepresented yourself to the Court and, in so doing, got a murderer out on bail."

"That's pretty awesome, Gran!"

"A lad *accused* of murder, and thank ye, me lamb. Not bad for not havin' taken the Leaving Certs, isn't it? Perhaps I should be askin' Bridget if she needs a hand. Speakin' of which, I saw our girl—"

"Mom, this is serious stuff."

"And she says she misses ye. Have ye ever considered callin' her up and takin' her out on an actual date? If she's not sweet on ye, then—"

"Mom, you impersonate a lawyer. In front of a judge. And fraudulently got a… an accused murderer out on bail."

"And ye wonder why the pneumonia isn't curin' itself. That would be enough to knock anyone flat on their back, never mind pickin' up the parentin' end of things for Max."

"That's enough!" Mike shouted. "Max doesn't need—"

"Well, I need another wee dram, and then I'll be headin' up to me bed. Max, would ye do the honors?"

"Mom! And don't you touch that bottle, Max!"

"Michael, instead of wastin' yer breath on how me day went and intimidatin' yer son, let's try to find the murderer. If this is how ye run yer investigations, I'll be nothin' but dust in the wind before ye become Police Officer of th—"

"It's not my case, and I don't give a—"

"Does Arthur still have the bones?" Max asked.

"I don't believe so, luv. I think they took them to the morgue. Marry them up with the head and all. Only fittin', really. Wonder when the funeral will be. Rather than riskin' losin' a limb while tryin' to pour yer gran some whiskey, will ye be a luv and go shine up me funeral shoes for me? I think we got most of the muck off them from the last one, but ye never know once that clay gets on them."

"Now?" Max asked.

"I think it would be wise," Mary-Margaret said, looking directly at Michael for a moment before reaching across Max to retrieve the whiskey bottle and pour herself a healthy shot. "They're in me closet upstairs."

"Why don't you just go up to your room for a bit," Michael said, handing Max a half-full box of pizza.

Max got up from the dining room table and disappeared up the stairs.

"If yer da was here, God rest his soul, he'd have said somethin' about all of this," Mary-Margaret said, her tone notably chillier as she gave Michael a disapproving look.

"If Dad was here—"

"God rest his soul."

"God rest his soul, we wouldn't be in this predicament."

"And just what predicament is that?" she asks sweetly.

"Come on, Mom. As soon as they find out that you're not really a lawyer—which should have been about two hours ago—they'll have an arrest warrant out for Arthur. And then they'll start typing one up for you as well, I imagine."

"Ach, we've got to warn the wee lamb!" Mary-Margaret said, jumping to her feet and racing to the front door. "Where's me purse? I've got to call him."

"Don't even...!" Michael shouted, unable to formulate any other words.

"And why not?' Mary-Margaret replied, cell phone at the ready, having retrieved it from her purse. "If what ye say is true, then 'tis me fault he's a fugitive, and if so, 'tis my responsibility to keep him safe. I'm havin' him come stay here until ye get things sorted out."

"What??"

"Arthur, luv, 'tis Mary-Margaret. I'm hopin' ye aren't out galivantin' or whatever it is ye do because there's an arrest warrant out for ye. After ye listen to this message, erase it. And then get yerself to me Michael's house. Come by the back door. Knock four times, pause, and then knock two more times. I'll let ye in, and ye can stay here until we get this sorted. Bye-bye bye bye-bye bye."

"Mom, we can't have him here," Michael snapped as he grabbed her cell phone.

"Well, where else is he supposed to be?" Mary-Margaret demanded, taking the cell phone back.

"In jail. Which is exactly where you'll be if—"

Before he could finish, there was a knock at the back door, and then another and another and another and a pause. And then two more.

"Does he just hang out in the back alley?" Michael asked.

"Not like yer neighbors don't, drinkin' from their tinnies," Mary-Margaret said, trying to get to the backdoor before Michael.

"But they live here, Mom," Michael said, his hand reaching the doorknob first.

"And so does Arthur, for the time bein'," she stated, pushing his hand away. "Now, go on downstairs and make up the spare bedroom."

"No, Mom. This isn't how it's going to go," Michael said, stepping aside for his mother to open the door.

"Michael, this will all be sorted. Yer makin' a mountain out of a molehill."

Max came into the kitchen with an empty pizza box.

"Is this a bad time?" he said, looking at his grandmother and his father.

"Not in the slightest, my lamb. Let me just open the door and let—"

"Sister Augustine at your service," Arthur, dressed in full nun's habit, said with a smile.

Chapter Seventeen

"What the…" Max began, dropping the pizza box.

"Blessings upon you, Max," Arthur smiled, gathering up the scapular and tunic as he strode inside. "And you, Michael. I mean…Mike."

"You have the right to remain—" Michael began, pushing past his mother.

"Michael," Mary-Margaret gasped. "What are ye doin', me son?"

"Mom, he's wanted. I have to arrest him."

"This is a bad time," Max said, looking for the least obvious way to get out of the kitchen.

"Ye will do no such thing, Michael. Now, sitcheedoon. All of ye," Mary-Margaret demanded, pointing them in the direction of the dining room.

Phil ran into the kitchen and began dancing at the back door.

"Max, luv," Mary-Margaret said, "can you pop out the back here with Wee Phil?"

Thankful for an escape, Max quickly bounded out the door, the dog barely ahead of him.

"This isn't going to end well, is it?" Arthur asked, glancing at Mary-Margaret as he began to move skittishly past Michael.

"There is an outstanding warrant for your arrest," Michael said, blocking Arthur's way. "Now, it is my duty to inform you—"

"Michael, calm yerself," Mary-Margaret said, pushing both Michael and Arthur into the dining room. "Ye are goin' to give yerself a—"

"Max was wrong. This isn't a bad time. This is a *horrible* time, isn't it, MM," Arthur said, slumping down into a chair at the table.

"It'll all be fine, luv. Just fine," she said, patting him on the shoulder.

Michael took a couple of deep breaths.

"That's better, me son. Take in the air and let out the stress," Mary-Margaret said, standing beside Michael as she breathed along with him. "Now sitcheedoon and we'll have a chat. That was quick, Wee Phil. Be sure to give him a treat, Max, and come join us. No need to stand in the kitchen with yer gob hangin' open."

Max stepped out of the kitchen and sat down in his chair at the table.

"Go to your room, Max," Michael said from his chair at the head of the table.

"Sitcheedoon, luv," Mary-Margaret countered, not yet having sat down at her chair at the opposite end of the table from her son.

Max looked back and forth from his father to his grandmother.

"If I were you—" Arthur began, reaching over to put a hand on Max's arm.

"If I were you, I'd keep my mouth shut," Michael ordered.

"Michael!" Mary-Margaret roared. "I shall *not* have that tone of voice at me table."

"Fine. Then go to your own table and do what you want," Michael said.

There was a silence, the likes of which had not been heard in Mary-Margaret's presence for a very long time.

"I'll just be a moment while I get me things," Mary-Margaret finally said in a low, steely tone. "Arthur, get Wee Phil's leash on and gather up his bowls."

She slowly got up and stepped away from the dining room table, her eyes fixed on Michael, who met her gaze. Max's eyes were almost bugged out of his head, looking around the table. Arthur was looking down as he wrung his hands in his lap.

"Sit down, Mom," Michael said firmly.

"I've made a great mess of it all and put the people I love in harm's way. 'Tis best I leave ye to do what ye do best, Michael. I am sorry."

Mary-Margaret went over to the stairs and then, as she slowly climbed each step, called back. "Remind me to give Sally-next-door a ring when I get home, Arthur. 'Tis about time she takes her wee dog back. I'm not fit for the company of man nor beast."

"Dad, do something!" Max said, his voice breaking, tears welling up in his eyes.

Michael took a deep breath and slowly exhaled but remained motionless.

"I think she might be serious," Arthur said.

"She's not serious," Michael replied. "Just give her a moment."

"And make sure ye put all of the empty pizza boxes out for the bin man tomorrow, Max," Mary-Margaret called from the top of the stairs. "God knows there are enough rats in the laneway already without leavin' anythin' more for them."

"Dad," Max pleaded.

"Wait for it," Michael said, his lips starting to curl in a knowing smile.

"And could one of ye lads give me a hand with me bags, unless ye want me to be breakin' me neck on these stairs, and then I'd be stayin' on another few months. This with a *Best Before* with yesterday's date stamp on me forehead."

"I'll help," Arthur said, getting up from the table.

"Stay where you are," Michael said more kindly than Arthur had expected. Arthur sat back down.

"What about the pneumonia?" Michael called up to his mother.

"No need to concern yerself, me son," she called back from her bedroom. "It'll likely be a broken heart that kills me now."

"What about the dram of whiskey on the table?" Michael called.

"Take it for yerself, Michael. Or best not. No need to smell of it if yer goin' to be makin' yer big career-makin' arrest."

"And I think there's some pizza left. What about that?" Michael said, taking the last slice of pizza from the box on the table, both Max and Arthur looking at him in disbelief.

"Ye take it, me eldest child. Ye'll need it to keep yer strength up," she called from the top of the stairs, an empty suitcase in hand. "Unlike meself. Likely die in me bed...me own cold bed...within the week."

Michael took a bite of the pizza, chewed it, and swallowed it. He took another bite. And then another with Max and Arthur watching with astonishment.

"Jesus, Mary, and Joseph, Michael," Mary-Margaret said from the landing, setting down the suitcase.

"What?" he responded, mouth full of pizza.

She tramped down the stairs and returned to the table.

"Were the lot of ye goin' to leave me standin' at the top of the staircase waitin' for an invitation while ye watched me Michael inhale the last of it?"

"Wha—" Arthur began.

"I told you she'd be back," Michael said, wiping his mouth with the inadequate napkin the pizza place provided.

"Well, I can't leave ye in this mess we're all in, Michael. Somebody's got to figure out who killed that girl, and 'tis likely me who's goin' to be doin' it," Mary-Margaret said, sitting down at the other end of the table. "Max, not a word beyond these walls. Michael, the same."

"I hardly think you're in a position to negotiate the terms, Mom," Michael said, his eyebrows lifted into his hairline. "There's a warrant for Arthur's arrest and one likely to follow for you."

"Give us until Friday. If we don't have it all sorted by then, we'll all pay the piper, won't we, Arthur?"

"Uh, sure," Arthur said.

"I don't think I can keep—" Michael began.

"Friday at midnight. If we've not caught the murderer, then ye can arrest Arthur and yer old mam yerself. Besides, I've put ye down as the surety for the two hundred thousand dollar bail yer judge lady was askin' for."

"How—?"

"Ask me no secrets, and I'll tell ye no lies. Ach, look at the time," Mary-Margaret said, glancing down at her watch. "Best get figurin' now, lads. We've got our work cut out for us. Max, go get yer gran some paper and a pen from the kitchen."

"I need to go lie down, MM. I feel a migraine coming on," Arthur said., getting up from the table.

"Ach, Michael. Ye never made the room up. No worries. I'm sure ye can handle it, Arthur. Clean sheets are in the closet. And there should be a robe downstairs for ye for the mornin'. If not, Michael will give ye his, won't ye, me son?"

"I've got pajamas, MM. I'm fine," Arthur said as he headed downstairs. "I'll see everyone in the morning."

"Are ye sure ye want to tuck in so early, luv?"

"If I can't avert this migraine…."

"Here's hopin," Mary-Margaret called after him and then looked back at the table. "Well, that leaves the three of us to sort this out, then."

"Two of us," Michael corrected. "Let's leave Max out of this."

"Yer da has ruled out Johnny and Maeve O'Leary, haven't ye, Michael?" Mary-Margaret said, ignoring Michael's direction as she jotted a few notes down on a pad of paper.

"I can't say whether they've been ruled out or not," Michael said. Mary-Margaret looked up from her paper at him.

"It's not my investigation."

"Well, I'm sure ye can rule out Johnny."

Mike tilted his head.

"Not that I'm one for tossin' someone under the bus, but we all know how tightly wound Maeve O'Leary can be."

"If being known for getting…tightly wound makes someone a murder suspect, you'd better put yourself on the list, Mom."

Max giggled.

"That leaves—" Mary-Margaret continued, ignoring her son's comment.

"Arthur's at the top of the list right now," Michael cut in.

"Hardly."

"Not according to—"

"Billy Gilly?" Mary-Margaret said with a snort. "Give yer head a shake, lad. Look at who he's arrested. Ye know our Arthur, Michael. Do ye honestly believe that he, a lad who's about as methodical as yer average five-year-old, could manage a murder like this?"

Michael considered for a moment.

"It's not my investigation," he said, pushing his chair away from the dining room table. "And I've got to get back to work. Don't you have homework to do, Max?"

"No," Max replied, not taking his eyes off the scribbles his grandmother had made on the pad of foolscap.

"Or friends to talk to or message or whatever it is you do all night long?" Michael continued, his right eyebrow rising.

"Oh. Right. Yes. Sorry, Gran."

"'Tis all right, me lamb. 'Tis likely best that ye not be too involved in this part of our investigation."

Both Michael and Max stood up, almost at the same time. Michael gave his son a curt nod, and the boy disappeared up the stairs.

"Michael, before ye go, can ye take Wee Phil out to the jacks again? And maybe for a bit of a walk? I don't think he got out—"

Before she could finish her sentence, the Jack Russell had appeared, seemingly out of nowhere, and was standing by the back door, his whole body wagging along with his tail.

"How much water does this dog drink?" Michael said and then, seeing the look on his mother's face, sighed and added, "Sure, Mom. And you're still going to call your friend tomorrow about taking her dog back, right?"

"Michael, the seconds are tickin' away. Arthur's freedom is at jeopardy as we speak. I don't have time to be callin' around to see if a dog stays or goes now. Lives are countin' on me. Now get the wee pup out before he piddles on yer foot."

Michael sighed as he unlocked the back door.

Arthur came back upstairs wearing a pair of striped pajamas.

"Practicing?" Michael said, glancing at Arthur.

"And take the leash with ye if yer takin' him for a walk, which ye are," Mary-Margaret said, ignoring Michael's comment. "Feelin' better, are we?"

"Much. By applying pressure points to my—"

"Grand," Mary-Margaret said, cutting him off. "Be sure to keep Wee Phil on the leash, Michael."

"Too late," Michael said as he opened the door and watched Phil run out.

"After him!" Mary-Margaret said, pushing Mike out the door. "I don't want the wee pup to get eaten by wolves. Go!"

"Wolves…?"

"Now," she said, turning to Arthur, "put yer thinking cap on, lad. Who else could have killed Cassandra?"

"Well, uh, there's always some weirdo from the pub," Arthur said.

"Have ye been to O'Leary's, luv?" she said with a laugh, walking back into the dining room, Arthur behind her. "Hardly the crowd for it, I'd say."

"What about a jilted lover or an angry former employer?"

"Now we're gettin' juicy. I'm thinkin' boyfriend," Mary-Margaret said as she sat down.

"I thought you said that was too easy."

"I've reconsidered."

"Why would he go to so much trouble to dispose of her body like that if he could just say it was an accident or something? And I'm imagining that a biscuit or two would go over well about now," Arthur said, looking around the table as if such imagining would make it so.

"Might not be the brightest star in the sky. And ye might as well get us a plate, then."

"What about Johnny's wife?" Arthur asked, going into the kitchen to load up a plate with McVities. "She seems like the type who could kill someone."

"Maeve? I'm not sayin' no, but she's got a lot to lose."

"She also has access to some pretty large pots," Arthur replied, setting the biscuits down in front of them both.

"Oh luv," Mary-Margaret said, bringing her hand up to her mouth. "Yer not thinkin'...?"

"I don't know but I am thinking that we might need more than a few days to sort this one out, MM," Arthur said, looking up at the clock on the wall before shoving an entire biscuit into his mouth.

"Lad," Mary-Margaret said, leaning over towards Arthur, "what did they do to ye?"

"What do you mean?" he asked, covering his mouth to prevent spitting chewed McVitie bits at her.

"Look at the state of ye. Takin' on the role of the disenchanted prisoner already."

"I think," Arthur softly corrected after swallowing the mouthful, "that would be disenfranchised, MM."

"Same thing. But what I'm tryin' to say is that ye seem to be givin' up the fight before it's even begun."

"I know, it's just that whole jail thing—"

"Was just a big mistake. Billy Gilly and his lot actin' the maggot is all. And it's up to us to not only solve a murder, but to show that poor excuse for a tax-payer's dollar bein' spent that he'd be better off writin' parkin' tickets than investigatin' anythin'."

"When you put it like that, MM—"

"Figured it out yet?" Michael said as he brought Phil in from his walk.

"That was hardly a run down the back lane, Michael. Are ye sure ye oughtn't to take Wee Phil out for a bit longer?'

"I'm sure. And I'd strongly suggest that you two call it a night sooner than later."

"And why is that?"

"With your pneumonia and all," Michael said, unable to suppress a chuckle.

"Never mind me pneumonia. I've got bigger fish to fry now. Regardless, if it's not the pneumonia, it'll be somethin' else that'll kill me soon enough."

"Mike's right," Arthur quickly cut in. "You need your rest, MM."

"And since when did the two of ye become cozy?"

"When it comes to your health, MM, we can't be too careful. I spend a lot of time googling things, and I know how quickly a common cold can kill. Or turn into cancer. Or—"

"Ach, the lot of ye. A night we'll call it, then. Sleep well, lads," Mary-Margaret said.

Chapter Eighteen

"You're up awfully early, Mom," Michael said as he came into the kitchen, pulling the knot up on his tie, his jacket left on the banister by the front door.

"'Tis the early bird that catches the worm," his mother replied, turning from the stove to look at him. "And don't ye look sharp this mornin'. Curious, me son. Do ye have anything other than a suit to wear?"

"Are you trying to tell me something?" Michael asked, reaching around her to pull the tin of coffee down from the shelf before turning the coffee maker on.

"Are you sure you don't want a cuppa? I'm just this minute makin' a pot," she said, ignoring his question as she lifted the kettle off the stove and poured most of its contents into the waiting teapot.

"No thanks. I'll stick with my coffee. I'm heading into work and don't have time to–"

"And that's what I was just sayin'. Is there ever a day when ye are *not* on yer way to work, or comin' home from work, or thinkin' about work?"

Micheal watched the caffeinated water drip into the decanter.

"It wouldn't hurt for ye to spend some time at home with Max," Mary-Margaret said. "They don't stay young forever, ye know."

Michael grabbed his travel mug from the dishwasher and poured the coffee into it.

Mary-Margaret began a series of breathy coughs, holding her hand to her chest.

"The pneumonia?" he asked, a twinkle in his eye.

"Indeed. It's gettin' the best of me," she said.

"I bet."

Michael reached past her into the fridge and pulled out some milk.

"Might be a good thing for ye."

"What might be?" he replied absently, putting the milk back in the fridge after having doused his coffee.

"Me dyin'. They can't prosecute a dead woman, can they?" she said, scooping the two Barry's tea bags out of the pot and dumping them in the sink.

"Oh. Right. About that."

Mary-Margaret began coughing louder.

"I think I'm in court most of the day today, but I can't promise that there won't be a knock on the door," he said, snapping the lid on his mug, refusing to give in to her antics.

"But ye said we had until—"

"I agreed that I wouldn't arrest Arthur before Saturday morning, but I can't promise that no one else will. And you might want to give some thought into how you're going to explain your actions in court when the officers come for him."

"*Explain* meself? I've got no explainin' to do. It's a poor excuse for a legal system that would allow an uneducated immigrant woman like meself to stand in as a criminal lawyer *and* be able to get bail for an accused murderer."

"This isn't like on TV, Mom. This is very serious business," he said, taking a sip of coffee and then realizing that the lid wasn't on properly as a stream of it drizzled down his chin.

"Speakin' of which, that Janelle Austin was in court when Arthur go let free," Mary-Margaret said, pouring herself a cup of tea.

"He was released on bail, Mom. He wasn't set free," Michael corrected, wiping his chin. "And about that—"

"I'm sure she'd love to do a story about how it was that an accused murderer got let out to wander the streets," Mary-Margaret continued, taking the milk pitcher back out of the fridge to pour a drop into her tea.

"You're kidding me, right?" Micheal said, stopping to look directly at his mother.

"Am I?" she said, looking back at him before turning to replace the pitcher.

"You're actually considering—"

"I might be."

"Really?" Micheal said, tightening the lid on the mug.

"I'm just sayin', Michael, that if ye want to play rough, ye'd best choose someone else to play with."

"Jesus, Mom," Micheal groaned.

"And if yer lads are bent on harassin' me client—"

"He's not your client. You don't have any clients. You're not a lawyer."

"Not accordin' to yer high and mighty courts. In any event, we'd best get Arthur moved somewhere safe if he and I are to solve this murder in," she looked at her watch, "eighty-nine hours and twenty-seven minutes."

She pushed past Micheal and hollered down the back stairs for Arthur.

"I want to keep out of this as much as I—"

"He's not answerin', Michael. Maybe they've already arrested him."

"Very doubtful," Micheal said, making his way to the front door, mug in hand.

"Can ye just go down and have a look?" she said. "Please."

"Alright," Micheal said with a huff.

"He may have been wearin' pajamas last night, but ye never know with Arthur, and I don't want to see somethin' I can never forget. Away ye go then," she said, practically pushing him down the stairs.

"Great."

"Well?" Mary-Margaret called down after a few seconds.

Michael waited until he was back upstairs to answer her.

"He's gone."

"Gone? Gone where? Oh, Michael," Mary-Margaret exclaimed, her hands at her mouth, "does this mean I've lost yer bail—"

"Holy crap! Are there ever a lot of cops out there," Arthur said, letting himself in the back door, donning a full nun's habit. "Like ants on a piece of raw—oh, hello, Michae...Mike."

"Arthur! Where were ye? Here I was, beginnin' to think I'd lost me

Michael's house and was stuck with him livin' at mine."

"Gee, that sounds kinda familiar," Michael grumbled, grabbing his coat and heading to the front door. "Now that you're back—"

"I was doing a little early morning recon, MM. I found out where that little guy who dumped the bag with the head works."

"Did ye now?" Mary-Margaret said, her previous concerns evaporating. "That's grand. So let's have it."

"He's at the convenience store attached to the gas station around the corner."

"And did ye have a word with him then?" Mary-Margaret asked.

"I'm off to work now. I'd suggest that both of you—" Michael interrupted.

"I would have, MM," said Arthur, ignoring Michael, "but the laneway was already crawling with cops when I made my way out earlier. I didn't want to push my luck. Or blow my cover."

"Before ye go, Michael, can ye just have a peek out the back? See if there's anyone ye know?" Mary-Margaret asked.

"As if a big fat guy dressed as a nun wouldn't draw attention," Michael said, dutifully going to the back of the house and opening the door to poke his head out. Phil skirted around Michael's legs and bolted down the laneway.

"At least he's not like yer neighbors and their tinnies," Mary-Margaret groused. "Grown men drinkin' in the laneway like that. 'Tis a disgrace, is that. Yer lads are probably back there now respondin' to a call for a bunch of old men drinkin' back there."

"And I don't exactly identify as male. I'm—" Arthur began.

"Gender fluid. I know," Michael said, watching Phil run to the police car parked at the end of the laneway, lift his hind leg, and pee on the back tire.

"Jesus," Michael said, shaking his head. "Can someone get that dog!"

"Yer the only one amongst us who's not currently wanted by the police, Michael," Mary-Margaret said amidst another round of coughs.

"Forty-eight hours!" Michael called as he stepped out the back door and then turned to face the angry glare of the officers standing by the car. "Sorry about that, boys."

* * *

"So what of this lad that ye saw depositin' the bag with our girl's head in it?" Mary-Margaret asked, pouring Arthur a cup of tea as she sat down at the dining room table.

"Do you have any McVities left?"

"In the cupboard. Ye know where they are. Me knees can't take all this up and down. Put them on a plate, and we'll call it breakfast. Don't tell me, Michael. Or Max. Speakin' of whom…"

"Micheal seemed really upset, MM," Arthur said as he plopped the box on the table between them.

"Ach, 'tis just his way, I'm beginnin' to think. Ever since I got here, he's been out of sorts. Likely the stress of the job. And here he is, on a day off, away to court. 'Tis no way to live. And 'tis no way to deliver biscuits. Could ye not find somethin' to put them on, luv?"

"Sorry," Arthur said, not making any motion to get up.

"Never mind. 'Tis done. And about our lad?"

"Oh, right. The guy who works at the gas station," Arthur said.

"Works there? I thought ye said ye saw him there."

"That would be so random. He's totally an employee. I knew it—"

"And ye didn't think to mention this about our lad earlier?" Mary-Margaret asked. She turned her head slightly and hollered with such intensity that the windows practically rattled. "MAX! 'TIS TIME FOR SCHOOL, LUV."

"I didn't know for sure. I mean, I knew he had a logo on his shirt, but I thought it might be a designer logo."

"But now?"

"I put myself into a state of hypnosis last night to try to recall—" Arthur began.

"But ye knew he had that logo on his shirt when ye first saw him. Did ye mention that when ye spoke to the police?"

"I'LL BE DOWN IN A MINUTE," Max shouted back.

"I was in custody," Arthur said, unfazed by the yelling. "And everyone knows you don't talk when you're in custody."

"But ye did speak to them, luv. And ye didn't think to tell them about–"

"They never asked."

"So you're tellin' me that Billy Gilly and his lads didn't have the wherewithal to ask ye what the lad ye saw in the laneway was wearin'?"

"Nope," Arthur said, shoving a biscuit in his mouth.

"And they wonder why I get involved in these matters." Mary-Margaret took a long sip of her tea. "GOOD, BECAUSE I'M NOT DRIVIN' YE TODAY," she yelled back to Max and then turned to Arthur. "And now, here we are, forced to live like a couple of fugitives in our own home. 'Tis not right, luv. 'Tis not right at all."

"We're only fugitives until we're cleared, MM."

"WHY NOT?" Max yelled down.

"I'm wondering," Arthur said, lowering his voice, "if the police have spoken to our gas station guy."

"I doubt they've spoken to anyone, knowin' how that Billy Gilly operates," Mary-Margaret said, and then hollered back to Max. "BECAUSE I'VE A MURDER TO SOLVE, SOME UNDERAGED MISCREANT TO CAPTURE, AND AN ENTIRE BOOK TO READ FOR ME BOOK CLUB THIS EVENIN' SO GET YERSELF DOWN HERE BEFORE YER LATE."

"Do you think you'll have time to make it to the book club tonight, MM?" Arthur asked.

"I doubt it, but if it puts a fire under me grandson," Mary-Margaret said, taking a sip of tea.

"And I thought you were going to give up—"

"Give up?" Mary-Margaret exclaimed. "Never. On what?"

"The book club."

"It's a good distraction," Mary-Margaret said.

"Don't you think you're spreading yourself a bit too thin, MM?" Arthur asked.

"Ye may be right, luv. Good thing there's a lot of me to spread around. And don't ye be repeatin' that!" She said as Max came down the stairs. "Ach, here's him himself. I picked up some danishes from the bakery just yesterday, luv. Grab one before ye go. Can't be startin' the day on an empty stomach.

And take a brolly. It's starting to rain."

* * *

"And what about you, MM?" Arthur said once Max was gone. "You're looking a little stressed."

"Do ye think, Captain Obvious?" Mary-Margaret said with a laugh.

"I think I might have put too much starch in this," Arthur said, disregarding Mary-Margaret's comment as he adjusted his wimple. "Anyway, as the empath you know me to be, I can tell that something's not right. I mean, beyond having a killer on the loose and this murder charge I'm up on and you being—"

"All right. All right. Ye've broken me," Mary-Margaret blurted out and then, in a barely audible voice added. "'Tis this business at me Max's school."

"I'll put the kettle back on."

After refilling their mugs and the plate of biscuits, Arthur sat down across from his friend and carefully crossed his legs at the ankles.

"Okay, dish. And why is this the first time that I'm hearing about this?"

"Ye've got enough on the go, luv. What with all that ye've said and now yer work at the church—"

"When you put it that way, MM, I can see why you've been holding back. But I am your rock, so lean on me!"

"Well, if ye must know," Mary-Margaret said, taking a slow sip of tea.

"I must."

She took a deep breath.

"There's an organized crime ring operatin' in me Max's school."

"Oh my, MM. Have you told Michael?"

She stared blankly at Arthur and sighed.

"Not interested?"

"Not in the least," Mary-Margaret said. "Honestly, luv, 'tis as if the lad's lost his will to be Police Officer of the Year the way he's disregardin' me tips."

"Well, he is getting older," Arthur reminded her.

"And what is *that* supposed to mean?"

136

"Men. They get older and get kind of like—"

"Neutered dogs," Mary-Margaret said, shaking her head sadly as she dipped a biscuit into her tea.

"I wasn't going to say that, but okay," Arthur replied, squirming in his habit. "So what about this organized crime ring?"

"I'm sure…well, I'm not sure, but 'tis not the organized crime that bothers me. 'Tis that the principal lady doesn't seem to care that her students are bein' terrorized. If it weren't for Old Bird—"

"Who?"

"The school secretary. Looks more like a tarted-up Stevie Nicks than a proper secretary, if ye ask me, but she's the only one who seems to know what's goin' on. Anyway, she's called the police—those that aren't me Michael, thanks be given—but they've no suspects, no video, and that Leona Zalinski, the school principal lady, doesn't seem to give a pig's foot. Scarred for life, will that cohort be."

"Wait a minute," Arthur said, his eyebrows almost touching his wimple. "Did you just offer me, master of disguises, an assignment?"

Mary-Margaret blinked slowly at Arthur.

"Come on, MM. Tell me my blind-guy disguise I used to help solve Jane Ann Hill's murder wasn't brilliant."

"It wasn't."

"And this?" Arthur said, reaching his arms out to display the fullness of the Benedictine habit.

Mary-Margaret shook her head slowly.

"Oh. We are in a mood today, aren't we?"

"I'm sorry, luv. I know ye mean well, but this is about me Max."

"And that's exactly why we need to get into that school and bust that ring wide open."

Mary-Margaret considered for a moment.

"What have ye in mind?"

"Well," Arthur said, popping a biscuit in his mouth as he leaned in towards her. "I say I go UC…that's undercover—"

"I know, luv. I'm up on the lingo. Me son is a police officer, as castrated as he may be behavin' at the moment."

"Right," Arthur said. "So, I say I go in as a student and, through brilliantly strategic lingering, am by the exact locker these Mafiosos are—"

"Who said anythin' about the Mafia? I'm talking gangs."

"Okay. So I'm right there when the Crips or the Bloods roll in, and we make a citizen's arrest."

"Sounds a bit dangerous, don't ye think?"

"MM, do I need to remind you that we catch murderers for breakfast?"

"Right," she said.

"Is there something in the air around here?" Arthur said, raising his head and giving a sniff.

She frowned and sniffed the air.

"Do ye smell gas? I've told me Michael that—"

"No, MM. I smell lethargy. And it's an ugly stink. Since when have you ever backed down from anything?"

"Ach," she conceded. "Aren't ye just spot on, luv. I suppose 'tis time to don me big girl panties and sort this out."

"That's the spirit! I'll get a disguise together, and we'll close this thing down."

"All right then. But I think we should get Old Bird involved. She seems to be in the know."

"I'm not so sure, MM," Arthur said, squinting as he leaned back in his chair. "Loose lips sink ships and all of that."

"I hear what yer sayin', luv, but if anyone's goin' to notice somethin' or someone out of place, it'll be her, so we'd best let her know what we're up to. Or, at the very least, that ye'll be there."

"Okay, makes sense." Arthur looked at the watch he had pinned on the inside of his tunic. "Oh my. Will you look at the time. If we're going to be doing anything on our real work—"

"Which is?"

"Finding out who murdered that barmaid, obviously. MM, I'm worried about you. Anyway, we need to get moving. Also, it may take me a while to get up. It's really hard to move in this thing. I don't know how Julie Andrews does it," Arthur said, pulling the habit skirt away from his body while trying not to step on the veil as he lumbered to his feet.

"She isn't a nun, luv. She's a—"

"She is, was, and will forever more be Sister Maria, just as I am, was, and will forever more be Sister Augustine. At least until further notice. Now pass me your mug, and let's get going to check out my lead at the convenience store."

Arthur took the tray and danced his way to the kitchen, humming 'The Hills Are Alive' while Mary-Margaret moved around him to let Wee Phil out the back.

Chapter Nineteen

"Honestly, I still don't know how Julie does it," Arthur said, hoisting up his habit to step over a puddle as the two of them stood outside the store attached to the gas station. "I think we would have been better to have driven, MM."

"This just bein' around the corner? The rain has stopped, and we wouldn't have melted anyway. Besides, we don't want to chance havin' the lad run the plates if he turns the tables and decides to start investigatin' us. No. It's best to walk. And Julie Andrews was not a—ach, never mind. Now remember, we are just away from the church lookin' to buy—"

"What, MM? What would an old woman and a nun who just happened to walk in off the street from God-knows-where buy at a gas station store?" Arthur said with a pout.

Mary-Margaret paused for a moment, overlooking Arthur's comment about her as she considered that he may have raised a good point.

"Lottery tickets," she blurted out. "That's it. Lottery tickets."

"Aren't I supposed to be a nun?"

"To give any potential winnin's to the Church. For the Unwed Fathers' Confessional Program."

"Reasonable," Arthur had to agree. "Now remember, I'm Sister Augustine."

"Right," Mary-Margaret said with a sigh.

The plump little Irish woman and exceptionally large nun walked into the gas station store, heads held high. Mary-Margaret glanced over at Sister Augustine.

"That's him," the faux nun whispered.

The two of them approached the cashier.

"Whah?" the scrawny young man said in a contrived Cockney accent, looking across the counter at the two of them.

"Have ye any lottery tickets for sale?" Mary-Margaret said in her best Church Fundraiser voice.

"I fink so. Yiz might see 'em yerself if yiz looked," he said, dropping his eyes to the glass counter between them, chewing his gum with a bit more vigor than Mary-Margaret thought was necessary.

"Right. Yes. Well. Which one would you suggest?"

"Not me job."

"What the lady is asking," Sister Augustine said, her jaw clenching as she carefully articulated each word, "is which ticket is most likely to win."

"If I knewed which ticket was the winnin' ticket, do you fink I'd be pissin' about 'ere, Sweet'eart?"

Another customer entered the store. She had purchased gas and was standing behind Mary-Margaret and Sister Augustine, credit card in hand.

"Go ahead," Mary-Margaret said, stepping aside.

"I tried to pay at the pumps, but—" the woman began.

"Yeah. It don't work. The Man's gettin' someone in t' sort it later today. Or tomorra. Just like it says on the sign on the pump," the attendant said wearily.

The woman smiled weakly as she passed him the card, looking back at Sister Augustine.

"Me...sister...*The*...sister...and I are just tryin' to figure out which lottery ticket is most likely to win," Mary-Margaret said. "On account of our purchasin' it to raise funds for the Unwed Fathers' Confessional Program. Ye wouldn't happen to know, would ye?"

"I don't purchase lottery tickets as a rule. But I've heard that this one is good," the woman said. "What did you say you were raising money for?"

"The Unwed Fathers'—"

"UFC program," Sister Augustine broke in loudly, noticing two other customers approaching the cash register.

"Well, it's about time the church takes on something like that. Here. Let me buy you a ticket. Can you add the price of one—make it two—of those tickets to my gas sale, please?" the woman said to the attendant, motioning under the glass at a row of brightly colored tickets. "As I said, I don't usually buy them, but my neighbor does, and he's won a few times with these ones, I think."

The attendant took the credit card and rang in the sale, returning the credit card to its owner, handing over two lottery tickets from beneath the glass to Mary-Margaret. He ended the transaction by blowing a rather large bubble that burst with a loud pop.

"UFC is running a lottery? Cool," the next customer said. "Add five tickets to my bill and give 'em to the sister here."

"UFC? UFC? What is this UFC?" the third customer asked.

"You know. The Ultimate—"

"Unwed—" Mary-Margaret tried to cut in.

"Oh, you mean *THAT* UFC. Well, of course. I will buy...how many did he buy? Five? I will buy *eleven* tickets and keep one for myself."

"Right," the attendant said, with a shrug, pulling more tickets from the tray. He handed ten of them to Sister Augustine, who already had her hand outstretched to receive them, and the other one to the customer, along with his receipt for the gas.

As the recipient of the lone lottery ticket put the receipt in his wallet and turned to the door, he passed another customer and said: "They're selling lottery tickets for the UFC. I just bought eleven and gave ten to the nun for good luck."

"Thanks for the tip," this latest customer said, reaching for the crucifix hanging on a gold chain around his neck.

"Give me twenty-two of those tickets everyone else is buying, bud."

Before anyone could object, the fourth customer had paid for his gas, purchased twenty-two lottery tickets, handed Sister Augustine twenty, and was out the door.

Sister Augustine shoved them in the pocket of her habit, along with the other seventeen tickets.

"I don't want the risk of the gov'ment comin' in 'ere and bootin' the door down cuz they thinks I done somehin' to fix the lotto," the attendant said. "So are yiz done now?"

"Not quite," Mary-Margaret said, unsure about the legitimacy of the series of transactions that had just occurred. "We actually came for a reason above and beyond encouragin' gamblin' in the name of unwed fathers."

"Recognize me?" Sister Augustine said, leaning closer to the attendant.

"I've never laid eyes on yiz or nuffin' like yiz in me life," he said, his chin up, eyes half-closed.

Arthur jerked back the wimple to reveal his full face and hair.

"Recognize me now?"

"I must say, Arth—Sister Augustine: ye do get a bit...aggressive...when yer in full garb," Mary-Margaret commented.

"I. Have. Issues. So, do you recognize me, you little punk?"

"What the livin'—?

"Yeah. You recognize me. And I recognize you. You dumped that bag in the laneway."

"And wha' if I did. Is tha' a crime?" the attendant said, stepping from the counter, his eyes darting around the shop, hoping for a customer to enter or some other distraction that would allow him to get away.

"Luv," Mary-Margaret said softly to the attendant, "what me friend here, is tryin' to say is this: we know ye dropped of a bag full o' bones the other day. We also know that another bag with...the rest of the business...was dropped off in or near the same area. The chances of two different people droppin' off body parts is as likely as a rabbit abstainin' from its natural tendencies for Lent. Now, what we're wonderin' is how a lovely lad like ye would end up with somethin' like that in his possession."

There was a long pause.

"Let me begin again, lad," Mary-Margaret said, a little less softly. "The police are scouring that laneway now. And to make matters worse for ye, me friend here is wanted. For murder. But he knows he didn't commit the murder and is desperate to find out who did. He's seen ye in the laneway with the bag of bones, and any idjit would link ye to the bag with the rest of it, so—"

The attendant looked up as a customer approached the cash. Arthur put the wimple back on his head to the best of his abilities, given the lack of a mirror and time to adjust as would normally be necessary.

"For the love of God, Arthur, do not get anyone buyin' us any more lottery tickets," Mary-Margaret murmured softly as they stepped aside.

The customer stared at the misaligned headdress and then looked Arthur up and down a couple of times before pulling out his credit card and passing it to the attendant.

"'Tis all right, lad," Mary-Margaret reassured the customer. "Ye aren't Catholic, are ye?"

"No," the man said, staring back at Arthur.

"Clearly. Which is why ye would have no idea that the Church is looking to allow men to become nuns."

The customer said nothing as the attendant rang his sale through.

"'Tis true," Mary-Margaret said, prepared to continue, but was cut short when the customer shoved his credit card back in his wallet and hurried out of the store.

"Listen, I don't know wha' yiz two is up to an' I don't care," the attendant said, his voice quivering despite his best efforts. "Yiz needs to leave now before I chucks yiz out wiff me own two 'ands."

"Well, here's the thing, luv," Mary-Margaret said. "If we leave here without ye, my friend, Sister Augustine—"

"I thought yiz said she was an 'e."

"Baby steps, lad. Baby steps. While the Church is considerin' men as nuns, they haven't quite come around to workin' out the pronouns."

"Get out," the attendant directed.

"I've got a fist full of—lottery tickets—that says you know who those bones and that...that...bag...belonged to, and that you murdered her," Arthur said.

"And I've got an alarm button 'ere what says yiz're both crackers, and the cops yiz say are 'round the corner will be 'ere in about two secs if I press it," the attendant responded, his courage regained.

"I've got a feelin' that both of ye will end up in jail if ye press that button before tellin' me where ye got that bag from," Mary-Margaret said with the warmest smile she could muster. "I know ye aren't a bad soul, luv. Ye just got yerself into somethin' a bit bigger than—"

"Oi! ʼOw can I ʼelp yiz?" the attendant said to a woman with cropped hair who was now standing behind Mary-Margaret.

"Twenty dollars on pump seven," she said.

Mary-Margaret stepped back from the counter. The woman handed the cash over to the attendant.

"Ta, darlin'," the attendant said, taking the cash without opening the till.

The woman turned and, once she was out of the door, Mary-Margaret approached the counter again.

"Was it for the money, then?"

"Whah?"

"That ye took the bag. Likely knew it held something other than a cabbage, didn't ye?, But ye were—"

"Piss off," the attendant scowled. "I don't know what yiz are talkin' about."

"I disagree, luv."

"Even if I knew what yiz were on about, why would I–"

"Well, I'm noticin' ye didn't put the cash from the last sale in the till, so I'm thinkin', given how few people pay with cash, that skimmin' isn't the business it used to be and ye have to make ends meet somehow, don't ye?"

Mary-Margaret gave the attendant the same look she had used numerous times on her own four children over the years.

"I-I was just gettin' 'round to it now, right?" the attendant stuttered, popping the cash register open and putting the twenty-dollar bill where it belonged.

"This outfit isn't nearly as comfortable as it looks," Arthur said, pulling her shoulders back to adjust the habit, "so let's get to the point. You dumped both bags. You knew there was a head in one of them. It's impossible that you wouldn't. Where did you get them?"

The attendant looked blankly across the counter.

"Listen, bub," Arthur said, reaching over the counter, grabbing the scrawny man's shirt collar, and pulling him closer, "the lady already told you I'm wanted for one murder. Another isn't going to make too much of a difference to me. Tell us what you know, or you could end up like that head in the bag."

The attendant's pale face got even paler.

"What Arth—Sister Augus—me friend is tryin' to say—" Mary-Margaret began.

"Right. Right. I'll tell yiz. Just let go of me so that I can turn off the pumps and lock the door, yeah?"

Rather than loosening his grip, Arthur hauled the scrawny man right over the counter and plopped him down on the floor at Mary-Margaret's feet.

"Oh, my," Mary-Margaret said.

"I've been working out, MM," Arthur replied and then looked down on the cowering little man. "Don't make me hurt you before the next customer gets here."

"Stop! I'll tell you whatever you want to hear," the attendant said, dropping his accent. "No need to get violent, okay? So yeah, I found the bag of bones in the washroom during clean up and was going to take it home—"

"As one would," Arthur said dismissively.

"Let the lad speak," Mary-Margaret said.

"I know, but I'm kinda into taxidermy," he continued, getting to his feet, "and thought it would be kinda neat to—"

"And now ye've lost me."

"I've never done a human before. Just squirrels and stuff I pick up when I'm out and about. So when this practically dropped into my lap—"

"And it never occurred to ye that these bones belong to a real person?" Mary-Margaret asked.

"Not anymore. They're just bones."

"So why did you leave it in the bushes?" Arthur asked, feeling a wave of nausea wash over him.

"Like I said, I was taking them home, but I had to take a whiz, so I stepped into the bushes," the attendant explained, resuming his place behind the counter, "and that's when I noticed you—or your brother or…so I just booted it and figured either you'd find it or I could come back later and get it."

Mary-Margaret and Arthur just stared at the attendant for a moment before a middle-aged woman came in. Cell phone crunched between her shoulder and head, she pushed past the two and plopped her clutch purse down on the counter. She then rummaged through the various credit cards to pick out one before looking up.

"Oh. I'm sorry. Did I butt in?"

"Not at all," Arthur said in a comically high voice, reverting to his Sister Augustine persona. "We were just talking to our friend here—"

"Good. Pump six. Yes, oh, absolutely. She has no sense of…no, I agree…but I wouldn't want to be the one to say…no, for sure…" the woman said into her phone, waiting for the attendant to ring in her sale.

"I shall say a prayer for you, my sister," Sister Augustine said as she turned and followed Mary-Margaret quickly out the door.

The two of them hurried through the laneway towards the back door of Michael's house, heads down, as they tried to avoid drawing any more attention to themselves than was necessary from the two uniformed officers patrolling the laneway, casually chatting on their cell phones.

"I don't think it's quite a confession, but we've got somethin' that we can take to the police," Mary-Margaret said as the Jack Russell bounced into the kitchen to greet them. "Too bad it wasn't recorded. Did ye think that lad's actually from London?"

"No. He just watches too much Brit TV. And about that," said Sister Augustine, removing a tiny video camera from one of the folds of her habit.

"Let's have a look then," Mary-Margaret said, her eyes sparkling.

"No time." Sister Augustine pulled up the sleeve of her habit to check her watch. "I've got to get over to the church. Let me just get myself put together before I head out."

"I don't think they expect ye to clean in yer outfit, luv."

"But Julie Andrews—"

"I think she was a novice. Didn't wear the full habit," Mary-Margaret said, giving up on this point.

"Oh," Arthur said, his eyes widening. "I never knew that."

"'Tis true. As such, ye may wish to…dress down."

"Right," Arthur said, nodding in agreement. "I think I've got just the thing at home."

"I'm sure ye do, luv, so away with ye. Best leave out the front door. And don't worry, Wee Phil. I'll be runnin' ye out the back in a moment."

Chapter Twenty

"Who are you?" Ashleigh asked, looking up from her computer screen at the hefty figure dressed in pink scrubs and a nun's veil, leaning over the half door of the secretary's office.

"I," the woman said, flicking her veils as if they were long locks of hair, "am Sister Augustine. And I'm assuming you're the new girl. Ashleigh, isn't it?"

"Uh, yeah. How did you know that?"

"Because your name is here on the door."

"Oh. Right," Ashleigh said, her mouth agape

"You may be wondering where my tunic and coif are," Sister Augustine said, sensing that this was the source of Ashleigh's expression. "Given that my dry-cleaning bills are already out of control, I decided to wear something a little more appropriée for the task at hand."

"Okay. Makes sense," Ashleigh said, returning to the images from the *Top Ten Nurseries to Create an Exceptional Baby Experience* on the website she had been scrolling.

"A little...direction...here?"

"I have no idea where the cleaning stuff is. You're just gonna have to look around until you find it, I guess," Ashleigh said, not taking her eyes off the screen.

"Perfect."

"And I have to go out in a bit. Midwife appointment. I'm pregnant. I'll leave my office door unlocked for you to clean."

"Outstanding," Sister Augustine said, the word so soaked in sarcasm

149

that anyone marginally less self-absorbed than Ashleigh would have been offended.

"And not that it's a thing with me or anything, but weren't you supposed to be here this morning?" Ashleigh asked, arching her back as she stood up.

"Yes, now that you mention it, I was," Sister Augustine said, looking down to admire her own fingernails. "Had an exorcism to do, and it took a bit longer than I expected."

"Don't priests do that sort of thing?"

"Not really. I mean," she sighed, "I suppose they can, but I like to get right in there, you know? You're probably just the same as me. Like to get right involved in all of that God stuff."

"I guess so."

"Guess? Well, honey," Sister Augustine said, going into full-on drag queen mode, "why else would a pretty little bit of a girl like you be sequestered within these walls unless you were all Girl For G?"

"You wanna know something, Sister...?" Ashleigh said, leaning towards her.

"Augustine, but you can just call me Sis," she practically whispered back.

"Wanna know something, Sis? I'm not even Catholic."

Sister Augustine leaned back from the door that divided them, clutching her wimple as if she had pearls over top.

"I know," Ashleigh said, also leaning back. "They never asked, and I never told."

"Kinda brings a whole new meaning to that *don't-ask-don't-tell* thing, doesn't it?"

"Huh?'

"Never mind. Have you got any coffee around this place, hun?"

"Yeah," Ashleigh said, unlocking the half door to invite her new friend in. "The first thing I did when I landed this job was toss the old kettle and get them to buy me a Keurig. Give me two minutes."

"So very drab," Sister Augustine commented, looking around the office.

"Tell me about it. And *this* is an improvement. The old woman who worked here before me had crucifixes and pictures of Jesus all over the walls. Very creepy."

"A couple of bright prints would just perk this place right up," Sister Augustine said and then, flicking the dark brown curtains on the dirty window, added: "And these definitely have to go."

Ashleigh said nothing as she handed Sister Augustine a cup of steaming coffee.

"So I hear your brother's in a band."

"How did you know?"

"Word. And I used to be in a band. Sister Augustine and The Nasty Habits. We did a lot of Clash covers. I still like to keep my hand in the community."

"Wow. I would never have thought…." Ashleigh said, her eyes wide open.

"Clearly. Ever think, I mean. But about your brother…?"

"He's the lead singer now. He used to just play the guitar, but their singer dropped off the face of the earth, so he stepped in. Do you want anything in your coffee?"

"Just some brandy," Sister Augustine said. When Ashleigh didn't respond, she continued. "Just black is fine, hun. Keeps my heart pumping. God knows something has to. So this band. I hear they're not half bad."

"They do okay. They're just in the process of restructuring because the lead singer got kinda messed up on drugs."

"Living La Vida Loca a bit too much?"

"Exactly."

"That's a problem with bands. Always has been. The drugs, I mean. I should know. The Nasty Habits sure had their share of drug problems. And boys, but we don't talk about that."

Ashleigh stared at Sister Augustine.

"How deep into them—the drugs, I mean—is your brother?"

Ashleigh shrugged.

"Oh, my. There I go again, forgetting my manners. I am so sorry and it is none of my business. I do drug counseling as a part of my community outreach, and sometimes I just forget where I am and who I'm talking about. But look at you: the non-Catholic working here in the heart of the beast. And expecting a baby. You *are* married, right? I mean, I can't imagine them being okay with…"

"Yes. Just."

"Quick out of the gate, eh?'

Ashleigh blinked a few times.

"Oops! There's me again, shooting off my mouth. God," Sister Augustine said, looking up, "are you sure there isn't a splash of brandy in this coffee? Don't we all wish. Again, not my business, but I also do a series of group counseling sessions for young…unwed fathers, so I'm used to just… well, never mind."

"No worries," Ashleigh said. "And if we're going to be completely honest with each other, it's not like I wasn't pregnant before the honeymoon."

"Oh, you vixen."

"Well, we've known each other for six months, so…."

"That long, huh?" Sister Augustine said, rolling her eyes.

"Right? I mean, I'm not getting any younger, so it was kind of like now or never and he wasn't too eager to put a ring on it." She wiggled the fingers on her left hand to show the garish diamond ring that now adorned the appropriate finger. "So I just turned up the heat."

"Well, that boy is nobody's fool, the poor bast—" Sister Augustine caught herself. "And all that with a bun already in the oven? Girl, you've got it going on."

"I know. I have no idea how he's going to pay for it and manage the payments on our new house. Wait until the baby comes! Oh well, not my problem. He signed up for it. He can look after it."

"You go, girl!"

The two clinked their coffee mugs together in agreement.

"So about this brother of yours. And the drugs. What's his deal?" Sister Augustine asked.

"He's kinda in a bit too deep if you ask me, but he's a big boy. What can I do?"

"And that's what girlfriends are for, right?" Sister Augustine said with a wink.

"I don't think she's good with the drugs."

152

"So why didn't she just give him an ultimatum? You know? Me or the drugs, sex, and rock and roll? Wasn't that kind of what you said to your man? Freedom or me, a baby, and a huge mortgage that you'll be working the rest of your life for and probably die trying to pay off?"

"You're too funny!" Ashleigh said with a laugh.

"Just because I'm a nun now doesn't mean I never got none before," Sister Augustine said with a wink and a snap of her fingers.

"OMG, I can't believe you just said that!"

"Honey, you ain't seen nothin' yet. If I didn't make it as a nun, I was going to go into stand-up, but there's more money in the church."

"What about your band?"

"No money in it. And it was taking up too much time to be just a hobby. I'm sure the guys in your brother's band feel the pinch."

"Hardly. None of them work."

"They're doing that well?"

"No. One lives in the basement of his mother's house; the other lives with his sister, I think."

"I get the mother part, but why would any sister let her punk brother sponge off of her?"

"Who the hell knows," Ashleigh said and then brought both hands up to her mouth. "Oh, I am so sorry. I shouldn't have said that."

"Hun, if a piece of my nun gear fell away each time I heard someone swear, you'd be seeing my..."

Ashleigh began to laugh.

"I have never had this much fun in this church. I don't know where you came from or whether or not you can clean, but you are worth five hundred bucks a week just for the laughs!"

"Oh. Right," Sister Augustine said, dropping her voice and her shtick. "Speaking of that, can I get paid on Tuesdays instead of Fridays? I have some...unpaid business to take care of."

"You can get paid whenever you want, Sister. In the meantime, I've got to get to my appointment. Let me just get you the money from Miguel's office, and I'll be right back."

* * *

"Can I—oh, it's you, Mrs. O'Shea," the school secretary said, momentarily glancing up from her computer screen before returning to her work. "If you're here to pick up Max, he had a spare last period and has already left for the day."

"No, 'tis not me Max, I'm here to see, but I must say, I'm impressed with your knowledge of his whereabouts," Mary-Margaret said, placing her purse on the counter that separated the public from the staff-only area.

"I'm the school secretary. It's my job to know everything. Hang on. I just have to fill out this form and send it off."

Mary-Margaret stepped away from the counter, noticing the stacks of papers on the secretary's desk.

And they said we'd be paperless, she thought to herself, recalling the similarities between this desk and her own when she was the secretary at St. Francis.

"There. Send. Done," the secretary said, pressing a button on her keyboard before giving her attention to Mary-Margaret. "Leona's out for the afternoon, and I'm the only one here, so what can I do you for?"

"Just as well the big boss is away," Mary-Margaret said, stepping back up to the counter, "because 'tis ye I'm wantin' to speak with."

"Okay. Here I am," she said, walking over to the counter.

"'Tis about the organized crime—"

"Locker thefts," the secretary corrected, lowering her raspy voice. "Leona prefers that we call them locker thefts, although, if you ask me, you're right. It's not just some random thing. It's organized. And it's a crime."

"I'm glad we're in agreement on that," Mary-Margaret said approvingly.

The secretary looked Mary-Margaret up and down.

"Why don't you come around? I'd invite you into Leona's office—I use it all the time to talk to the kids—but end-of-day can get a bit busy here with helicopter parents calling when their kid doesn't come home at exactly the right time. You know," she said, swinging open the gate that separated them, "they sit at work, watching their nanny-cams or Nests or whatever, waiting

154

for the kid to walk through the door. Whatever happened to personal space? A totally different world. Anyway, come on around."

Mary-Margaret followed the secretary's direction and sat in a wooden chair by the desk.

"Old Bird, just in case you forgot," she said, extending her hand. "I mean, Sue Bird, but everyone here except Leona calls me Old Bird, so call me—"

"Pleased to make your acquaintance, Old...Bird. Mary-Margaret," she said, shaking the woman's hand. "That's the name I was given and that which me friends call me by."

The two women smiled at each other before drawing their hands away.

"Forgive me for askin', but ye seem a bit...long in the tooth to be workin' here."

"Ha!" Old Bird squawked in a manner that suggested there may be more than one reason why they referred to her as Old Bird. "You can say that again. I was eligible to retire about seven years ago, but who's counting? That's what happens when you spend your—what do they call them? Foundational years?—playing clubs in a band instead of boring yourself silly in a suit."

Mary-Margaret's eyebrows raised.

"Oh, yeah. We were really something back in the day," Old Bird said, smiling as she took a deep breath, her eyes seeming to focus on somewhere far away. "Opened for a lot of big acts back then. This was a really big music town in the '80s."

"I wouldn't know," Mary-Margaret said. "I was at home evenin's, raisin' me family. Didn't get out much."

"Everyone came through here. They probably still do, but it's not my thing anymore. Not like I'm turning down gigs these days, even if it was. Ha! We were more into electro-pop and those brooding ballads back then. Depeche Mode, Human League, Roxy Music...ah, those were the days."

The phone on the secretary's desk rang. Old Bird looked up at the clock on the wall.

"H. V. Opticians. Give it two more minutes," she said to the phone rather than picking up the receiver to speak to the person on the other end. "Veeth will be walking through the door, and you'll see him on your cam."

"So what happened?" Mary-Margaret asked once the phone had stopped ringing. "With the bands?"

"Nothing. Ha!" Old Bird screeched again. "And that's why I'm here. That and Sid, my guy, dumped me after Bowie's *Serious Moonlight Tour*."

"I see," Mary-Margaret said as the phone rang again.

"Hello, Mrs. Bornstein," Old Bird said when she picked up the phone. "Amanda has violin lessons after school on Tuesdays, remember? She'll be home at 4:30.... You're welcome."

Mary-Margaret smiled. *'Tis the secretary who keeps the ship afloat.*

"Yeah, so after the final chords of *Modern Love*, Sid walks away, and I discover that I'm beyond broke, but I could type, so I got a job with the Board of Ed, and here I am."

"Did ye remarry?" Mary-Margaret asked, finding herself more involved in this conversation than she had anticipated.

"Remarry? Ha!" Old Bird threw her head back as she let out a laugh. "I never got married to begin with. Not my thing. But don't get me wrong. After Sid, there were a few winners, but no. Marriage is definitely not my thing."

"So no smallies."

"What?"

"Smallies. Little ones. Children."

"Only about two thousand of 'em every year. Ha!" She stretched her arms towards the entrance of the office, her billowing sleeves flapping before she pulled herself back in again. "But enough about me. What can I do for you?"

"It's about this...these...locker thefts. I've got a plan to catch these malefactors."

"I like it. Keep going."

Mary-Margaret proceeded to tell the secretary how Arthur would be coming in as a student and would catch the thieves in the act.

"Is this guy a psychic?"

"I don't recall ever askin'," Mary-Margaret said, her eyebrows knitted as she tried to recall all the things Arthur had told her he was. "But likely."

"Good, because I've been sending kids out during class to try to catch someone for weeks with zero success. Hopefully, you're guy'll be able to shut this thing down before it hits the papers. Leona hates negative press."

"If anyone can do it," Mary-Margaret said with the hollow confidence that was the cornerstone of her relationship with him, "me Arthur can."

"We've got nothing to lose, do we? When will he be here?"

"Is tomorrow too soon? If 'tis, not a problem. And, in fact, I may actually have misspoken. Me friend may still have some unresolved business to attend to."

"Tomorrow is perfect if he can swing it," Old Bird exclaimed. "Leona's at some staff development retreat for a couple of days. I'll just let Joe the Janitor know."

"Ye've only got one man cleanin' a place the size of this? He's surely a wonder," Mary-Margaret said, looking approvingly around the office.

"No, there's a crew of them. I call them all Joe the Janitor. Anyway, I'll let all of them know, and we'll go from there."

"Grand. Although who would be havin' unlimited access...." Mary-Margaret began, recalling Arthur's words.

"You can't be serious," Old Bird said.

"About...?"

"About a janitor risking his job to steal some kid's—"

"Ye can't be too careful," Mary-Margaret said.

"True that," Old Bird said. "If I had been more careful...ha! Water under the bridge."

"Indeed, luv. We've all got things we wish were different."

The phone rang. Old Bird picked it up on the second ring.

"Nothing to report, Leona," the secretary said. "No, but I don't think that supply teacher you have in for Harriet is working out too well. Kids think he's an idiot.... I know, but I'm just letting you know.... And Mr. Vanier called to make an appointment to see you...Pippa is his kid...Yes, *that* Pippa. Anyway, I put it in your calendar for next week. Hopefully, things will cool down before that.... Okay. And you've got that thing tomorrow.... Okay. Bye." She hung up.

"Leona's a lovely woman, honestly, but if she spent more time doing her job and less time trying to become a superintendent...." Old Bird's words trailed off.

"Father Miguel is the exact item. Wants to be the pope, that one. And him bein' barely out of his deacon's robes," Mary-Margaret said.

"Ain't that the truth?" Old Bird said, giving Mary-Margaret a knowing look. " Hey, I've got an idea. Why don't you and I go for a drink or something after your friend catches the bandits? A little celebration party. Would you be cool with that, or am I being too forward?"

"Not in the least. I'd like that. A tremendous lot," Mary-Margaret said, sensing she'd just made a new friend. "And a drink at O'Leary's, me local, would be grand."

Chapter Twenty-One

"Where's th' young one?" Frank asked, putting his coat on the knob by the front door.

"Out with his lads. Can I get ye a cuppa?" Mary-Margaret said as Phil ran around the two of them.

"It's like that, is it?" Frank said with a slight smirk as he crouched down to pat the dog.

"By which ye mean?"

"Well," Frank said, straightening up again, "I can count on the fingers of me third hand the number of times I've seen ye on a Tuesday night here with neither Michael nor Max about. For just this moment, I was startin' t' think—"

"And therein lies yer problem, Francis. Now, cuppa or a wee dram of whiskey?"

"If yer offerin' me a wee dram, it must be bad news," Frank said, slouching into the familiar chair by the front door. "Best keep me wits about me, then. I'll have a cuppa."

"Ach, yer a regular worrier, are ye. 'Tis neither good nor bad. Hold that thought, luv. I've got the kettle on the boil, and I'm hearing it callin' for me."

Mary-Margaret walked back to the kitchen and returned a few minutes later with two mugs of tea in one hand and a plate of biscuits in the other, Phil at her heels the entire time.

"Not even a tray. Must be important," Frank said with a smile.

"'Tis about the murder of the thievin' barmaid from O'Leary's," Mary-Margaret said, setting the plate down on the small table in front of her before passing him his mug of tea.

"I figured as much. Sometimes, me pet, I wonder if ye just like me because, or it's me slicin' and dicin' skills ye fancy."

"That's not the only reason, Francis, but it helps," she said, with wee Phil hopping onto her lap the moment she sat down. "Now, about the murder. The bones, to be exact. How long would it take a body to, you know, become just bones?"

"A lot longer than our girl has been dead, I can tell ye that."

"So is there a chance that we've got two murders on the go then?"

"There could be."

"Well then," Mary-Margaret said, taking a slow sip of her tea. "This changes everythin'."

"But 'tis unlikely."

"And why is that then?"

"Well, let me start again. 'Tis as likey t' be so as not, technically speakin'."

"Luv," Mary-Margaret said, her eyes sharpening, "contrary to what yer eyes are beholdin', I am not a young woman and I'm agin' before right ye. Get to the point."

"'Tis not me area of expertise, but I am of the opinion, without any formal report in me hand, that the bones and the skull came from the same body."

"But ye just said—"

"If I had to swear on a stack of Bibles, I'd have to say it was possible that the two are not related because it would take longer than our girl's been dead for those bones to come to be as they are now if 'twere up to nature's own time. But there's more than one way to skin a cat, if ye will."

Mary-Margaret took a biscuit from the plate.

"Tell me more."

"What I'm gettin' at is that there are a number of acids and whatnot that can be applied t' remove the flesh from the bone."

"Whatnot?" she said, a look of disappointment in Phil's eyes as he watched her nibble the cookie without a crumb making its way down to him.

"Aye. Things ye can pick up from the hardware store around the corner, even."

"And ye think that would be the case here?"

"I'm not sayin' that 't'all."

"Honestly, Francis, ye've got me chasin' me tail on this one. Let's get back to me original question: are the bones ye have at yer work belongin' to Cassandra Lewis's head?"

Frank paused for a long moment.

"Likely. But we won't know for sure until we get the samples of the bone we sent off t' the tox labs. They'll be checkin' for DNA and t' see if there are traces of chemicals that would indicate the flesh didn't just come off natural-like, if ye know what I mean. In any event, don't go tellin' anyone. That's information not intended for the general public."

"Good, because I'm not the general public. And when will ye know for sure?"

"When the pathologist tells me." Frank took a sip of tea.

"Don't ye work shoulder-to-shoulder with the pathologist?"

"Indeed, I do. But I don't get involved in the bodies after they leave me tray. 'Tis not me job."

"If the whole world operated on that premise, Francis, nothin' would get done, which is likely why Billy Gilly can't catch his man."

"I think I'd best be goin'," Frank said with a yawn.

"That was a short visit," she said, the dog jumping from her lap as she stood up. "Tea not to yer likin' or was it somethin' I said?"

"The tea was grand, luv, and I could listen t' you until the cows came home. But I've an early mornin' tomorrow and I like to be as sharp as me scalpel, even if I don't catch murderers like ye apparently think I do."

"I never said anythin' about ye catchin' murderers, Francis. Ye are an important cog in the machinery of me life."

"I'm not sure if that's a compliment or not. Regardless, I'll consider it so. Now, unless ye have anythin' else I can do for ye, I'll be on me way."

* * *

"Arthur, are ye still awake?" Mary-Margaret said, having called him just as

Frank was walking down the front walkway.

"Of course I am, MM. It's only 8:30."

"Right. So have ye been contacted by the police yet?"

"No."

"Good. Have ye got that video confession handy for when ye are?"

"Yes, but they'll never find me. I've on the very *d l*."

"It's not me business what ye substances ye are ingestin', luv. I just want to make sure that ye—"

"No. I'm on the D-L. You know: the down low?"

"I don't care what yer on. Ach, can ye give me a minute, Wee Phil? I've just this moment got Arthur to bring down off of some acid trip he's on."

"MM. I am in hiding!" Arthur shouted into the phone.

"Well, ye'll not be in hidin' long if ye keep yellin' like a banshee. Now I'm thinkin' the best thing for ye to do is get yerself down to me Michael's police station first thing and turn yerself in."

"What?"

"Yes. Turn yerself in at Michael's. Be sure to have that video with ye. Show it to the lads there and ye'll be a free ma— free person in no time. And then after that, I need ye to get to Max's school to catch the criminals that have been terrorizin' them all."

"And what about you?"

"What about me?"

"How are you going to get out of this impersonating-a-lawyer thingy."

"Ach, I think Bridget and her lads will be all too glad to just let it go into the wind once we bring in the real killer."

"Not that I'm siding with Michael on this, MM, but you did kind of probably break a lot of laws."

"As I said to me Michael, ye will recall: the courts themselves should be embarrassed that a woman with as little formal education as meself could so adequately defend an accused killer. Nothin' will come of this. Trust me."

"I don't know—"

"Ach, the logic behind it is too complicated for me mind to unravel to ye in this moment, and we have a murderer on the loose besides. Get yerself out of the mess yer in, and then come by Michael's house tomorrow, and we'll go from there."

"Okay, but before I go, let me tell you about Ashleigh's brother," Arthur said.

"We've no time for that."

"He's a suspect, MM. And if they don't let me out once I turn myself in, it's important that you're up to speed on everything."

"Let me guess: her brother and all of the lads in the band are a bunch of drunken layabouts thinkin' they'll be the next U2."

"Uh, yeah. Pretty much. Except it's drugs, not booze for them."

"Grand. Now get yerself cleaned up for the mornin'. Ye've got a big day ahead. Call me if ye need me once ye get to the police station. Remember, yer lawyer's name is Tara Rafferty."

"I don't have a lawyer, MM."

"Has someone completely let the air out of yer tires? Between ye, Michael, and Francis, 'tis a wonder I can keep us on an even keel. And no more of that 'd l' or whatever 'tis yer takin'. Ye have to be clean and sober as a church mouse for the mornin.'"

"Okay, MM," Arthur said. "There's just one thing."

"And what would that happen to be?"

"I'm in hiding."

"So ye said."

"And I'm not at home."

"I'll see ye here at Michael's after ye turn in that tape," Mary-Margaret said, clicking off her cell phone before she said something she knew she'd regret.

Chapter Twenty-Two

Mary-Margaret figured there had to be a rut in the floor between the living room and the kitchen by now, given how many times she had paced back and forth on it since she woke up this morning. It was mid-day and even Phil had stopped following her and was now curled up, exhausted, on one of the wingback chairs.

She was just about to turn the gas off under the burner of the boiling kettle and make herself another cup of tea when she heard a light knock on the stained-glass window beside the back door.

"Jesus, Mary, and Joseph," Mary-Margaret said, pulling Arthur inside and giving him a big hug. "I was beginnin' to fear—"

"I'm okay, MM. You were right."

"Of course I was, luv. Now, what is me Michael goin' to do about catchin' the murderer?"

"Nothing," Arthur said, reaching around Mary-Margaret to make the tea. "You're almost out of McVities. Not to worry. I've got a stash at home that I'll bring over next time."

"What do ye mean nothin'? Ye've all but led him to the murderer, and the lad's still sittin' on his duff? Where's me phone? I'll give him a ring."

"MM, it's not his case, remember?"

"'Tis not ours either, and look where we've come with it. We found the bones. We found the head. We found the accomplice. What else do these lads need?" she said, throwing her hands in the air. "Never mind the madness of yer band boy dreamin' of becomin' Bono: I'm beginnin' to think Michael and the lads he works with all sit at their desks imaginin' themselves to be—"

"If I had a choice, I'd be Angie Dickinson in—"

"Focus, lad. Focus," Mary-Margaret said.

"Right. Okay, let's map out what we know. Oh, and I almost forgot," Arthur said, pouring the boiling water into the teapot, "Michael said you still need to sort out your impersonation thing before tomorrow."

"Ach, always lookin' at the trees, that one. Never seein' the forest. I love him like a limb, but I do wonder if he's not a genius on the installment plan some days." Mary-Margaret pulled a pen and pad of paper out of the junk drawer. "Here. If we have to give them a ruddy map to their killer, then let's get writin'."

Arthur stared at her as she gave the teapot a swirl.

"I never thought I'd see the day—"

"I know," Mary-Margaret said with a sigh. "But, we've a lot of work ahead of us. No time to wait for the tea to steep. Now, are ye goin' to pour us a mug or not?"

Once the tea was poured, Mary-Margaret took her mug and plunked herself down at the head of the dining room table. Arthur followed behind a mug in one hand, the plate of biscuits, and the pad and pen in another.

"We know Cassandra Lewis is dead," Mary-Margaret said, pointing to the chair to her right. "Don't be fumblin' the ball now, lad. Take yer seat and get writin'."

"Hang on," Arthur said, setting everything down on the table in front of him.

"Ye've never worked as wait staff, have ye," Mary-Margaret said, flinching at the awkwardness of his movements.

"Not officially, but there was this one time—"

"Never mind. Just get writin'," she directed. "And we know it was her head that was in the bag behind the house here. We know the bones are also Cassand—"

"Do we?" Arthur asked, looking over at her, his eyebrow arched.

"Almost," she replied.

"I don't think this is a detail we can gloss over, MM."

"Well, I'm sayin' they are, and Franci—me sources—tell me that they've got chemicals—"

"Of course. Chemicals that a taxidermist would have," Arthur said, his eyes narrowing.

"Which means that our lad at the gas station was lyin'."

"You mean about finding the bones in the washroom?"

"I've been in a lot of public toilets in me day, Arthur, and I've never found a bag of bones in any of them, so I'm wonderin' if he found the whole body in the jacks."

"That makes more sense," he said, taking a couple of biscuits from the plate.

"Right around the corner from me own grandson's home." Mary-Margaret shook her head. "Ach, what's the world comin' to?"

"Maybe she OD'd."

"And," Mary-Margaret added, "that emaciated young profligate couldn't get the body out in one piece, so he decided to take it home. But couldn't do it in one go, so he brought the chemicals for the bones to the shop."

"That makes no sense, MM."

"Have ye started sharin' a brain with Billy Gilly, lad?" Mary-Margaret exclaimed. "Let's go over it again: our lad finds Cassandra Lewis dead in the bathroom. Wants to do whatever 'tis he does—"

"Taxidermy."

"Indeed," Mary-Margaret said, curling her lip. "But can't get the body out. Decides to clear the bones and take the head whole. But he's goin' to need to do it in two trips. And—"

"And I happen to intercept him both times," Arthur finished.

"Just as well. Can ye imagine if Michael's Tinny-Boys had seen him? Likely offer him a can and carry on."

They both paused to have a sip of tea.

"So we're not lookin' at a murder per se. Just a lad who fancies himself a taxidermist for humans."

"Stranger things have happened," Arthur said, shoving another biscuit in his mouth.

"Which lets Maeve off the hook. This time."

"That was harsh, MM," Arthur said after he'd chewed enough to speak.

"Ye have never met an Irishwoman who feels she's been taken advantage of, have ye?"

"And she has no connection that we know of with our guy," Arthur said, choosing not to wonder what had happened to anyone who had ever crossed Mary-Margaret.

"So we've no murder at all," she concluded, the tone of her voice betraying her disappointment.

"If we agree that she was found dead in the washroom of a self-induced overdose, then no."

Mary-Margaret took a long sip of her tea.

"What if," she said, perking up again, "what if she was found dead in the washroom because her body was dumped there?"

"It's possible," Arthur said with a shrug, taking another biscuit.

"What if her body was dumped there, and our lad was tasked with gettin' rid of it as he saw fit?"

"Sure. Why not?"

"Then let's look a little closer into that idea before we shut the door on this bein' an overdose."

"Without anyone willing to say they saw someone dump a body—" Arthur began to object.

"Perhaps ye should give up yer job cleanin' and consider a career with the police department if that's yer attitude," Mary-Margaret scoffed. "Did ye not see the video camera starin' at us when we were speakin' to the lad? And did ye not notice that the jacks was just off to our left, which means anyone usin' it would have been filmed?"

"No. I was too busy. And how did you notice where the washroom was anyway?" Arthur asked, not sure if he should be impressed or concerned.

"I've had four children, luv," she replied, nibbling on a biscuit she'd taken. "Between rearin' them and me body agin', I've made it me business to know where to find the jacks, no matter where I am. Now, if we can look at the video on the day Cassandra's body ended up where it did, we'll know how it got there."

"And you think DJ Beats—"

"Who?" Mary-Margaret asked.

"The gas station guy. You think he's just going to hand over the video, assuming it even exists?"

"Well, he's either handin' it over to us or to the police. And if I go on me own, I'm thinkin' I'd be treatin' him a wee bit better than Billy Gilly's lads would."

"I don't know, MM. If this guy could cut off someone's head, I don't think you should be going in alone."

"Angus Corrigan is always buyin' gas for that foreign car of his. I can always give him a ring and have him fill up while I'm talkin' to our lad."

"I don't think we have time. And we don't want too many people involved. Too risky. I've got a better plan. How about we do this sooner than later and I cover you. You won't even know I'm there."

"But what about goin' to Max's school?"

"Hmm. Determine whether or not a woman was murdered or catch the kid who's been stealing his classmates' textbooks. Which one should I do today?"

"No need to be sarcastic. 'Tis organized crime, Arthur. In me own grandson's school. Hardly somethin' to be triflin'over."

"I do many things," Arthur said pointedly. "But I *never* trifle."

Mary-Margert took a sip of tea to stop herself from responding.

"Before we get ourselves too focused on this wannabe Carl Akeley—"

"Come again?"

"Carl Akeley, only the most famous taxidermist ever."

"Of course," Mary-Margaret replied, sighing deeply and rolling her eyes. "How could I ever have not known that?"

"Don't be too hard on yourself, MM," Arthur said, taking the last biscuit from the plate. "I have a remarkable mind for trivial information. My point is: have we for sure ruled out your friend at O'Leary's or anyone linked to the pub having anything to do with Cassandra's death?"

"Well, Michael hasn't said, but honestly, lad, as if the likes of them would be involved in this sordid business," Mary-Margaret said with a sniff.

"We can't rule anyone out, MM."

"Yes, we can, and we have. Maeve, as temperamental with the emphasis on mental as she can be, is definitely not the type."

"Okay, but let's keep thinking."

"I've not completely ruled out the possibility that there's some sort of an English connection," Mary-Margaret said.

"Is there whiskey in your mug, MM?" Arthur said, trying not to laugh at her suggestion.

"Ye heard the way that lad spoke at the gas station," Mary-Margaret exclaimed with pitch piercing enough to cause Wee Phil's ears to perk up despite having been dead asleep at the other end of the house.

"MM, he's not—"

"Really? So he's just a crazy-arsed lad who likes cutting dead bodies up and there's where we stop, then. Is that what yer sayin'?" she asked, crossing her arms resolutely in front of her.

"Not quite. Remember, Ashleigh's brother was Cassandra's boyfriend."

"But ye told me before that it couldn't be the boyfriend. Too easy," Mary-Margaret said and then leaned down after Phil hopped off the living room chair and came over to her. "Is it a walk ye need, or are we bein' too loud in here?"

"No, you said that. And reconsidered. And we now know that he's quite involved in drugs."

"Quite involved?" Mary-Margaret said, scratching behind Phil's right ear. "And how would ye know?"

"She told me," Arthur said, looking at the empty plate. "I wish *you'd* have told me you needed more McV—"

"Well, that does shine a bit more of a light on her brother then, doesn't it? And if he's as involved as ye say, I wonder if the other lads in the band are also wrapped up in them. They're all on them these days, aren't they? The drugs. Not like in my day."

Arthur rolled his eyes.

"Well, maybe some were," Mary-Margaret said. "But 'twas just after the '60s. No comparison. Anyway, if the lads in the band are all into the drugs, do ye think Cassandra was as well? Maybe the girl got murdered on account of some drug deal gone bad."

"So, where does the gas station guy come in?"

"All ye have to do is take one look at him, luv. He's all about the drugs, that one."

"I thought you said—"

"Stay close. The plot's evolvin'. 'Tis a shame, really, the way they get these young ones hooked, and then they're off their pins for life."

"It's not quite like that, MM."

"And ye would know this how? Don't be tellin' me yer into this rubbish, Arthur Lukowitz, because if ye are," Mary-Margaret scolded, her blue eyes blazing, "I can't have ye around me Max until ye get yerself sorted out. Now, I'll pay for rehab if that's what's—"

"Don't worry," Arthur cut in. "I'm not. I just know a lot of people—"

"Just ye mind who yer associatin' with, luv. The strength of a man is found in the measure of his five best mates."

"I don't have five *best mates*."

"Oh," Mary-Margaret said and then added after a long pause. "Well, ye've got me, and I'm as good as five. Now, back to mappin' out our investigation."

"Right," Arthur said, taking a deep breath. "So we've got Ashleigh on the far end. And we've got the brother."

"Motive?"

"Drugs, MM. A very expensive habit."

"And what about the other lads in the band? Or maybe it was all of them." Arthur looked at Mary-Margaret with surprise.

"Since we're lookin' at all possibilities, why not? Maybe they just killed her and dumped her body. And what about their drug dealer? We have no idea how far up the chain this—"

Just then, Mary-Margaret's cell phone rang. She got up to retrieve it from the counter in the kitchen.

"Hello?" she said.

"Oh, thank goodness you answered," Louise said and then gave a sigh.

"And why wouldn't I?" Mary-Margaret demanded.

"Because you missed your appointment."

"Ach, and so I have," Mary-Margaret said, her demeanor shifting from indignation to remorse. "I'm so sorry, luv."

"And Eleanor Corrigan says she hasn't heard from you all week," Louise continued.

"I can't get into the explanation of me absence with ye now, luv, but pencil me in for the same time next week, and I'll see ye then. And how do ye know Eleanor?"

"You referred her to me just a couple of weeks ago. It's not like you to not remember. Is everything alright, Mary-Margaret? Is something wrong?"

"No, no, luv. Nothin' 'tal. Just the usual. So next week, then. Be sure to bill me for missin' today. Bye-bye bye bye-bye-bye." Mary-Margaret quickly clicked off the phone.

"All good, MM?" Arthur called to her.

"Grand. Just grand. Missed me massage appointment, is all. Ach, yer practically doin' a jig, are ye, Wee Phil," she said, noticing the little dog running around in circles at the back door. "Arthur, start figurin' out where we're goin' to find this drug dealer while I take Wee Phil out the back."

Chapter Twenty-Three

"I see you've come to join us!" Doug called out.

"Have I now?" Mary-Margaret huffed, unable to avoid the neighborhood men gathered in the laneway.

"Good thing that dog's little," Charles said. "Otherwise, I'd blame you. I found a mountain of dog poop right by my car this morning."

"How do you know it's not his?" Johnny, a small man who always looked like he'd just rolled out of bed, asked, pointing with his beer can at the dog just emerging from the nearby bushes.

"Because the pile was about as big as he is."

There was something dangling from Phil's mouth.

"Don't tell me ye've found somethin' in the bushes," Mary-Margaret said, her shoulders dropping.

"It's just a leaf, Mary-Margaret," Doug said, reaching down for a beer. "Here. I'd offer you a whiskey, but it's in the house."

"Well, thanks be for this," Mary-Margaret said, taking the beer before bending down to pull the leaf off the dog's muzzle. "Ta, luv."

"I'm surprised to see you take that, Mary-Margaret," Charles said with a laugh.

"We're all here now, so we might as well make the best of it," she replied, looking at the unopened can. "I'll replace it for ye by tomorrow."

"What, you didn't even open it for the lady?" Johnny laughed.

"That's not how we operate back here, Mary-Margaret," Doug said.

"Ta. And don't ye worry, lad. I can still manage openin' a tin," Mary-Margaret said, holding the can of beer away from her as she awkwardly snapped the tab. "Sláinte."

"Sláinte," the three men said, raising their beers. They all took a sip.

"Any updates on the murder?" Doug asked.

"I'm surprised you're not a part of this now, Doug. You found the head, didn't you?" Charles asked.

"No, and I want no part of it," Doug stated, stepping back.

"I don't blame you," Charles said.

They all nodded in agreement and took another sip of beer.

"Ye lads have lived here a good while, haven't ye?" Mary-Margaret asked.

"Going on twenty years for me," Doug said. "You've been here almost as long as me, haven't you, Charles?"

"Oh, no. We moved in way after you. The place was a dump," Charles replied. "I don't know how the previous owners even lived in it."

"That's grand," Mary-Margaret said, already tiring of her companions' banter. "And I'm thinkin' there's been a fair amount of criminal activity in this laneway over the years."

"Oh, you can say that again," Charles said.

"I used to chase the hookers out in the morning on my way to the shop," Johnny added, his eyes lighting up. "Good times."

"But I don't think anyone's ever found a head in a bag. You've topped us all," Charles said with a laugh.

"That's why we got the city to put in lighting back then. To stop the hooker traffic. It's not much, but it's something," Doug said.

"But there's still likely drug dealin' goin' on back here?" Mary-Margaret asked.

"Hey, I buy my drugs at the pot shop around the corner," Johnny said with a laugh.

"You know, I think the government should just decriminalize it all," Charles said. "I mean, what business is it of mine if—"

"But there is still dealin' goin' on, no?" Mary-Margaret persisted.

"Not as much as there used to be. I'm out here a lot with the dog, and as you know yourself, the laneway is pretty well used nowadays," Doug said.

"Oh, I get it," Johnny said. "You're thinking the girl was caught in some drug thing. I would have said prostitution, but I don't know of anyone who would go to the trouble of cutting a hooker's head off."

"Hmmm," Mary-Margaret said. "I'd not considered the sex end of it."

"That's because you're a woman," Charles said with a laugh. "No offense, of course."

"None taken." Mary-Margert looked at the open can in her hand, then took a sip.

"You coulda got the lady a cup at least," Johnny said.

"No, lads, I'm fine. I'm just thinkin' about the time and how I've got to get dinner goin'."

"What? Can't Mikey make his own dinner?" Johnny laughed.

"It's not quite like that," Mary-Margaret replied. She looked at the tin again.

"I'm sure he'll be fine if his dinner's a bit late, Mary-Margaret," Doug said. "Finish your beer with us."

"Truth be told, I'm not a big beer drinker."

"Not that I don't believe you, Mary-Margaret," Charles said, "but, if that's so, you're the first Irish person I've ever heard say that."

"Well, be that as it may, I've got to get home. Thanks for the tinnie, Douglas."

* * *

"I was starting to worry," Arthur said while rummaging through Michael's kitchen cupboards.

"About?"

"You. You said you were just taking Phil out, and I thought the cops might have picked you up."

"If they'd been back there, the paddy wagon would have been full, what with all the alcohol flowin'. Now, what do ye know about prostitutes?"

"Pardon?" Arthur sputtered, turning to stare at his friend.

"Ladies of the evenin'. Hookers. Ye know—"

"Yes, I know what they are, but why would I know anything about that?"

Mary-Margaret raised an eyebrow.

"I don't know anyone who pays to play, if that's what you're asking."

"Do ye think our girl might have been involved in it somehow?" Mary-Margaret asked, reaching down to pull the cast iron frying pan out from the bottom cupboard. "Oof, I don't know why Michael doesn't just store this in the oven."

"Maybe he'd forget and turn the oven on?"

"Me Michael?" Mary-Margaret pushed past Arthur to get to the fridge. She pulled out some stewing beef and carrots. "I don't think he's ever used an oven. By the way, grab me some potatoes from that bin over there. So what if our girl was a prostitute? Ach, 'tis no wonder they got rid of her. Can ye imagine? At O'Leary's? That'd be the end of the business and all."

"I can add that to our list of things to find out."

"Do ye honestly believe—" Mary-Margaret said, washing the vegetables in the sink.

"Why not? O'Leary's wouldn't be the first bar—"

"Pub."

"To run prostitutes."

"I can't imagine it. My local. A brothel."

Arthur shrugged. "Why not?"

"Because I know," she said, cutting the potatoes and carrots into pieces.

"And maybe Maeve found out that Cassandra was a prostitute and didn't want her type in the pub."

"So she just made up the story of the thievin' to get her sacked?"

"Exactly. As you've said, O'Leary's isn't that kind of place, but it only takes one or two bad apples to bring a place down."

"Indeed."

Mary-Margaret grimaced when she saw that the large pot she wanted was at the back of the upper corner cupboard.

"Clearly, was Carmen who set up the kitchen. Doubt she was much of a cook, either. 'Tis a wonder they all didn't starve in this house," she said. "Can you reach up and grab that for me, luv?"

"Have you noticed a change in the clientele over the last few weeks?"

Arthur asked as he scrambled up on the counter and got it down. "That's a sure sign."

"Now that ye mention it…" she considered, filling the pot with water and setting it on the stove to boil.

"I rest my case. And now that I'm a free man, I'm going home."

"Yer not stayin' for me stew then?" Mary-Margaret asked, putting the cubed meat in the frying pan.

"I'm a vegan, MM, so no."

"So that means ye don't eat meat or anythin' good?"

"I don't eat meat or anything that comes from animals or fish."

"What's left?" Mary-Margaret asked. "Away with ye then. But don't go wanderin' off too far."

* * *

"Are ye comin' or goin', me son, and is it breakfast or dinner I'm makin' for ye?" Mary-Margaret asked when Michael came into the kitchen.

"It's Wednesday, so it must be day shift," Michael said with a laugh. "Although I'd eat whatever you put in front of me right about now."

"Grand. I was just makin' a wee bit of a stew. Tryin' to get some veg into Max, which between yer lack of veg on hand and all the comin's and goin's around here…"

"Oh, don't worry about him. He's out tonight."

"What, and on a school night? Will he be needin' a ride home, and why wasn't I told?"

"He's fine, Mom. He can make his own way home. Smells good."

"With a murderer lurkin' out our back step?" Mary-Margaret said, taking the lid off the pot to give the stew a stir.

"I don't think there's a murderer lurking anywhere, Mom," Mike said, grabbing a spoon from the drawer to sample his mother's cooking.

"Well, ye saw the evidence Arthur brought into yer work today," Mary-Margaret said. "What do ye think? Does it stand up?"

"Mmm," Michael said. "Pretty good. And no, I didn't see anything. It's not my case."

"Then let me enlighten ye," Mary-Margaret said, turning to face Michael, holding the pot lid in front of her like a shield. "The lad at the gas station around the corner confessed to droppin' the bones in the laneway. And I'm sayin' the head. So…"

"I don't need to know any of this, Mom," Michael said as he dropped the spoon in the sink and began to walk away.

"What about community safety?" Mary-Margaret asked, following behind him after putting the lid back on the pot. "I'm surprised yer lads haven't released some bulletin or somethin' warnin' us all."

"About what?" he said, not stopping.

"Ach, Michael. Are ye willfully slow to the races this evenin', or are ye workin' at it? And why didn't ye tell me about the sex trade that goes on in the back."

"What?" Michael said, turning around to look at his mother.

"Ye heard me. Put a roof on it, and ye'd have a brothel out back."

"Hardly," Michael said, shaking his head. "Who've you been talking to?"

"It matters not."

"And since when do you drink beer from a can?"

"What?"

"I saw the can on the counter in the kitchen, Mom. What's up?"

"Well then, clearly ye know who I've been talkin' to, don't ye?"

"They got you having a drink with them, did they?" Michael smiled, then turned to go up the stairs.

"Hardly. Just findin' out that yer back lane is riddled with ladies of the evening and always has been."

"There are no ladies back there, Mom," Michael said as he ascended the stairs. "And it's been a long time since we've had hookers. Drugs, yes. Hookers, no."

"So ye do admit that there is criminal activity in the laneway, then," she called up to him.

"There's criminal activity everywhere. You know that," he called back, walking towards his bedroom.

"And our server at the pub's head ends up back there, too. Do ye not see any connections, Michael?"

"I'm sure Homicide has it well in hand, Mom."

"Billy Gilly, ye mean? Hardly." She heard something in the kitchen. "Ach, and there's me stew boilin' over. Michael, come down and talk to me."

While Mary-Margaret removed the lid, turned off the heat, and gave the stew a stir, Michael reappeared in the kitchen, leaving his jacket and tie upstairs.

"Look, you're in enough trouble as it is, Mom." He took a couple of bowls out from the cupboard. "Can you just focus on that before—"

"Before ye arrest me? What do you think I'm doin' now, lad?" She slammed the wooden spoon down on the counter beside the stove. "I've not been to me yoga in a week. I've not gone to me book club. Me massage therapist is callin' to make sure I'm not dead. I'm livin' undercover. On the *down low*. I've not even gone to the pub for lunch."

"But you've been poking around," Michael said, setting the bowls down on the counter.

"Tryin' to solve yer murder, yes," Mary-Margaret said, scooping the stew into them.

"It's not my murder, and I would spend my time trying to sort out how you're going to explain yourself in court," Michael said, getting two large spoons out of the drawer.

"*Explain meself?*" Mary-Margaret exclaimed, topping up the bowl so forcefully that the stew splashed all over the counter. "Ach, Michael. We've covered this, lad. When I hand over the murderer to ye, and when that judge—a nice woman, but she seemed a bit tightly wound—hears what's happened, it'll all be yesterday's news."

"Well, until that time," Michael said, wiping the counter with a dishcloth, "I'd be laying low if I were you."

"Ye said I have until Friday. And here we are at Wednesday. And now that Arthur's got his affairs sorted..."

"Yeah. About that," Mike said, picking up the bowls. "I wouldn't exactly say they're *sorted*. He still has to—"

Mary-Margaret put her hand to her chest and began to cough. It was a slow, deep cough at first, but it quickly escalated into something that sounded more like she was choking. Michael set the bowls down and took his mother by the arm, leading her to her chair at the dining room table.

"Are you all right, Mom?" he said, a look of genuine concern on his face.

"Ach, 'tis just the pneumonia, lad. I'll be fine," she replied, pulling a tissue from her pocket to wipe her eyes.

"Have you heard anything more from the doctor?"

"Michael, when ye get to be a woman of a certain age, there's not much a doctor can do for ye."

Again, before he could respond, Mary-Margaret burst into a volley of coughs.

"Perhaps I'd best just get meself up to me bed. Can ye just bring up me bowl with perhaps a bit of a bun or some bread and be sure to get Wee Phil out a few more times before ye head off to bed yerself."

With that, Mary-Margaret headed towards the stairs. Then, hearing Michael stepping out the door after the dog, she returned to the kitchen, took a glass from the cupboard, retrieved the tin of beer, and went upstairs to her bedroom.

Chapter Twenty-Four

Mary-Margaret opened her eyes. She had heard something. She flicked on her bedside light and looked at her watch resting beside the lamp. Five past eleven. Voices. It was voices she was hearing. She put a robe on over her pajamas and headed down the stairs to see who was talking so loudly at this ungodly hour.

"Ach, me son," she said softly as she quietly stepped past his sleeping body and turned off the TV, but not before seeing Janelle Austin announce that the police had positively identified the bones Arthur had found as those belonging to Cassandra Lewis.

"Michael," she said, gently shaking his shoulder, careful not to startle Phil, who was curled up on his lap.

"Huh? Wha—?"

"'Tis alright, son. 'Tis just yer mam."

"What's this—"

"'Tis only Wee Phil, luv. He'll jump down, won't ye, pup?"

Phil jumped off Michael's lap, shook himself, and made his way to the back door.

"What time is it?"

"Time to be headin' up to bed. But did ye hear what that Janelle Austin woman was sayin' on the telly?"

"Oh no," Michael moaned.

"Yer lads have identified the bones. 'Tis our thievin' barmaid."

"I wish you would stop calling her that, Mom," Michael said, rolling his neck. "Not that it matters, I suppose."

180

"Well, 'tis either that that got her sacked, or she's involved in the drugs," Mary-Margaret said, her eyes on the TV screen.

"Drugs? I thought you were hot and heavy about her being a hooker."

"No, I'm not seein' it. Drugs is more likely."

Michael sighed.

"In the meantime, I think ye had better get Wee Phil out and, while yer at it, I'll get me list of suspects to show ye."

"Mom," Michael said, stretching his body as he slowly got out of the chair, "it's late, it's not my case, and you've been cautioned—"

"Not this time," she corrected.

"I believe the caution from the first murder stands."

Michael walked slowly to the back door.

"'Tis easier to ask forgiveness than to ask permission," his mother called after him.

"Wish I'd known you felt that way when I was a kid," he called back.

"Which is to say: do ye want this murderer caught, or shall we all just live in fear?"

"I'm standing by with bated breath." He opened the back door to let the dog run out on his own.

"I'll just pop upstairs to get me notes. Put the kettle on while yer standin' there with yer gob hangin' open, will ye?"

* * *

"Sticheedoon while I make us a cuppa," Mary-Margaret said, dropping two Barry's tea bags into the teapot before filling it with the water from the kettle that had just come to a boil. Michael sat down and put his head in his hands.

"Here. Take a look at this," his mother said from behind, passing an open steno pad over his shoulder.

"What is it?"

"Suspects. Did ye not hear me say I was goin' to go over me suspect list with ye?" She headed back to the kitchen.

"Right. Sorry. I forgot."

"Honesty, me son, I think ye need to be gettin' more sleep or somethin'. Yer not runnin' on all cylinders these days."

Michael rolled his eyes.

Mary-Margaret returned with the tea tray. "Here's yer tea and a few biscuits. Now, what do ye make of the list."

Michael looked at the pad and then took a biscuit from the plate.

"Well?"

"Well, what? It's a list with names on it. Doesn't mean anything to me."

"Ach, me son. No wonder yer not—"

"No, that's not why," he said, passing the pad back up to her. "It's because I spend my time trying to keep you out of trouble."

"Trouble? Here I am, likely solvin' another murder, and ye say I cause trouble. Not on all cylinders at all." Passing the pad back to her son, Mary-Margaret remained standing as she proceeded through the list.

Once she had finished, being sure to point out that Maeve O'Leary couldn't possibly be a serious suspect, she sat down at her spot at the end of the table and waited for Michael to nod in agreement. When he did not, she continued.

"And then there's yer drug dealer and yer pimp."

"I'm not seeing drug dealer or pimp here, Mom," Michael said with a smile, scanning the list she'd given him.

"I canna be doin' all yer detective work, lad," Mary-Margaret exclaimed. "And I've only just uncovered that possible connection recently."

She took a sip of tea.

"I have to go to bed, Mom," Michael said, pushing his mug away.

"And then there's the possibility that she wasn't murdered at all. Just overdosed in the gas station washroom."

"And where did you hear that?"

"But we can't rule out murder or foul play at the very least first. Let's consider Occam's razor."

"Mom," Michael said, standing up, "I'm tired, and I'm concerned that you're getting too inv—"

"What if she was murdered, and it was the boyfriend, and he tasked the lad at the gas station to get rid of the body?"

CHAPTER TWENTY-FOUR

"A huge leap, but okay," Michael said, stretching his arms out in front of him.

"Why? The two lads are likely the same age. Likely involved in the same sort of things. Likely know each other."

"And where are you drawing all of these inferences from?"

"Logic, me son."

"What logic? Do you know how many young guys live in this city?"

"Ach, clearly I do not, and 'tis a logic too complicated for me mind to unravel to ye in this moment."

"Clearly. I'm off to bed now," Michael grabbed another biscuit from the plate.

"'Tis the drugs," Mary-Margaret said. "That's the connection we've been lookin' for."

"What?"

"The lads in the band. All addicts. And the gas station terrorist. He's a dealer. And Cassandra was gettin' in the way. So he OD'd her. Haven't considered that, have ye?"

Michael shook his head as he ate the biscuit.

"Listen, me son. Ashleigh told Arthur—"

Michael froze.

"Arthur was talking to Ashleigh? When? How?"

"'Tis a long story, the endin' of which I'm about to tell ye."

"Go on," Michael said, sitting back down.

"Ashleigh told Arthur her brother and his lads were all heavily into the drugs. The girlfriends didn't like it. But the lads were too far gone. And maybe the other girls left, but Cassandra, bein' tied to two lads, couldn't."

"So why would anyone kill her, much less—"

"Ach, yer the big city detective, lad. Ye should know better than I why people kill. Maybe she was givin' them ultimatums or threatenin' to contact the police."

"Yeah, but then to…" He took a sip of the now-tepid tea.

"Our killer got scared. Didn't know what to do with the body. After all, they're only young lads."

"I don't know, Mom," Michael slowly said. "There's a lot of speculation involved here."

"Well, there doesn't have to be if yer lads would get off their duffs and do some investigatin'."

"I'm sure they're doing plenty of investigating, just not following your theory."

"Do I have to connect all the dots for ye, then?"

"I tell you what. Why don't I get Detective Sergeant Gi—"

"Why do ye waste yer breath? Is there no one else ye can call right now?" Mary-Margaret said, suddenly getting up.

"No."

"What about our Mandy?"

"No."

"So ye mean to tell me that there's not a single homicide detective available at the moment?" she said, taking her mug into the kitchen.

"Not for this, no," Mike called after her.

"Well, if ye won't make the call, then I'm calling our Mandy."

"Mom, you can't. You're wanted, remember?" Mike joined her in the kitchen.

"Ach. God must be testin' me. Then find me someone else that ye can call. Surely a lad with as much clout as ye do would know someone."

Realizing that he had no choice, Michael pulled his cell phone out of his pocket.

"You working, Joe? It's Mike O'Shea. You got a minute?"

* * *

"So," the paunchy detective said as she opened the front door to him. "This is the famous Mary-Margaret O'Shea,"

"Well, I wouldn't say famous," Mary-Margaret began, bringing her hand up to her mouth and lowering her eyes as her cheeks reddened a little.

"No need to be modest, Mrs. O'Shea. Everyone in Homicide knows about you." Smiling warmly at her, he undid his suit jacket and hoisted up his black pants before pulling his tie closer to the straining top button of his white shirt. "My name is Joe D'Angelo, and I understand you may have some information that will help us."

"Come in, lad. Sitcheedoon at the table, if ye don't mind. Can I get ye a cuppa, or would ye prefer a coffee? I understand ye lads like yer coffee here in America."

"Really, Mom?" Michael said, standing up to shake his colleague's hand. "Thanks for coming by, Joe. I appreciate it."

"Tea would be fine, Mrs. O'Shea. That is what you Irish drink, isn't it?"

"Ye mean when we're not drinkin' whiskey?" Mary-Margaret asked, giving him a wink before going into the kitchen.

"I'm sorry to bring you out," Michael began.

"No problem, buddy. I'm working anyway, as you can see," Joe said, motioning at his suit. "And your mom *has* been the talk of the unit for a while now."

"I bet," Michael said with a sigh.

Mary-Margaret returned and placed a mug of tea where Michael had been sitting.

"Ach, such a lovely lad, are ye, Joseph. Michael, where are yer manners? Step over so yer friend can sit down."

Michael shuffled over to the next seat and sat down as Mary-Margaret dropped herself in her spot and looked up at the detective.

"Sit, luv. And be sure to help yerself to a wee biscuit or two. I can see that ye don't hold back as a rule, so there's no point startin' now."

Michael cringed.

"Ha. You've got that right, Mrs. O'Shea. I'm Italian, as you probably figured out, and we Italians like our pasta." Joe took a couple of biscuits from the plate. "Now, Mike says you have some intel that might lead us to our murderer. Is that correct?"

"Well, I wouldn't say intel, per se, but I've got a feelin'"

"Great," Joe said, pulling his memo book from his pocket.

Michael pushed the steno pad Mary-Margaret had been using towards Joe.

"How about you just write things down on this," Michael said. "Might be easier than using your memo book."

"Okay. Sure," Joe said with a knowing look, putting his memo book back in his pocket. "I get it. So let's start at the beginning, shall we, Mrs. O'Shea."

After Mary-Margaret repeated the information that she had given her son, Joe put his pen down, took a sip of the tea that had gone cold, and stood up.

"I really appreciate your sharing all of this with me, Mrs. O'Shea. I'll be sure to have someone follow it up in the morning."

Mary-Margaret opened her mouth to object.

"Oh, believe me, Mrs. O'Shea, if it wasn't two a.m., I'd have officers speaking to everyone now, but, given the time...." He let his words trail off.

"Ach, of course. And two in the mornin', is it? Michael, ye've got to be up in a few hours. I don't know how ye lads do it, workin' day and night like this. And I've got to get me beauty sleep. And where's Max? The lad has school to—"

"He came home a couple of hours ago, Mom. Snuck up the stairs," Michael said.

"And me not hearin' it? I don't believe ye."

"He's very good at it."

"I remember doing that when I was a kid. Except I was sneaking out. My poor folks," Joe said, reaching his hand out. "Well, I won't keep you any longer. It's been a pleasure, Mrs. O'Shea, and thanks for all of this."

"Ye will let me know..." Mary-Margaret said as she shook Joe's hand vigorously.

"Of course. In the meantime, while I'm sure I don't have to tell you to be very careful with these people. If I were you, I'd just keep my nose out of it from here on in."

Mary-Margaret nodded.

"You've given us some good—I mean great—leads, Mrs. O'Shea," Joe said, folding up the paper and stuffing it in his jacket pocket as Mike led him to the front door. "Now, let us do our jobs. 'Night, Mike."

"Did you hear that, Mom?" Michael said once the detective had gone. "Let them do their jobs."

"What I heard is that I gave him some grand leads. And if they were doin' their jobs, we wouldn't have to be havin' these midnight meetin's, would we? Now, I'm away to take me face off. If yer needin' the bathroom, best get in now because it'll be takin' me a while. Beauty costs, me son. And the price I pay gets steeper every year."

Chapter Twenty-Five

There are very few people who can pull off wearing black flats, a short pink dress with a white apron attached, and a '60s flip hairstyle wig, including Arthur. There are even fewer people who believe they can. Arthur was one of those people, so he arrived at the back door of Michael's house dressed as such.

"Ach, ye scared me," Mary-Margaret said, freezing in the kitchen entranceway just as Arthur sashayed in.

"Sorry, MM. I assumed you'd still be asleep, so I just let myself in with my cleaner's key."

"Right.'Tis Thursday, isn't it? But did ye honestly think I'd be asleep? At this hour of the day? Although, with that detective over last night, 'tis a wonder—"

"There was a detective here? Have they caught the murderer? Have they caught you?"

"Drop yer gear, put the kettle on, and we'll have a wee catch-up."

After she filled him in over tea and biscuits, Arthur scratched his wig.

"The lad last night said they'd be workin' on me leads straight away this morning. Did ye see them in the laneway then?"

"No. But we're the ones who have to catch the murderer, remember? To keep them from arresting—"

"That's all said and done," Mary-Margaret interrupted.

"So you've sorted out that lying to the courts thing?"

"Oh, that. Right. Well, no," she had to admit. "But I don't believe that I was exactly lying, if push comes to shove."

"You said you were my lawyer, MM."

"I don't think I actually did, come to think of it. In which case, the egg's on them for not checkin', not me."

"MM, we have to act fast. You're still in a lot of trouble, and we've only got one day before…" Arthur let his words drop, bringing his wrists together as if in handcuffs.

"If they want to push it, I suppose yer right," Mary-Margaret conceded with a sigh.

"I say we do what you said yesterday."

"Which is?"

"You go in and shake down the gas station guy while I keep six outside."

"Let me think on it. So much has changed. In the meantime, I'll just let Wee Phil out for a piddle," Mary-Margaret said, taking the mugs into the kitchen with the dog bouncing behind her.

"It's our only hope," Arthur said, following her. "We're one step ahead of Michael's boys, and they're circling fast."

Mary-Margaret considered this for a moment and then looked closer at Arthur.

"Do ye think yer dressed for it?"

"Oh, don't worry, MM. I can transform into a ninja in the snap of a finger."

* * *

"There are security cameras everywhere, so don't try anything," the scrawny gas station attendant called out when Mary-Margaret entered the gas bar, his Cockney accent gone.

"I'm just here to talk to ye, luv."

"Unless you're buying gas, get out."

"Unless," Mary-Margaret said, looking at the rows of junk food, over-priced essential groceries, and cheap toys that could be found in every gas bar shop, "ye want this place crawlin' with policemen, I think ye'd best to be talkin' to me."

The man, who today looked even more to Mary-Margaret like the rodents he preserved for posterity, narrowed his eyes, lifted his chin, and slowly nodded. She approached the counter.

"If there was a time when ye'd like to turn yer pumps off, this might be it," Mary-Margaret continued, her voice firm but warm.

Without taking his eyes off of her, the young man reached below the counter and flipped a switch. At the same time, there was a loud thump.

"What was that?" the man asked, a slight glow that became a patch of sweat appearing on his forehead. He looked to his right out of the huge window that overlooked the pumps before hurrying around the counter to the glass doors.

"'Tis yer shop, lad. Not mine. Could it be yer pumps shuttin' off?" Mary-Margaret asked, knowing full well that it was not.

"Dunno. Maybe. But I thought it was from the roof."

"Likely just some squirrels, then," she said, a sinking feeling that the noise likely had something to do with Arthur beginning to wash over her. "If yer lucky, maybe one or two of the mangey rodents will fall off, and ye can take them home."

The attendant leered at Mary-Margaret as he locked the glass doors and returned to his perch behind the counter.

"Talk. I'll give you five minutes, and then I've gotta turn the pumps back on. They check the receipts. My boss will go for a five-minute lull in customers, but not much longer at this hour of the day."

There was a scratching sound from above now, as if something was being dragged. The attendant looked up.

"Likely birds. Peckin' away. And gettin' into it with the squirrels," Mary-Margaret said.

"I've never heard that before."

"Because ye've never listened. Got all this buzzin' and bingin' goin' on with the pumps, and ye've likely got yer ears stuffed with those things ye all use now, listenin' to the rubbish ye call music. But that's of no mind to me. I want to talk to ye about those bones."

"What about them?" the attendant said, crossing his arms.

"I'm thinkin' that Sister Augustine might have…intimidated ye a bit last time, such that ye might not have been as forthcomin' as ye'd have liked to be. Am I right, or am I right?"

The scraping sound from above seemed to be migrating from the back to the front of the building.

"Those aren't squirrels," he said, uncrossing his arms to place his hands on the counter that separated him from his inquisitor.

"And I'm sure ye would know, but 'tis none of our concern at the moment. What I'm askin'," Mary-Margaret continued, standing her ground while her voice got louder to drown out the noise from overhead, "is where those bones actually came from."

"I told you—" he said, leaning across the counter.

"Ye told me a story. That ye did, luv. Now, how about the truth?"

The attendant looked at Mary-Margaret, unmoved, his eyes flat.

"Me name is Mary-Margaret O'Shea," she began. "Me son is Police Detective Michael O'Shea. His lady friend is Bridget Calloway, the prosecutor who'll likely be presidin' over this matter once it gets to court. If ye start comin' clean, maybe we can all help ye out."

The young man didn't flinch, but sweat marks were becoming visible on his shirt.

"Let's start with yer name, shall we?"

The young man stepped back and looked her up and down before answering.

"Terry. My name is Terry."

Mary-Margaret saw something at the edge of the huge windows out of the corner of her eye. A hand appeared from the roof. An arm, covered by a black sweater, followed. The hand waved.

"Grand. So now, Terry," Mary-Margaret said, quickly turning her attention back to the young man. "Ye seem like a good lad. Ye've got a steady job, an…interestin' hobby. I'm thinkin' ye've got a place to lay yer hat and perhaps someone who's sweet on ye. So why get yerself involved in somethin' like this?"

Terry began biting his lower lip.

"I know a lad, Father Miguel is his name, who also bites his lip," Mary-

Margaret said, not wanting the conversation to stall. "Ye might consider droppin' by the church one day to have a wee talk with him. St. Francis of Assisi. It's a bit away from this neighborhood, but it might do ye a world of good."

"I know where it is," Terry said. "I live near there."

"Ah, so we're practically neighbors, then. When I'm not at me Michael's—the police detective son I was just mentionin'—that's where I live, too."

Mary-Margaret glanced quickly over at the window again and saw Arthur hanging upside down, peering in. "Raised me children in that house just around the corner from where ye likely live."

Mary-Margaret looked back at Terry, but not before noticing that he, too, might have seen something dangling from the roof.

"Listen, lad, here's what I'm thinkin'," she continued. "Yer not a bad sort, but ye've found yerself in somethin' that's gone a wee bit pear-shaped. By the looks of ye, yer goin' to have a terrible go of it with the police, but if ye come clean with me, and I'm not promisin' ye anythin'…."

Terry didn't respond.

"Or ye can wait for the police to track ye down and hope for the best. What'll it be, luv?"

A few seconds passed. And then a minute. And then another minute.

"I-I didn't kill anybody," he blurted out.

"I know you didn't, luv. So what happened?"

Terry gave a big sigh.

"I was out looking for dead things—squirrels, birds, you know—and thought I'd check the dumpster behind my building…"

"Yer in those old low rises right near the church, then?"

"Yeah. The units are falling apart, and the landlord sucks, but the rent is cheap."

"Well, there's somethin' to be said about that then, isn't there," she said with a nod. "So there ye are, doin' a little dumpster divin' and…?"

"So I figure I might get lucky and find a dog or a cat to work on. Kinda up my game, you know? I've come across them before, but never had the guts to restore one."

CHAPTER TWENTY-FIVE

"And on this particular day?" Mary-Margaret said, trying not to wince.

"Yeah. I'm standing on the side of the dumpster, and I see what looks like a hand, and I'm thinking either it's a mannequin or a really good score."

Mary-Margaret forcibly swallowed the bile that was building up in her mouth.

"I grab a stick and start pushing away the garbage bags, and I see that it's an entire body."

"And it didn't occur to ye to call the police?"

"Uh," Terry said, his brow furrowing, "no. I was thinking more about how I could get it up to my place without anyone seeing me and then how I'd, you know, position it once I got it, you know…."

"I see," Mary-Margaret said, even though she could not.

"Like, would I have it as my fake girlfriend, sitting on the couch, or—"

"I get the picture, lad," she said quickly. "So then what?"

"So then I hop in and grab the body out of the dumpster and just haul it up to my apartment."

"How?"

"I just kind of hold it as if it was my girlfriend who passed out."

"Because ye've done this bef—never mind. So there were no signs that she'd been murdered or…?"

"Oh yeah. The hair at the back of the head was matted in blood, but—"

"And ye still didn't think ye should call the police?" Mary-Margaret asked, reaching out to steady herself on the counter.

"No. To be honest, I was pretty pumped about the idea of restoring her. And I might have been a bit stoned at the time."

"Indeed. But how did yer…body end up as bones in me son's laneway?"

"Well, I kinda didn't take into consideration that this was going to be a massive project and would take time. I've only done little stuff and I just shove the specimens into my fridge or freezer to keep them, you know… when I'm working on them. I guess you could say I kinda didn't think it through."

"What I'm hearin' ye say," Mary-Margaret said, trying very hard not to let her face betray her disgust, "is that ye had a corpse that was decomposin' and...?"

"Yeah. And then I sorta realized that this was way beyond my abilities, so I had to break the whole thing down and get rid of it."

Mary-Margaret looked over to where she had last seen Arthur and noticed that he was still there, but his face looked a little purple.

"I see," she said, turning her attention back to Terry. "So why didn't ye just return it to the dumpster?"

"I thought of that, but the cops had been around at my buddy's place, probably around the time I found the body, now that I think of it, and I guess I kinda got nervous."

"Knowin' that buildin' as I do, I'm sure the police are by quite a bit. And them stoppin' in on yer mate had nothin' to do with this, I'm thinkin'."

"Well, it kinda does."

"What do ye mean?"

"The body I found in the dumpster was his girlfriend."

Chapter Twenty-Six

Mary-Margaret gasped. At that very moment, there was a short scream and a loud thump outside. Without thinking, both Mary-Margaret and Terry rushed out the door.

"Don't worry about me, MM," Arthur moaned, splayed out on his back on the cement in front of the large window. "I've fallen further before and been fine."

"Holy crap!" Terry said. "That was epic!"

"I think we should call the paramedics," Mary-Margaret said. "Ye don't know what kind of internal injuries ye could have."

"I anticipated this," Arthur said, rolling over onto his hands and knees before pulling something from the back of his turtleneck. "I layered my back with foam padding."

"Epic," Terry repeated, this time nodding like a bobblehead.

"Well, let's at least get ye home and get a good cuppa into ye."

Together, Mary-Margaret and Terry got Arthur to his feet. As he had predicted, he didn't seem to be too much worse for wear.

"We're just 'round the corner, luv. Can ye give us a hand?" Mary-Margaret said, looking at Terry.

"I can't leave the ga—"

"Yer pumps have been locked for a while. A few moments more won't make any difference," Mary-Margaret continued.

"I don't know," Terry said, looking at the gas bar.

"Arm over him," Mary-Margaret instructed Arthur, thereby conscripting Terry into the rescue mission.

Arthur attempted to throw his arm over Terry's shoulder but stopped when he almost knocked the much smaller man to the ground.

"I think I can walk on my own," Arthur said, straightening up as much as he could, considering that he'd just fallen twenty feet. "And," he whispered to Mary-Margaret, "we don't really want this weirdo knowing where you live, do we?"

Mary-Margaret gave him a nod in agreement.

"Never ye mind then, luv," she said to Terry, who looked rather relieved. "Go on back to work. We'll manage from here."

With a shrug, Terry turned back to the gas bar.

"One more thing," Mary-Margaret called over her shoulder. "Ye might be gettin' a call from the police. Just tell them everythin' ye've told me, and ye'll be fine."

"Not a chance," Terry said with a laugh from the gas bar doorway. "I'm not saying anything."

"Too late, luv. Yer security video has already recorded ye."

* * *

"What were ye thinkin', hangin' upside down over the roof like that?" Mary-Margaret scolded as she turned the burner on under the kettle, Phil dancing around at her feet.

"How else was I going to keep an eye on you without being seen?" Arthur asked, leaning against the kitchen wall across from the stove.

"Oh, I don't know...perhaps just standing off to the side of the buildin'?"

"Too obvious. And far too amateur for me."

"Amateur, me ear. Yer lucky ye didn't break yer neck. Now let's have a bit of somethin' before I gnaw me own arm off, and then we've got to check out that apartment the lad was speakin' about."

She checked the cupboards and the fridge for a suitable snack before settling on some stew from the night before.

"What happened to being the fugitive?" Arthur asked.

"The what?"

"Fugitive. You know. You're wanted."

"I'll take me chances. And if they happen to stop me, then the police can come with us. Sitcheedoon while I heat this up on the stove."

"Why don't you just use the microwave, MM?"

"Are ye judgin' me cookin' now, too?" Mary-Margaret turned on the burner and motioned for Arthur to set the table in the dining room. "And what can I get ye, luv?'

"Just some McVittie's are fine," he replied.

"Ye can't live on biscuits alone, luv. Let me see if I've got some fruit or—"

"Biscuits are fine, MM. I had a big breakfast."

"Suit yerself," Mary-Margaret replied.

Once they had finished eating and Mary-Margaret felt confident that Arthur hadn't broken anything or given himself a concussion, the two of them headed off in Daphne. It hadn't been a practical option as a family car when Jimmy purchased it years ago, and now it seemed even smaller with Arthur stuffed in the front seat beside Mary-Margaret.

"I'm thinkin' ye've put the idea of poppin' around to Max's school on the back burner," Mary-Margaret said as they made their way across the city.

"Hardly. I've got a plan in place, and expect this whole mess to be sorted before your first court date."

"I've not got a court date. They haven't charged me with anythin' and likely never will."

"Oh," Arthur said, then pointed to a couple of dingy little buildings. "I think one of those is our building, MM."

"So I see. I'm supposin' the dumpsters are at the back, although by the looks of the place, a dumpster out front might be an improvement."

She turned onto the narrow driveway between the two low-rise buildings and proceeded into the back parking lot. Surprisingly, the lot was full of new, higher-end cars.

"'Tis not just the latte factor that's keepin' the young ones from ownin' a place of their own, is it?"

"They're probably all leased," Arthur said. "And I think we should call the police, MM."

"What?" Mary-Margaret turned to stare at Arthur. "Since when are ye the givin' up sort?"

"Since I don't have a disguise or any of my gear with me. Can you watch where you're going, please?"

"Ach, we'll be fine," she replied, squeezing Daphne in between a shiny black Lexus and a monstrously huge Land Rover, pulling the parking brake up before she got out of the car.

"Wait for me," Arthur said, struggling to get out of the little car. Mary-Margaret yanked the broken metal fire door beside the dumpster open and disappeared inside the building before Arthur managed to catch up with her.

Not surprisingly, the hallway of the apartment smelled rancid. The carpeting was of an indiscernible color and had likely never been cleaned since it had been laid down decades before. The walls may have intentionally been painted a burnt orange at one point, but it was impossible to tell for certain. Too many handprints, scuff marks, and stains that could have been anything covered them now.

Mary-Margaret was just rounding the corner towards the front entrance-way by the time Arthur, gasping for air, caught up with her.

"Glad ye could make it," Mary-Margaret said with a smile, opening the broken glass door to let them out into the building's small lobby. "If I'd known the door was smashed, we could have just let ourselves in the front like regular folk."

"What are you doing?" Arthur whispered, glancing around for security cameras.

"Checkin' for names. Here," she said, running her finger down the list of occupants on the board, stopping at one. "Pike. Do ye suppose that's Ashleigh or her brother?"

"Or neither. But you certainly don't think she'd live in a place like this, do you?"

"All that glitters is not gold, lad," she replied, looking at the greasy build-up on her index finger. "But it has to belong to one of them because we know it was Cassandra's body our lad found in that dumpster out back. This was the buildin' she was murdered in."

"We don't know that, MM. Maybe she was killed somewhere else and just dumped here. The possibilities are endless, really. And even if they weren't, we don't know that her boyfriend did it, and you said—"

Just then, Mary-Margaret was startled by the sight of a young man stomping out a cigarette before opening the door to the lobby from outside.

"Christopher?" She blurted out, recognizing him from the other night at O'Leary's.

He looked the older woman up and down before answering. "Uh-huh?"

"Christopher Pike, is it?" Mary-Margaret clarified.

"Maybe. Sure. Yeah. Why?"

"'Tis me, Mary-Margaret."

The young man looked at her without showing any signs of recognition.

"Ach," she said with a sigh, realizing that she didn't have a plan for this meeting and hoping something would come to her. "Yer sister, Ashleigh—"

"I think he'd know who his sister was," Arthur whispered.

"Havin' only one sister is a glitch in God's plan where I come from," Mary-Margaret whispered back, then turned her attention back to the young man standing impatiently in front of her, "works at me old job. I've somethin' to drop off to her, and here's me thinkin' our girl was the Pike on the wall. I must have gotten me info wrong."

Seeing nothing in her hands, Christopher looked Arthur up and down before giving a shallow cough.

"Never mind. I'm just thinkin' this moment that I've left what I was goin' to drop off to her sittin' on me kitchen counter anyway. I'll just be on me way."

Mary-Margaret began to push past Christopher in the tiny entranceway, Arthur in tow, when she turned back.

"And sorry for yer loss, luv," she said, lightly touching his arm as she looked up at him.

"What loss?" Christopher asked, shaking her hand away.

"Yer girl," she replied, reaching out again and now holding his arm.

"What about my girl?" he asked, again shaking her hand off of him.

"What she's trying to say," Arthur cut in as Mary-Margaret stepped back, "is that we're sorry that she's dead."

While it lasted only a moment, Mary-Margaret felt that the weight of the silence in that tiny lobby could have crushed them all.

"How'd you know she was dead?" Christopher said, his demeanor souring as the size of the lobby seemed to be shrinking.

"'Twas in the papers," Mary-Margaret said.

"*I* didn't see anything."

"Well, clearly ye have been so wrapped up in yer grief that ye likely missed it," she said, pulling Arthur in front of her as she pushed past Christopher and out the door. "Regardless, we're off now, and while the circumstances are poorly, 'twas nice meetin' ye."

Mary-Margaret gave Arthur another push as she hurried down the couple of steps that led to the walkway.

"And it was grand hearin' yer band the other night at O'Leary's. Ye and the lads clearly have a gift," she called back over her shoulder, coming as close to a run as was possible for her as she and Arthur disappeared around the building towards the parking lot.

"There was nothing in the paper, was there?" Arthur said, strapping his seatbelt on.

"Not a peep. But I had to say somethin' to get us away. Clearly, young Christopher knows somethin'."

"But isn't that why we came here? To find out what he knows?"

Mary-Margaret revved the car engine, skipping first gear and dropping the engine into second before roaring out onto the main road without stopping to check for traffic.

"I've got to give me Michael a call when we get home."

"But—"

"Ach, I'd explain it all to ye, but the logic behind it is far too complicated for yer mind to grasp at the moment," she said, pushing Daphne to her limits as the little car wove in and out of traffic. "Now, are ye goin' to sit there and argue with me, or are ye goin' to reconsider the possibility that the most obvious choice might be the right answer?"

Chapter Twenty-Seven

The phone rang several times before he picked up.

"Michael. 'Tis yer mother."

"Oh no," he groaned.

"And what sort of a way is that to answer yer phone? No wonder ye aren't—"

"What do you want, Mom? I'm very busy."

"Since we're bein' so direct with one another," she said, "I need ye to check somethin' for me."

"I'm at work. And I'm very bu—"

"I know yer at work. *I* called *ye*, remember?" she said, shaking her head. "I do worry about ye, me son."

"What do you need?"

"I need ye to check to see if yer lads attended an address the other day."

"Sure. I'll get right on it."

"Grand."

There was a pause.

"Get me a paper and pen, luv," she whispered to Arthur, who was sitting kitty-corner to her at the dining room table munching on a biscuit. "He's just gone off to see when the lads were there. Mustn't have put me on hold, on account of I'm not hearing any of that horrible music they play when he does."

Arthur got up, retrieved the items from the side table in the living room, and set them in front of her.

"Ta, luv. He'll just be another minute, I'm sure of it," she whispered.

Another minute passed.

"Michael?" Mary-Margaret said loudly into the phone when she could wait no longer. "Is that you I'm hearin' breathin' this whole time?"

"I was only kidding, Mom," Michael said with a chuckle.

"And ye find this sort of behavior funny, do ye?"

"Even if you gave me more details, I wouldn't be able to give you that kind of information. You know that."

"Even if it has to do with a murder?"

"As long as you're not the one that was murdered, no."

"That makes no sense, lad," she said with a frown. She looked over at Arthur, taking her index finger, and rotated it around her other ear.

"Neither does your ask of me. Now, if there's nothing else, I have to go."

"Right," she said with a sigh. "And I suppose ye'll be workin' late this evenin', too."

"Likely."

"And therein lies yer problem, Michael. If ye were home more, ye'd have time to—"

"Goodbye, Mom."

And with that, Michael hung up.

"What did he say?" Arthur asked.

"He said he couldn't give me the information on account of me not bein' dead."

"That makes no sense."

"Exactly. Well," Mary-Margaret said, looking at her phone again, "he's left me with only one other option."

She pressed a single button on her cell.

"Detective Sergeant Black. Homicide."

"Mandy, 'tis me, Mary-Margaret. Mary-Margaret O'Shea. Michael's mother."

"Yes, I know who you are, Mary-Margaret."

Mary-Margaret beamed.

"Can she help?" Arthur asked, mouthing the words. Mary-Margaret held up her hand to silence his already silent questioning.

"Hang on a minute," Amanda continued. "I'm in the car, and I just dropped a piece of a carrot on the floor and—"

"Ach, look at the time. Ye must be famished. And eatin' a bit of carrot won't help. How be ye and I get a bit to eat at—"

"O'Leary's, isn't it? That would be perfect. I'm just leaving a scene around the corner from there, and I could use something more than this container of carrots for dinner tonight."

"Grand. O'Leary's it is."

Arthur frantically waved his hand across his neck in a slashing motion, mouthing the words 'No. No.'

"I'm at me Michael's," Mary-Margaret continued, "so I'll likely be there within the hour."

"No problem, Mary-Margaret. I have some notes to get caught up on, so I can wait in the car in the parking lot until you get there."

Arthur began crisscrossing his hands in front of him, shaking his head violently.

"And ye don't mind if I bring our Arthur along?"

"Great. See both of you in about an hour?"

"Indeed. Bye-bye bye bye-bye-bye." Mary-Margaret clicked off her cell phone. "And what would be the matter with ye, then?"

"We can't meet Detective Sergeant Black, or any other cop, for that matter."

"And why not?"

"Because you're wanted, remember?"

"Ach, right. I forgot."

"You have to call her back and cancel. It might even be a trap."

"A trap?"

"Absolutely. I know how these cops work: they lure you to a place under one pretense and, before you're even out of the car: BAM! Semi-automatics pointed at your head from all angles."

Mary-Margaret's eyes narrowed. "I hardly think—"

"I've seen it before, MM. These cops are slippery."

"This is me Mandy we're talkin' about here. I hardly think anyone would call her slippery."

203

"Nonetheless, you can't leave this house."

Mary-Margaret thought for a moment.

"Unless…." Arthur said, reconsidering.

"Unless what?"

"You go in disguise."

"Oh, for the love of—"

"Do you want her help or not?"

"I do."

"So give me a minute to think, and I'll have you so done up that not even your own son would recognize you."

"No worries about that, given how little he sees of me as I am now."

* * *

"Arthur, luv," Mary-Margaret began, looking at herself in the mirror, "did ye have any particular thought in your head when you put this together for me?"

"Oh, absolutely, MM! When I see you," he said, stepping back to admire the outfit he'd provided her with, "I see Norma Desmond in Sunset Boulevard."

"I'm not thinkin' the old girl was at her best at that point in her life," Mary-Margaret grumbled.

"If that image doesn't resonate with you, what about seeing yourself in something Coco Chanel would have–"

"Unlikely. In fact, truth to be told, and told with great appreciation for yer efforts, lad, I think I look more like I should be goin' to the homeless shelter a few doors down from the church than the mucky-muck you were shootin' for."

"I realize that disguises are not, as they are to me, a strength of yours," Arthur said, unfazed, "but rest assured that no one will recognize you."

"Let's hope not," she said with a sniff. "Away we go, then."

* * *

"Everythin' all right, Mary-Margaret?" Maeve said from behind the bar as Mary-Margaret and Arthur walked into the pub. "And who's the ninja ye've got comin' in after ye?"

"Just fine, luv. And this is me friend, Arthur," she answered before looking over and scowling at Arthur. "I'm so used to yer getups that I don't notice anymore. And clearly, whatever it was ye had me made up to be hasn't fooled anyone."

"She's a pub owner, MM. Trained to recognize regulars. Don't worry. You'll be fine."

"Mary-Mar—" Amanda began. "What happened to you? Has Mike kicked you out?"

"Ach, 'tis no use, I'm afraid," she said, pulling the wig Arthur had used in one of his earlier disguises off before plopping herself down in the chair Arthur had pulled out for her. "I'm wanted, and I thought this ridiculous getup would put ye off me trail."

"Stop right there," Amanda said with a smile. "You've lost me."

"What MM is saying, Detective Sergeant," Arthur said as he sat down, "is that you guys have a warrant out for her arrest because she represented me at the bail hearing on my murder charge. And the outfit is not ridiculous, MM. It's just that the first two people to see you are both trained observers who–"

"Whoa!" Amanda said, throwing her arms up while leaning back in her chair. "And I thought my life was complicated."

"'Tis no joke, Mandy," Mary-Margaret said, shoving the wig in her purse. "But that's not what I'm—we're—here about."

"You can't make this stuff up, can you?" Amanda said with a smile.

"Apparently not," Mary-Margaret replied, taking a deep breath before continuing. "So, here's the high and low of it."

As she recounted what had just happened at the apartment, with Arthur adding details about the found bones and head, the server took their orders, brought a half-pint of a crown float for Mary-Margaret and a soda each for Amanda and Arthur, and then laid their dinners out in front of them.

"Have you told all of this to Detective Sergeant Gill?" Amanda asked.

"Clearly not," Mary-Margaret replied sharply. "Although me Michael did put me in touch with a Detective D'Angelo. Lovely man."

"Joey D? Yeah. He's a great guy. A floater now. Should still be off on stress, if you ask me, but they let him come back to Homicide. They pretty much have him working permanent nights now, going around picking up documents, checking on victims' family members, or going on coffee runs."

"I don't follow," Mary-Margaret said.

"He isn't assigned to a team because," Amanda said, glancing over at Arthur, "and I shouldn't be saying this, but he's really not fit for the road anymore."

"I see," Mary-Margaret said, the pieces starting to fall into place.

"His psychologists convinced our medical bureau that it would be healthier for him to come to work than to sit at home, so we made a spot for him."

"He's not a real detective then?" Mary-Margaret asked.

"Oh, he's a detective, but he's not active. In fact, I don't think they even let him carry a gun."

Mary-Margaret looked down at the food on her plate. She took a couple of deep breaths and then looked at her two dinner companions.

"So what I'm hearin' is that me Michael is makin' a mockery of me. I see."

"I don't think—" Amanda began.

"No, 'tis fine. Just fine. And a clear indication that me Michael doesn't believe me. Us," she corrected, looking over at Arthur.

"I can't speak for Mike, but if I were you, I'd be more concerned about the charges you may be facing than running a parallel homicide investigation, Mary-Margaret," Amanda said. "Detective Sergeant Gill and his team are working this one and—"

"And they've arrested the wrong lad."

"No offence intended, but," Amanda continued, choosing her words carefully, "based on what I've been told, I'd have to disagree."

"Are ye callin' this lad a murderer?" Mary-Margaret said, perhaps a bit louder than she had intended, causing the hum of the other patrons' conversations to stop. All eyes were on their table.

"I didn't do it!" Arthur said, sitting up as straight as his huge frame permitted.

In a manner that suggested that scenes such as this were not an unusual occurrence for her, Amanda smiled and nodded to no one in particular and then waited. As expected, the pub returned to its regular bustle, starting with the sound of a draft being pulled from behind the bar.

"It's not my investigation," Amanda began, "but Arthur—"

"Mandy, luv, they've got the wrong man. And he's been cleared. It's just a matter of time before the charge is withdrawn."

"As I said, Mary-Margaret," Amanda continued, "it's not my case. I'm sure Detective Sergeant Gill is doing a very thorough—"

"So thorough that he arrested Arthur, leaving the real murderer roamin' around the streets, likely plannin' his next attack," Mary-Margaret said. "I've...we've got suspects with real motives, Mandy. We've spoken to the lad who admitted to having found the body and then disposin' of it."

"And we know that Cassandra was a drug dealer," Arthur added.

Amanda pulled her cell phone out of her purse.

"Detective Sergeant Black. Yes. Okay. I'll be right there," she said, dropping it back into her purse. "I'm really sorry, but I've got to go. And it's not magic. I've got my phone hooked up to my watch, so my wrist vibrates when it rings. Crazy, isn't it? Sorry. I'll pick this up. Talk soon."

Before either of them could respond, Amanda was at the bar, credit card in hand.

"I can't believe the girl was dealin' drugs out of me local," Mary-Margaret said, looking around the pub. "No wonder Maeve wanted to kill her. But who would she be dealin' to in here? Look around. Hardly the crowd for it."

"Cassandra was a drug dealer, not a barmaid," Arthur said. "And didn't Maeve say that Cassandra wanted to have bands in on a regular basis?"

Mary-Margaret stopped for a moment to consider.

"I think ye might be right, luv. I remember her talkin' about havin' bands in. And about how keen Johnny was on the idea, likely because the girl probably told him it would bring in more of drinkin' crowd. Oh, me stars. This is worse than I thought."

Mary-Margaret looked past Arthur over to the bar where Maeve was wiping down the counter.

"And she and Johnny livin' just upstairs with a smallie. The place is rampant with drugs. Maybe the death of the girl was a blessin' in disguise."

Mary-Margaret crossed herself. "Forgive me for sayin' so, Father."

"So now, what do we do?"

"Well," she said, taking a deep breath, "as Mandy's said, yer still on the books for murder—"

"Accused of murder," Arthur corrected as he looked around them, his voice lowered.

"And I'm only hours away from joinin' ye in the Big House unless we can sort this mess out. I don't suppose the crayons Billy Gilly's currently usin' are sharp enough to connect the dots on this one, and even with the tape ye gave him, we still don't have a murderer to drop in his lap. I'd say we best get our skates on and sort it out for him before the lazy sod decides that it's easier to pin this thing on you."

"What?" Arthur exclaimed. "But I thought it was all—"

"Nothin's a done deal until the deal is done, luv, so let's get on our way."

Chapter Twenty-Eight

I f Phil was walked once, he was walked a dozen times the following morning. The on-again off-again drizzle reminded Mary-Margaret of the Ireland she'd left almost fifty years before and she wondered how different her life would have been had she stayed put.

Doesn't matter now, me girl. Here ye be and, if ye don't sort this mess out, ye'll be rottin' in a jail cell for the rest of yer life. And so will Arthur. Ach. What a mess I've made of it all. There has to be a way out. There's always a way out.

Mary-Margaret went through the rest of the morning, well into the evening, in a funk. Between what could only be seen as a betrayal on the part of her own son and what she feared would surely be the inevitable outcome of Detective Sergeant Gill's incompetence, the sparkle in Mary-Margaret's eye was dimming. And Max's news at dinner didn't make her feel any better.

"There's a perv at my school," he began.

"A what?" Mary-Margaret said, his words bringing her into the present.

"A perv. You know. Pervert."

"And ye know this how?"

"There's posters warning us about him all over the school."

"Where was he seen?"

"Hanging around the lockers."

"Could be part of that organized crime lot," Mary-Margaret said.

"I don't think so. Someone said that he was telling everyone that he was a new student, but if he was, he must have flunked grade twelve about twenty times."

"And he was hangin' around the lockers? For no reason?"

"Not unless he really did fail grade twelve twenty times," Max said, glancing down at the cell phone he'd pulled from his pocket.

"Not at the table," Mary-Margaret said.

"It's Dad," Max said.

"What's he doin' textin' ye durin' dinner?"

"Says he won't be home for dinner."

"Good thing he's the detective. The rest of us wouldn't have figured that out," she said with a grimace, looking at her son's empty chair. "And why didn't he call me to say so?"

"I dunno. Want me to ask?"

"No textin' while yer at the table," Mary-Margaret snapped.

Max put the phone back in his pocket and continued eating his spaghetti.

"Ach, 'tis yer da. Best text him back," Mary-Margaret said.

"Should I tell him about what you said about him being a detective?" Max said with a grin.

"Leave that part out, Clever Clogs," Mary-Margaret said. "And the part about the sexual deviant roamin' the halls of yer school. Ach, what's it all comin' to?"

As Max typed his response to his father, the penny dropped for Mary-Margaret.

"Arthur," she said under her breath.

"Huh?" Max asked, his cell phone back in his pocket.

"What did the lad in your school look like?" Mary-Margaret asked, perking up.

"I don't know. I didn't see him. I'm just telling you what I heard."

"But the posters. Ye must have seen them."

"I didn't look too closely," Max said, looking down at something else on his phone.

"Did anyone tell the school secretary?"

"Must have because she's the one who put up posters warning us about him."

Surely she would have recog—no, she's never met him.

"'Tis nothin' for it but an early night," she announced, getting up from the

210

table.

"It's six o'clock, Gran."

"So 'tis. And it'll be 6:05 by the time ye finish on whatever else yer doin' on yer phone and get the plates cleared away. Don't forget to put some plastic wrap over that bowl before ye put it in the fridge. Yer da can heat it up whenever he gets home."

Wee Phil leapt off one of the living room chairs and scampered towards her as soon as he heard her chair being pushed away from the table.

"Ach, I should probably get ye out again before turnin' in," she said, instinctively taking her plate with her into the kitchen. Max continued texting with his thumb while clearing the table with his other hand. After setting her plate down on the counter, Mary-Margaret slipped on her shoes and unlocked the back door. She clipped the leash to Phil's collar, checking the small container attached to it for bags.

She opened the door and jumped back, suppressing a scream.

"MM!"

Her initial instinct was to slam the door on the figure that was standing on the step, but recognizing the voice and then the man in the outfit, she did not.

"This may be my best disguise yet," Arthur said as Mary-Margaret pulled him inside and quickly closed the door.

"If yer goin' for the 1970s pimp look, I'd have to agree," she said, looking him up and down while Phil pulled on the leash.

"New Age drug dealer, MM," Arthur said with a slow nod, the oversized brim of his hat flopping in agreement.

"New Age somethin', I'd agree. And I'm sure the lads in jail will just love the look. Shall I put the kettle on, then, or are ye on yer way to somewhere I don't want to know?"

"Oh, hi, Arthur," Max said as he came into the kitchen, cell phone in one hand, a cup and his cutlery on top of his plate, all balancing on the bowl of pasta in the other.

"Mind yerself, luv," Mary-Margaret said to Max.

"Don't worry. I've got thi—" he began before the plate slid just enough for the cup and cutlery to come crashing to the ground, causing Phil to jump.

"'Tis yer lucky day, me lamb," Mary-Margaret said, noticing that the cup had not shattered.

"Sorry."

"I was at your sch—" Arthur began.

"Not a word!" Mary-Margaret cut in. "Loose lips sink ships, if ye'll recall."

"Right," Arthur said with a knowing nod.

"Wait," Max asked with a grin, picking up what he'd dropped. "Are you the perv?"

"I am many things, Max, but I am *not* a—"

"It was you!" Max cried out. "What were you doing there?"

"I was—"

"Not!" Mary-Margaret said, opening the back door again to take Phil out.

"It's okay, MM. I solved the crime."

"Ye what?" Mary-Margaret said, dropping the leash, letting the little dog run wild down the laneway.

"I solved the locker theft crimes. It wasn't organized crime at all. At least, not in the way you were thinking."

"It was those girls, wasn't it?" Max asked.

"What girls and ye know this how?" Mary-Margaret said, looking from one to the other.

"The two girls in my grade."

"And now I'm hearin' that me own grandson is cavorting with criminals?"

"I don't *know them* know them. I just sort of…know them. And yeah, all of a sudden, they started dressing really well," Max said. "We figured they were probably turning tricks."

"Oh, me stars!" Mary-Margaret said, her knees buckling. Arthur grabbed her before she could fall and guided her to her seat at the dining room table.

"I was kidding…sort of," Max said, his face suddenly as white as a clean porcelain plate.

"Put the kettle on, Max," Arthur instructed. "I'll explain everything, MM. And it's not like that at all."

Without waiting for the tea to arrive, Arthur explained how he had, indeed, been lurking around the lockers. And how he had, indeed, been suspected of glancing at two of the older girls in the school.

"Ye may have to pour me a wee dram, luv. I don't think me tender constitution can take this," Mary-Margaret gasped.

"But it wasn't like that," Arthur said as Max came in with a cup of tea for his gran. "They were looking at me."

"I don't follow," Mary-Margaret said. "And the whiskey, lad. Pour me a whiskey."

"I was watching them break into the lockers, MM. One of them kept six while the other one manipulated the combination lock," Arthur explained.

"So what yer tellin' me is that they picked the locks?" Mary-Margaret asked while Max handed her a shot glass full of whiskey. "Ta, luv. Sláinte."

"Not exactly, but kind of," Arthur said. "There's a hack anyone who knows anything about combination locks—"

"I'm sure there is, but we need not go into it now," Mary-Margaret said, upending the glass. "And what of the girls?"

"Oh, I listened to them long enough to get their first names, noted the lockers they'd broken into while I was watching them, and then called Mike."

"Michael? Me Michael?" Mary-Margaret asked.

"Of course. Who else? Anyway, he told me to keep an eye on them, which I did. Hence the perv designation."

"I'm not followin'."

"The girls, Jessica and Kate—"

"Jessica Hansel and Kate…I don't know her last name," Max added.

"The two of them," Arthur continued, "went into the office and *reported* me. While they were in there, those cops who ride around on bikes came. I spoke to them outside the office first, and then they went in and did their thing."

"So why are there posters about ye bein' a…" Mary-Margaret couldn't make herself say the word.

"Pervert? Because I didn't want to burn my cover, just in case."

"So what I'm hearin' is that it's these two girls that've been terrorizin' the school, and it'll just be a matter of a phone call to yer Old Bird to get those posters removed?"

"Exactly."

"Well, that's a relief," Mary-Margaret said as Phil came running in the back door, his leash fluttering after him. "Let's hope it's as easy to have Billy Gilly get ye off the accused list. Get yerself a cuppa, and we'll—"

"No time, MM. I've got something to sort out. And you're coming with me."

"Me?"

"I have a plan."

"Dressed like that? Never mind. Let's be off, then. Max, be a luv and pop down the laneway to look for landmines, will ye?"

"What?" Max said.

"Ye know what I'm meanin'. The last thing I want is for those drunkards in the laneway to come knockin' at me door, sayin' that I can't manage a wee dog."

* * *

"I am *not* going to wait in the car while ye risk life and limb," Mary-Margaret stated as they drove to Christopher Pike's apartment.

"He's a very dangerous guy, MM," Arthur said.

"And what's to say he won't try any funny business on ye? Or are ye suggestin' that I'm not fit to handle meself in such situations?"

"I don't mean to sound condescending or ageist, MM—"

"Then don't," she said, turning onto the laneway between the two apartments. "I've already got me Michael placating me. I don't need it from ye."

"I was with you when you practically ran away from him the other day, MM. You obviously realized that he was too much for you."

"I just wasn't prepared for him to come at me like that."

"He walked through the front door, MM."

"Exactly! How could I have prepared myself for that kind of attack?"

"He lives there, MM. How else would he come in?" Arthur said. "And it was hardly an–"

"He startled me. Caught me off me guard, alright? Feel better now?" she said, turning the car off in the back lot. "Ach, no wonder there's so much crime back here. Not a light to be seen."

"Because they've been shot out," Arthur said, pointing to the lamp posts.

"All the more reason why I should come in with ye."

"Here," Arthur said, pulling an earpiece out of his pocket. "I've wired myself up. You can hear everything that's going on. There's also a record feature on my bodypack, so everything that's said—"

"I know what a recordin' is, luv," Mary-Margaret said with a huff, taking the earpiece.

"If things go sideways, call the police. Otherwise, I'll give you a cue just before I bring Christopher out through the front door. You'll meet us there, and we'll take him to the police station."

Mary-Margaret looked in the back seat of her car.

"He'll fit. Don't worry," Arthur said, getting out of the car and adjusting his hat.

"And if things do go…sideways, what's yer plan until the police arrive?"

"I haven't thought that far yet," Arthur said as he closed the car door and walked towards the apartment.

As he disappeared inside the building, Mary-Margaret looked at the earpiece that he had given her. Not seeing any place to turn it on or off, she placed it in her ear. Nothing. She removed it and looked at it again but couldn't find any sort of switch or toggle or button to turn it on. She momentarily debated whether to stay in the car to wait for Arthur or not before hopping out to follow him, but he was already out of sight.

Not having an apartment number, Mary-Margaret considered that Arthur couldn't be that much further ahead of her, so, she reasoned, if she just stopped at each floor, she would likely see him in the hallway. Then, it occurred to her that he didn't have an apartment number either.

We'll either make short work of this, or I'll be callin' me Michael before the night is through.

She waited at the elevator door for what seemed like an eternity. Finally, a gaunt woman pushing a bundle buggy full of unidentifiable items came up behind her.

"Still not working, eh? The super said he'd have it done by now. Guess I'm going to have to haul these up the stairs. Again."

And with that, she was gone.

Mary-Margaret considered doing the same, but then decided that walking up several flights of stairs was beyond her scope of interest. She went into the so-called lobby and sat down on the least filthy part of the ledge to wait, reasoning that Arthur or Christopher or both would be coming out this way. Before she could think of it, the door that separated the lobby from the hallway clicked shut, locking her out of the building.

Nothin' ye can do about it now, me girl. Just wait it out.

And so she waited. And waited. And waited.

"What are you doing here?" a voice said, startling her.

"Ach, I must have dozed off. 'Tis ye I am here to see," she replied.

"Why? I don't know you," Christopher said.

"Yes, ye do. We met the other day. I'm Mary-Margar—"

"So? What do you want?"

"To talk about Cassandra," she said, standing up and taking a deep breath.

"I've got nothing to say. The cops already asked me a pile of questions. If you're so interested—"

"Luv, I know ye had somethin' to do with it."

Christopher froze, looking like a mouse cornered in a small glass jar.

"And I might be able to help ye."

Christopher did not move.

"Is there someplace we can go? To talk. Just you and me?" she asked.

Christopher did not answer.

"Or we can chat here," Mary-Margaret concluded, settling herself back on the ledge, patting the spot beside her. "Would ye care to join me?"

Christopher sat down beside her, not knowing what else to do.

"Grand. Now we all know that Cassandra was yer girl. And we all know that she was involved in drugs."

Christopher opened his mouth to speak.

"And," Mary-Margaret continued, not waiting for him to say anything, "we all know ye and the lads in the band were…are also pretty hard into the drugs. Am I right, or am I right?"

"Maybe."

"And I'm thinkin' that, drugs or no drugs, yer girl likely spent more time with ye and understood ye better than anyone else ever had."

Christopher looked down slightly and licked his lips nervously.

"I know what 'tis to be in love, lad," she said, reached over and put her hand on his knee. "I wasn't always this old bag of bones ye see sittin' beside ye."

The two of them sat in silence for a few moments.

"Poor choice of words, I'm just now thinkin'," Mary-Margaret said, looking straight ahead. Christopher said nothing as he looked down at her hand on his knee.

"But yer girl was into the drugs," she continued, removing her hand while looking back over at him. "She was the one supplyin' them to ye and the lads, wasn't she?"

Christopher didn't answer.

"And like any of them in that world, she answered to someone above her, didn't she?"

Christopher nodded.

"Drug dealin'. The ultimate multi-level marketin' scheme. Ach, luv," Mary-Margaret sighed. "So I'm thinkin' that her dealer had to meet her somewhere to deliver the drugs, and ye, bein' the good lad ye are, likely had him meet her at yer place, yeah?"

"Yeah," Christopher said. "I hated it."

"Hated what, luv?"

"The drugs. That she dealt. That she was a part of that world."

"But ye use. I don't understand."

"That's different. I just pay my money, and I'm done."

"So was she yer girl because she was yer dealer or…?"

"She was my dealer, and then she became my girlfriend."

"So ye knew she was a part of that world before ye—"

"I thought she'd keep it out of our lives."

"Are ye daft, lad? Yer lives *were* the drug dealin'."

"She said she'd keep it out of our place."

"Ach, luv," Mary-Margaret said, putting her hand back on his knee. "Sounds like ye really cared about her, lad. Like ye wanted to make a go of it, despite her...occupation."

"I guess."

"Love is a blessin' and a curse sometimes, isn't it?"

Christopher sat silently as Mary-Margaret rubbed his leg.

"And I know," she continued, now patting his knee, "from the stories me neighbor, the Avon lady who lived four doors down, used to tell me that not everyone pays up. So what happened when Cassandra's clients didn't pay?"

"He'd beat her."

"Who'd beat her?" Mary-Margaret asked, pulling her hand back.

"Her dealer would beat her."

"Jesus, Joseph, and Mary, luv!" she said, a look of horror on her face. "Did ye not call the police?"

"And tell them what? That my girlfriend, the drug dealer, just got beaten up by *her* dealer?" Christopher said with a bitter laugh. "What do you think?"

"Ach, I see what yer sayin'," she said, shaking her head sadly. "'Tis a tough spot ye were in, luv. A tough spot. Okay, so let's go back to where we were. Ye hated that she was a dealer. Ye hated that her dealer came to yer place to get his money, and ye hated that he beat her when she didn't come up with the cash. I'm also thinkin' ye hated that he always dropped off more drugs for her to sell, puttin' her in an endless loop of drug dealin'. So what did ye do about it?"

"What do you mean?"

"Did ye and yer girl argue? Did the two of ye fight? Did it come to blows?"

"No!" Christopher said. Now it was his turn to look horrified. "Never. Not with her."

"So the two of ye never had words?"

"Well, yes, but—"

"When was the last time her dealer was over?"

CHAPTER TWENTY-EIGHT

"A few days ago."

"And did ye…have words with her then?"

"Yeah."

"Did ye have more than words with her?"

Christopher looked down.

"Sometimes, luv, things happen that we don't mean to have happen."

There was a pause.

"Sometimes, words lead to a push or a shove." She paused before continuing. "As ye might surmise by me age, I've lived a bit of a life, and I know how things can sometimes go too far, especially when ye really care about the other person."

Christopher said nothing.

"And sometimes, we do really horrid things that we would never have thought we were capable of doin'."

Christopher remained silent.

"They're goin' to notice if her skull was fractured, luv. The pathologist, I mean. And ye know they're goin' to come runnin' back to ye. Ye might have thought that, by choppin' her head off—"

"I never did that!" Christopher yelped, jumping to his feet. "What kind of a—"

"But ye did kill her, didn't ye," Mary-Margaret said, slowly standing up beside him.

"I didn't mean to," he said with a sniffle.

"Was it a wee shove? Knocked her off her pins, and she hit her head? Ye should have called for an ambulance, but ye knew it wouldn't look good on ye, so ye just…?" She looked over at him and, reaching into her purse, pulled out a Kleenex and passed it to him.

"I thought she was okay," Christopher sobbed, wiping his nose.

"I know, luv," Mary-Margaret said, sitting back down on the ledge. "Here, sitcheedoon. I'd offer ye a cuppa while ye tell me everythin', but…."

"After her dealer left," Christopher said, sitting down beside her, "we got into it. I told her that I never wanted that guy at my place again. I probably told her that I never wanted her at my place again, either. She started to leave. I followed her to the stairwell. We were screaming at each other. She pushed me. I pushed her back. Except I was on the landing, and she was on the stairs."

Mary-Margaret nodded as she looked out of the grimy front window of the lobby at the traffic passing by.

"I was so mad that I just went back to my place and did some of the drugs her dealer dropped off. I don't even know what I took. I just zoned out. I never even thought to check on her then. And by the time I did, she wasn't there, so I figured she'd gone off somewhere and was fine."

"But she ended up in yer dumpster," Mary-Margaret said.

"The dumpster?" Christopher asked.

"The lad at the gas station said he found her body in the dumpster."

"I-I don't know."

"C'mon, lad. I'm tryin' to help ye here, and yer playin' games with me. The police already told ye—"

"I don't rememb—"

"And how did she end up...in the condition she was?" Mary-Margaret asked.

"I honestly have no idea," Christopher said, lowering his head into his hands.

Chapter Twenty-Nine

When Arthur jerked open the glass door that had kept Mary-Margaret from re-entering the building several minutes earlier, he found her sitting beside Christopher on the narrow ledge, her arm around his shoulder.

"MM!" he shrieked as he rushed towards her.

"'Tis alright, Arthur. Our man here is just havin' a moment," she said, holding Christopher as if he was one of her own.

Christopher looked up, causing Arthur to step back.

"I know what happ—" Arthur began.

"I don't think ye do, luv," Mary-Margaret said. "He's not a killer, or if he is, he's more of an accidental murderer."

"Oh, he's the killer, MM. Accidental or not," Arthur said adamantly. "But I was more concerned about you. I thought he was attacking you."

"Me? Did ye not see me tryin' to console the lad?"

"I wasn't really taking in the subtleties of your gestures," Arthur admitted. "I was too busy thinking of everything I just heard."

"Now ye've certainly got my attention. Out with it."

"I'd rather not say in front of…" Arthur nodded towards Christopher.

"I think we're all beyond that at this point, luv. In fact, let me fill ye in on the story as I know it to this point."

Arthur sat down beside Christopher, the three of them side-by-side on the slender piece of wood. Mary-Margaret narrated most of the story, with Christopher clarifying a few details.

"Well," Arthur said, "that fits right into my story. As you can see, I didn't find you, Christopher, but I did find Terry, our friend who works at the gas station."

"Terry?" Christopher asked. "He has a job?"

"Yes. And he said he was coming up the stairwell that night and saw Cassandra passed out on the stairs. He wanted to call 9-1-1, but his cell phone was dead, so he carried her up to his apartment. Once inside, he checked her again, but she was dead."

Christopher let out a cry.

"Yeah. So technically, that makes you the killer," Arthur said matter-of-factly, "although it could be argued that if Terry had called for help, she'd be alive today. But I doubt anyone would buy that."

"Yer bein' a little harsh, aren't ye? Look at the state of the man," Mary-Margaret said, rubbing Christopher's back. "Never mind, luv. These things happen."

"MM!" Arthur said, leaning forward to look across Christopher at her.

"We're a little prone to...volatility...once in a while, aren't we, luv," Mary-Margaret replied, hoping to keep Christopher calm until she could figure out a way to call the police. She nodded and grinned, hoping Arthur would realize how precarious their position was at the moment. "Get on with yer story, Arthur."

"Oh. I get it. Okay," Arthur said, giving her an obvious wink. "So anyway, Terry figures it wouldn't look too good on him if he had a dead body in his apartment, so he carries her down to the dumpster and tosses her in."

Christopher put his head in his hands and began to weep.

"Here. Take another Kleenex," Mary-Margaret said, passing him another.

Christopher took it and blew his nose several times and then leaned back, resting his head on the wall behind him.

"How did he get into dismemberin' her, then?" Mary-Margaret asked. Christopher snapped his head forward and made a choking sound. "Sorry, luv."

"He has no idea," Arthur replied. "Said he got really high and must have decided then that it would be a good idea to try to do his taxidermy stuff on her or something because the next day, he woke up to find bones all over the place and her head in a bag in the fridge."

Christopher leapt up and, pushing the front door to the building open, threw up in the bushes on the right.

"Sorry!" Arthur called out and then turned to Mary-Margaret. "You're right. He is very emotionally unstable."

"I'm sure it's all just a bit much for him, what with him killin' likely the only girl he's ever loved and now hearin' this," Mary-Margaret said and then switching gears with the ease of someone who has managed small children on her own. "So our man Terry has no strong recollection of what happened, then."

"Apparently not. Except that, he knows he brought a living body to his apartment and took a dead one out."

"Is he still up there, in his apartment?"

"Yeah, I think so. I mean, he hasn't passed by here, has he?"

"And yer forgettin' that there's a back door—the door ye came in through—as well?"

"Holy crap, MM. You're right," Arthur said, smacking his forehead as he sprang to his feet. "He might have gotten away."

"If so, we'd better figure out where he went. We'll be in real trouble if the police get involved at this point," Mary-Margaret said as Christopher stumbled back into the building. "Christopher, we're looking for the lad that butch...disposed of yer girl. Any ideas where he might have gotten to?"

"I'd check the storage lockers," Christopher said, his face still white.

"Why?" Mary-Margaret asked cautiously.

"Because if he thinks this guy called the cops, he's going to want to clean out a lot of illegal stuff he has down there."

"How do ye get to the lockers from here? Oh, me legs," Mary-Margaret said, looking at the ledge she had just gotten up from. "Not built for comfort, was it?"

"Follow me," Christopher said.

Arthur followed closely behind Christopher, who was sprinting to the stairwell, while Mary-Margaret lagged considerably behind them both. Nevertheless, they all ended up in the basement where the lockers were.

And there was Terry, tossing various small shopping bags into the hallway from the four-by-six cage that was his storage space.

"You scared me," he said with a start.

"Good," Christopher said, hauling off and sucker-punching the much scrawnier man.

Before anyone could react, Christopher was on top of Terry, both fists plowing into his face.

Mary-Margaret grabbed Christopher by the hair and pulled him back, giving Arthur enough time to drag Terry out of harm's way.

"Don't get in the middle of this, lady," Christopher said, sweat dripping into his dark eyes. "This is between me and him."

Christopher lurched towards the pile that was Terry, but Arthur grabbed and pushed him back, pinning him against the wiring.

"Look, Christopher," Terry began, wiping the blood from his face. "I don't know what your deal is."

"Are you kidding me, Terry?" Christopher shrieked, his eyes bulging. "You killed my girlfriend!"

"No, you killed her, dude," Terry said, his eyes equally wide, but in fear. "She just died when she was with me."

"If you had have—"

"Me? If you hadn't have—"

With that, they dove at each other.

"Lads!" Mary-Margaret hollered, grabbing the closest one to her and pushing him into the storage locker. She quickly closed the wire door and pushed the lock down on it. "Arthur, call the police."

Arthur pulled out his cell phone.

"I've got no service down here," he said.

"Christopher, have ye got a locker down here as well, lad?" Mary-Margaret said to the young man she had not just captured.

"Yeah. Over here, but—"

"Open it up," she commanded.

Stunned by the recent turn of events, Christopher complied.

Before anyone had a chance to think, Mary-Margaret pushed him inside the cage and locked it as well.

"Now," she said after taking a deep breath, "be a luv, Arthur, and go upstairs and call the police. I would say call me Michael, but we all know how he feels about all of this business."

Chapter Thirty

"Do me eyes deceive me, or is it me Mary-Margaret I see before me?" Frank said as she and Arthur approached the bar. "And this not bein' a Friday night. What's the occasion?"

"Indeed, 'tis me, in the flesh," Mary-Margaret said. "And I'd murder a pint of—"

"A pint?" Maeve said with a smile from behind the bar. "And to what do we owe this indulgence to? And what about yer friend here? Just off the Dalgleish film set, are ye, lad?"

"I'll have a sparkling water, please," Arthur said, glancing around the near-empty pub. "Alcohol doesn't agree with me. It makes me break out in a—"

"Not Irish, is yer lad?" Maeve said, pouring a half pint of Strongbow before carefully pulling the Guinness to fill the glass. "So don't keep us on tenterhooks, Mrs. O'Shea. Let's have it."

"Sláinte," Mary-Margaret said, taking the glass and raising it to her lips. "I don't even know where to begin."

"By the looks of ye, luv, I'm goin' to need another pint meself," Frank said, raising his hand to order another.

Rather than take a table as she usually did, Mary-Margaret remained at the bar, balancing herself on the bar stool, the legs of which were just a bit too high for her compact body and the seat just a bit too small for her plentiful behind. Despite these deficiencies in the furniture, she managed to tell the story of the thieving barmaid, her jealous boyfriend, and the inept taxidermist, careful not to put too much emphasis on what would have surely been the introduction of illegal drug dealing at O'Leary's Pub. Nor how close Maeve came to being the primary suspect.

"I've just got to run upstairs to get wee Nolan off to bed. Johnny should be just finishin' givin' him his bath. When he comes down, can ye tell it again?" Maeve asked.

"I've not got the strength," Mary-Margaret conceded, feeling a numbness in her lower legs.

"I'll give him the abbreviated version if ye'd like," Frank offered. "Why don't ye and the lad go sit at the table by the side there, and I'll order us another round."

"Ach, I don't think I could manage it," she said as she climbed off of her perch. "Gettin' down, not another pint. Ta, luv. I think that would be grand. Arthur, give me yer arm."

"Sure thing, MM. And I'll have another sparkling water, please."

As Arthur and Mary-Margaret got to the table, Mary-Margaret's cell phone rang.

"Mom, where are you?" Michael demanded.

"And what business is it of yers?" Mary-Margaret asked in a tone that matched his exasperation. "And shouldn't ye be workin'?"

"I am working, which is why I'm wondering where you are. They brought a couple of guys in—"

"And I've got a second pint comin' on account of Arthur and me havin' caught the lads."

"I'm drinking sparkling water. Alcohol doesn't agree—" Arthur hollered in the background.

"They've just put a warrant out for your arrest, Mom. You're wanted," Mike said. "And Arthur's on conditions not to—"

"About that," Mary-Margaret said. "Now that we all know it's been a horrible mistake, I'm thinkin' ye could take us both off yer criminal-catcher system."

"It doesn't quite work like that."

"Well, as ye've pointed out numerous times, me son, I'm not a police detective, so it's of no concern to me how yer system works. I'm sure ye can sort it all out. In the meantime, I'm at O'Leary's with Arthur and Francis, if ye must know, and I'll be needin' a ride home. I'm beyond me usual half and am in no condition to operate a motor vehicle."

"I don't know if—" Michael said, his voice breaking.

"Or I can just call our Mandy, and she'll no doubt tear herself away from whatever gruesome murder investigation she's got on the go to make sure yer mam gets home safely."

There was a pause.

"I take it I'll see ye when I'm finished me second pint, then."

She could hear the sigh at the other end of the line.

"And since we're discussin' it, make a note on yer system that we sorted this murder out ahead of schedule, just in case I need a credit another time."

"Mom," Mike began.

"Sorry, luv," Mary-Margaret said, smacking her cell phone. "Can't. Hear. Breaking. Poor. Conne...."

She clicked the phone off, nodded as Frank sat down beside her, and leaned back in her chair while Johnny came by with another round.

"In memory of Cassandra," Johnny said, taking the last pint off the tray for himself.

"God rest her soul," Mary-Margaret and Frank said, crossing themselves.

"While I'd love to hear the whole story," Johnny said, "I've no one to watch the bar, so it'll have to keep for another time. In the meanwhile, tonight's drinks are on the house. I take it Michael's coming to pick ye up, Mary-Margaret, so feel free to enjoy any of our fine whiskeys from the top shelf over there."

"Ach, yer a good man, Johnny," Mary-Margaret said with a smile, "but I'm afraid me partyin' days are long gone. With a full pint behind me and another before me with me name on it, I'm callin' it a night."

"Suit yourself," Johnny said, turning back to the bar.

"And besides," she said to Arthur and Frank, "I'm sure me Michael's still goin' to need me help runnin' his life for a while longer. Can't let meself go now."

"Not a chance of that, luv," Frank said.

"Sláinte," she said as they all raised their glasses.

About the Author

Desmond P. Ryan was born and raised in Toronto, Canada. He completed an honors Bachelor of Arts Degree in English Literature and Political Science at the University of Toronto before spending the next thirty years as a detective with the Toronto Police Service.

He now resides in a neighborhood in Toronto known as Cabbagetown, where he spends his time writing, teaching, and wandering off to the pub.

AUTHOR WEBSITE:
https://realdesmondryan.com/

SOCIAL MEDIA HANDLES:
https://x.com/RealDesmondRyan
https://www.instagram.com/desmondpryan/?igshid=MzRlODBiNWFl
ZA%3D%3D

Also by Desmond P. Ryan

The Mike O'Shea Series
10-33 Assist PC
Death Before Coffee
Man at the Door
Blind Spot

The Pint of Trouble Mysteries
Mary-Margaret and the Case of the Lapsed Parishioner